GODS & GANGSTERS 2

AN ILLUMINATI NOVEL

SLMN

Kingston Imperial

Gods & Gangsters 2 Copyright © 2020 by Kingston Imperial 2, LLC

Printed in the United States of America

Rights Department, 144 North 7th Street, #255 Brooklyn N.Y. 11249

First Edition:

Book and Jacket Design: Damion Scott & PixiLL Designs

Cataloging in Publication data is on file with the library of Congress

ISBN 9780999639016 (Trade Paperback)

1

Rubber burned.

The air filled with tar and fumes.

The MPV rode straight up onto the curb, coming out of the night like the shadow of death, blacker than black. The five guys hustling on the corner didn't see it coming until it was beyond too late.

"Don't fuckin' move!" Othello barked out of the minivan, before it came to a stop. He had a chrome nine in each hand. The gleam, razor-sharp, sliced through the black air. He was vengeance and wrath wrapped in one, ready to strike down.

The five dudes were all high on that Wet; none of them were in any shape to react, guns tucked into their waistbands or not.

Cash hopped out of the backseat with a Draco while Mac, the driver, rounded the car with a Desert Eagle to play with.

"Yo! The fuck wrong wit' you niggas?" one dude bassed, not bothering to raise his hands, making like he wasn't about to be intimidated by the show.

Buck! Buck!

Two head shots silenced his bullshit, dropping him where he stood.

The other four got the message real fast, drugged up or not, and started reaching for the sky like they were trying to grab God's robe to haul their asses up out of there.

"The money's in the alley," the second dude blurted out, hating the feeling of the warm piss running down his leg. He was smart enough not to flinch, as Othello got up in his grill.

"Fuck that short shit. I came to ask y'all one question: whose block is this?" Othello growled, his gun barrels as black as the abyss, staring them down.

The second dude scowled, confused by the question. He told Othello, "Ours."

Buck!

A single-head shot red dotted him like an Indian at 7-11. He slumped to his knees like he needed to pray.

Othello turned the gun on dude number three.

"Ima ask you instead. See if you got the right answer: whose block is this?"

"Don's," three answered without hesitation, sure in his truth.

Buck!

He died with another dome check.

The smell of blood had the block reeking like a pig farm. The mist settled like a red fog over the night air. Othello turned his guns onto the fourth dude. He didn't need to ask. "Yours!"

Othello laughed.

"Smart nigga. Too bad your friends didn't get it before they got it! Bottom line, I'm Othello, but my friends call me O. Another question for you: You wanna be my friend?'

"Yeah yo, I do," the fourth dude stammered.

"Then call me O. G'head, let me hear you."

"O."

"Whose block is this?"

"Yours, I mean, O. It's O's block."

Othello smiled.

"You catch on quick. What's your name?"

"Benny," he answered.

"And what happens to muhfuckas who violate, Benny?" Othello questioned him.

Before he could answer...

Buck! Buck!

Two more shots blasted through the fifth nigga's brains into a dash for the back of his head, like a moneybox waiting for some little kid to put his dimes and nickels in, and splattered against the window of the store.

"Oh God!" Benny exclaimed.

Othello got up in his face real close, and spat, "Exactly. O is God, got me? And I don't forgive. I'll be in touch." With that, the three-man team got back in the MPV and disappeared just as quickly as they came.

Two days later, they struck again.

In the daytime, to the naked eye, the nondescript building in the back of an even more nondescript alleyway, was nothing. Nowhere. A small garage. Just big enough to fit two cars side by side, but anyone paying attention when they walked past would've noticed that the guys in there seemed to be working on the same two old ass Buicks every day, one red and one brown.

It was at night that it came to life for anyone in the know.

It wasn't some backstreet chop shop. It was a private gambling spot frequented by some major hustlers, primarily from the Southside. This was an area that fell under the control of Rome's clan, who unlike Don, *were* feared in the streets.

So feared, that no one ever dream of hitting *his* gambling spot...

Until Othello, Mac and Cash walked in.

There were six hustlers shooting craps on the pool table that night. Their lucky number. Usually, there would be upwards of twelve. The pile of money in the middle of the table was a small mountain. Serious money. With some hands, that pot would grow as much as fifty thousand. A few, it would scale higher.

To the naked eye, the stack looked to be at least that much.

The music blared in the background, pounding out the beats relentlessly. Two butt-naked bitches danced, grinding their asses, teasing their lips open like wet smiles, flirting, fucking and bringing drinks to the crowd. Both females were top choice, one Cuban and the other white. The white girl was every bit as nasty as Amber Rose, but her ass was much juicier. And it was *real*. None of that implant shit. The Cuban girl would've put Black Chyna to shame. They had the whole place smelling like money, honey and lust, which was about as heady a mix as any liquor. The white girl had a trick that the guys loved: she squatted over a beer bottle, sinking down on it until her pussy lips gripped the bottle top, then she flipped forward into a handstand and her pussy guzzled the whole bottle. It was right up there with a Thai ping pong show.

"Goddamn that bitch got a grip!" one hustler laughed.

He would be the first to die.

They were all so captivated by the bitch and her thirsty snatch, they never heard the three-man team enter.

BBBBBRRRRRRRRAAAAAAPPPPP!

They announced themselves with the fully automatic Mac-11's. That got their attention. The laughing dude went for his gun.

BBBBBRRRRRRRRAAAAAAPPPPP!

The bullets made him twerk like the Cuban stripper, until the quarter ran out on his jukebox called life.

"Anyone else got the urge to dance?" Othello quipped, ice cold.

Everyone in that room knew just how fucked they were the second they realized the three gunmen weren't wearing masks. It was a bad sign in any robbery. Nothing to lose, another dude decided to say to himself, *fuck it, I'ma die anyway*, and reached for the piece laying on the edge of the table. Maybe he was psychic. He was certainly right.

BBBBBRRRRRRRRAAAAAAPPPPP!

Mac laced him from navel to neck, the bullets splitting him as precisely as a surgeon's scalpel.

He was dead before he hit the ground.

"Y'all niggas think this a game? Serious?" Mac barked, waving death back and forth, like he was its master. The smell of fear had him amped on 1000.

No one spoke.

Othello eyed the money on the table.

"What's the pot?"

The four remaining dudes looked from one to the other, no one eager to open their mouths and invite a whole new set of lead fillings. Reluctantly, the shortest hustler in the room, Lil' Mike, answered, "Forty large."

Othello whistled, then added, "What's point?'

A beat.

"Six," Lil' Mike replied.

Othello smiled.

"You a gambling man? What am I saying, you're here, ain't you? Course you a gambling man. Okay, so here's the deal. Roll the dice. You crap, you die."

Lil' Mike looked down at the dice, sweating bullets. He picked up the dice.

"You gonna kiss 'em for luck?"

He was shaking so bad, he didn't have to shake the dice, he just rolled them.

He rolled a four.

"Shit out of luck, nigga."

BBBBBRRRRRRRRAAAAAAPPPPP!

Cash gunned down the dude standing next to Lil' Mike.

The blood splattered all over Lil' Mike's face and mouth. He couldn't help himself, he swallowed some. He gagged. Retched. Bile and puke and blood spat up.

"Come on, bitch ass nigga, you wastin' my time," Othello huffed. "One thing I hate is wasted time."

"Please man, just take the money," Lil' Mike begged, blood flecks on his chin.

"Roll!"

Lil' Mike was crying real tears. He was thinking about the baby daughter he knew he'd never see. He was thinking about the fact that before he left, his girl told him to stay home, and how different it would have been if he'd just listened. But most of all, he was thinking, like a prayer: *don't crap out.*

He rolled double fives.

No hesitation.

BBBBBRRRRRRRRAAAAAAPPPPP!

Cash gunned another dude down. This one melted like hot butter as those slugs tore through him.

"Point, nigga!" Othello demanded.

Lil' Mike didn't even shake the dice.

He was past the point of caring.

He rolled a six.

"Lucky you," Othello smirked, then blew the last dude into the next life.

The two naked bitches held water the whole time, looking on in amazement, but not fear. This wasn't their fight. They were just the decoration. As long as they kept the place looking good, whoever ran the joint would keep them around. Such was life.

"Now. Call Rome," Othello instructed him.

With shaking hands, Lil' Mike speed dialed Rome.

"Put it on speaker," Othello said.

The ring of the phone amplified, filling the room with anticipation, over and over, until the other end was picked up.

"Yo."

"Nice to hear your voice. It's been awhile," Othello didn't bother to mask the sarcasm.

A beat.

"Who this?" Rome asked, but he knew exactly who it was. Of course he did.

Othello chuckled.

"Nigga, you know *exactly* who I am. Needless to say, I'm baaaack!"

Mac, Cash and the bitches laughed like it was the funniest fucking line in the world. It wasn't. But fuck them.

"Where the fuck is Mike?"

"R-r-right here," Lil' Mike stammered.

"What the fuck is goin' on?" Rome thundered, his voice filing the room like the voice of God, only it was twice as fucking useless. "They dead. Everybody, the whole team." Lil' Mike blabbered, not caring that Othello got to see the bitch under his gangsta facade.

Othello's laughter boomed like James Earl Jones going full Dark Side.

"Nigga, fuck you askin' him for? You know what the fuck is goin' on. Don't need to be no psychic to see I'm here to take back what's mine!"

"Oh yeah? What's that?"

"The streets, muhfucka!" Othello bassed, then put the gun to Lil' Mike's head and blew it all over the iPhone in his dead hand. Lil' Mike slumped on the table, blood slowly spreading like one of them Rorschach blobs looking for context.

"O! O!" Rome exclaimed, but Othello didn't answer.

He picked up the phone and smashed it against the wall.

He turned to the two bitches.

"Ladies, help yourself," he nodded subtly toward the pile of money. "Consider it a reward for all your hard work. Can't be much fun riding that pussy."

The two bitches looked at each other, greed clouding their

vision. They stuffed the money into their over-sized bags hand over fist. It was more money than either one of them had held in their lives. It was life-changing money for a couple of basic bitches like them. Not that they'd change. Their kind never did.

Othello chuckled, then turned for the door.

He took a few steps then realized Mac and Cash weren't with him.

When he turned back, they each had one of the bitches over their shoulders.

"What the fuck y'all doin?"

"Shit, did you see what this bitch did with that bottle?" Mac exclaimed, shit-eating grin plastered across his face.

Othello laughed and they all walked out.

A week later, they struck again.

This time, the whole city bore witness to their wrath.

The anchor, one of those beautiful talking heads they like to employ to make the bad news seem more bearable, looked earnestly at the screen. "Yes, Bob, I'm here on the scene of what police are already calling a mass murder. Behind me you will see firemen and the rescue squad battling desperately to put out the blaze raging through what was, until tonight, a popular night-club. Reports are already coming through that the front, back and emergency exits were chained from the outside, condemning everyone inside the inferno a hellish death." She let that sink in for a moment, the camera silently watching the men beaten to their knees by the sheer heat of the blaze behind her. "I'm hearing reports that Leroy Austin, known in certain circles as Big L, is among the victims. He may have been the intended target. At this moment, it is too early to know. Police have no suspects, but—"

Black Sam snapped off the TV.

He wanted to slam the whole set through the floor.

"You seeing this shit? You *see* what I'm saying? No respect! No goddamn respect!" Sam fumed.

Joe Hamlet sat at the bar. He nursed an expensive cognac. He had been nursing it for the last hour. They were in one of Joe's legitimate businesses, a bar on the Southside named Sharkey's. Joe loved to hold court in this place. It was his Carnegie fucking Hall. Tonight, the place was closed. He and Sam were the only people in the place.

Black Sam was his lieutenant. He has been with Joe Hamlet for over twenty years. Joe trusted him implicitly. Joe was an old school gangsta, a towering muscular black man, with a shaved and oiled scalp. His clan was by far the most respected and well-established within the infrastructure of the city. In other words, they might vote-in the politicians, but he had the real power.

Joe shrugged, "Don't complain. Play the game."

"I'm tellin' you, Joe. We can't let this shit slide. It's time we start cleaning house. You want my wisdom? It's pretty simple; all these gangbangin' ass niggas, we just kill 'em before they become a problem."

"Think for a moment, my trigger happy friend. Just say we did that. Just say we went to war. What would happen? No, let me tell you...we'd drive the murder rate sky high. And what would happen then? Again, it's a rhetorical question, Sam. The mayor would come down on us so hard we'd be shitting blood. We'd lose business. And, that, my friend, is the real problem."

Black Sam walked back over to the bar, refreshed his drink and replied, "Fine, then what do you suggest?"

Joe thought for a minute, rolling the cognac around the glass and watching it stick to the sides, then slide slowly down the glass. "It's obvious that this nigga, whoever he is, ain't moving on his own. Somebody on The Commission is backing him. He's a piece of shit. A pawn. A knight a best. He ain't no fucking king. So the question is: who is behind him? Because that's where shit gets interesting. Not in this show; all this violence is just theater."

Black Sam nodded.

"Okay. I can see that... But that don't change the fact that if we don't get to the bottom of this, shit in this city is gonna explode!"

Joe downed his drink.

"That it is. What did you say his name was again?"

"Othello. Othello Moore."

Joe's brow furled and he looked in his empty glass, mind turning, as if he could find the answer in the last teardrops of cognac.

"Moore... Moore... It feels like I should know that name from somewhere."

Black Sam chuckled.

"Damn nigga, you getting *old*."

Joe laughed. "And if I am, you gettin' *older*! Shit, you got two years on me *old* man."

"And fuck you for remindin' me," Black Sam returned.

The two men were like brothers in a war that never ended. The Street Life. They'd come up together, and now, both in their fifties, they were at the top of their games. So many of their generation hadn't lived to see the way the game had changed, but Joe and Black Sam hadn't just survived, they were the originals, the ones who changed the game.

"Get the clans together. The Commission needs to meet. I want to look each and every one of the bastards in the eye and see who's behind this bullshit," Joe instructed.

Black Sam nodded, then downed his drink like a shot.

"Consider it done."

Joe's phone rang.

He saw Mona's picture on the screen and smiled as he answered, "Hey, babygirl."

"Hey, Daddy," she sung in a syrupy sweet voice.

Joe laughed. She wanted something.

"Spill it."

"What?" she replied, feigning innocence.

"Mona, don't bullshit me," he said, indulgently.

Mona giggled.

"Okay. I-umm- kinda... messed up."

"How much?" Joe cut to the chase.

"How do you know it's money?"

"Because that's the only thing you mess up. Constantly."

Mona could only laugh, because she knew it was true.

At 22, she was a good daughter. Far from perfect, but definitely on the right side of the scales. She'd finished school without giving her parents grief over boys, pregnancies or drug issues. And she was most definitely Daddy's Little Girl.

"*Wellllll*," she stretched the word out so long it nearly snapped. "Remember that money you gave me to pay my car note?"

"I do."

"I sort of spent it," she cringed, then quickly added, "but it was on this hot pair of Louboutin's that I knew would be gone if I didn't snatch them up on the spot!"

"You are your mother's daughter."

"And for an extra five hundred, I won't tell her you said that," she snickered.

"And your father's daughter as well," he chuckled.

Mona had him wrapped around her pinkie and she knew it.

She was Joe's only indulgence. Well, one of two, but his beautiful wife paled beside his babygirl.

"You keep this up, you're gonna have to get a job," Joe said.

"Well, you know I can always work for you. It would be cheaper."

"Goodbye, Mona."

"Love yoooooooooou! Mwah!"

Mona hung up and turned to her brother, Adonis.

He was looking at her funny.

"What?"

"You actually told him the truth?"

She shrugged as she got off of her bed, her body saying, *why wouldn't she*? She walked over to her vanity mirror and sat down to apply her makeup. "I never lie to Daddy."

"Never?" Adonis pressed, not buying the bullshit she was selling.

She looked at him through their reflections in the mirror.

"Well, almost never."

They both broke into spasms of laughter.

"Shit, we're like, whaddya call it? That black and white swirl thing?"

"Yin and yang."

"Yeah, that's it. I'm the exact opposite. I never tell him the truth if I can help it," Adonis admitted.

Mona eyed her older brother sadly, shaking her head.

She knew perfectly well why Adonis lied so much to Joe.

He didn't want their father to know he was gay. It certainly wasn't obvious. No one would guess from just looking at him. Adonis, living up to his name, was a woman magnet, just like his father. He had Joe's ruggedly good looks, along with an athletic build, wide shoulders and a V-shaped back. He was darker than Joe, a trait he got from their Cherokee grandfather on their mother's side, with good "Indian" hair, like black folks call it.

Their father had big plans for Adonis.

He wanted him to take over the family business when he retired, but Adonis was not cut out for the gangsta life.

Mona sighed.

"You'll have to tell him sometime, Don-Don," Mona said.

"That's easy for you to say. You're Daddy's little girl," he huffed, a hint of barely concealed resentment in his tone.

"No, you are. Daddy just doesn't know it yet," she joked.

Adonis laughed. "You're crazy, Sis."

"Seriously though, it isn't about him or how he feels. It's your life."

Adonis looked her in the eyes and nodded. "So you're telling me, if you had a secret that you knew would upset daddy, you wouldn't hesitate, you'd just tell him?"

"Like I said, I never lie to Daddy."

"Well good for you, Sis. I say be careful what you ask for."

"What would happen if I asked for that fine ass boy toy of yours?" Mona teased.

Adonis grabbed her around the waist and tickled her until she was howling and begging for mercy through laughing screams.

"Okay okay okay!"

"That's what," he cackled, adding, "Speaking of boy toy, I've got a taste for some of that good-good right now."

Adonis took out his phone as he walked out onto Mona's balcony.

He thumbed through his contacts and called Devante.

He picked up on the first ring.

"Let me find out you were waiting for my call?" Adonis flirted.

"Always, baby, but I can't talk now. My uncle is spazzing out over Dazzle's," Devante explained.

"Dazzle's? The club?"

"Is there any other Dazzle's worth talking about? You haven't heard?"

"No."

Devante grunted with sassy gayness. "Hmph, this shit is crazy! They said three guys rolled up in like, some type of SUV, with big guns, big like that dick of yours."

Adonis chuckled.

"Flattery will get you *everywhere*."

"They forced inside everybody that was in line outside. People were going crazy, but you know how hard it is for some people to get into Dazzle's? I'm sure they were thanking these niggas at first."

"Sure."

"But then, word is these muhfuckas locked all the doors with junkyard chains and torched the place." Adonis couldn't believe his ears. "Nobody made it out, man. No one. Everybody burned to death, including Big L," Devante gossiped, breathlessly.

"Big L? Fuck me."

"Exactly. Oh my God, can you *imagine?* Burning to death. Fuck. We got angels on our shoulders, bro. I'm so glad we didn't go to Dazzle's tonight," Devante sighed, then added, "Anyway, like you might guess, the whole clan is on alert."

"Can't you get away? I'm missing you like crazy," Adonis remarked, cupping his hardening crotch. He worked his palm over it, a small sigh escaping his lips. It was completely wrong, given everything they'd just talked about, but sex and death, death and sex, they were inextricably linked. Always have been. Always will be.

"Mmmmm, I bet you're grabbing yourself right now. You thinking about this pretty, juicy ass, ain't you? Well, gimme a sec to go somewhere more private, you just lay back and let mama take care of you like this...."

The Cuban bitch was named Venus. The white bitch was named Milk, and her pussy was so sweet and came so thick, that it could make a man forget he was lactose intolerant.

Together, they could curl the average nigga around their little pinkies.

But not Cash.

Viagra had nothing on Cash.

"Nigga, you shoulda been a fuckin' porn star," Mac joked, and he definitely wasn't lying. Not only was Cash one mighty fine specimen, he had a ten-inch dick that was known to put a bitch into a coma when he was done pounding it out.

As soon as they got back to the apartment, the bitches were back on it, picking up exactly where they'd left off, stroke for stroke. Their girl-on-girl action got the party started nice and smoothly. Karma had a tongue like a lizard. As soon as she slid it up in Milk's pussy and began to tongue fuck her, Milk did just that all over her tongue.

Cash pulled his shirt off, then unbuckled his belt, unbuttoning his jeans, and stepping out of them.

"Goddamn, pussy that creamy got to be good!" he said as he bent Milk over on all fours. He grasped each cheek and parted it, then plowed all ten inches, balls deep into her.

His back shot was so good, she came a second time just off penetration.

Mac grabbed a handful of Milk's hair and slapped her across the face with his dick, grinning as he face fucked her until she gagged up a froth of saliva and bile around his cock, and kept on going until it sounded like she was gonna puke.

"What's up, Daddy, don't you want to have some fun?" Karma cooed, unbuttoning Othello's jeans and reached inside.

It was the slight stutter of a pause that reminded Othello why orgies just weren't his scene.

He was a big, ugly nigga, standing 6'2, and black as midnight, blacker than Biggie, and just as ugly. But he didn't have the type of dick you could sport. It wasn't some little needle dick. It was just over seven inches, but in the shadow of that fine ass, big dick Cash and fine ass, good dick Mac, he knew any girl going down on him was scraping the bottom of the barrel.

"Naw, I'm good," Othello he said, but Karma wasn't taking no for an answer. She had his dick out and was sucking his balls so good he couldn't help but throw his head back and enjoy the good life that came with all that good Karma he'd been building up.

Milk was a squirter, which scared the shit out of Cash, but once he knew what the fuck was going on, he only had one thing on his mind: making her squirt again.

He did.

Mac wasn't as long-winded.

"Besides, if I don't get home, wifey gonna kill me," he chuckled on his way out the door.

Othello got head from Karma, fucked her once, taking his own sweet time to do it right, then went into his bedroom.

He took a quick shower to wash her shit off him, then laid down on his unmade bed.

"Oh God oh God oh God," Karma moaned deliciously through the walls. Her voice was as sweet as her pussy had been, and it made Othello hard all over again.

He closed his eyes.

It didn't take long for her lustful cries to carry his mind to a zone and before he knew it, he was jacking his dick, imagining he was the reason she was screaming so loud.

The feeling of staring at the ceiling, his dick in his hand, toes curled, dreaming, fantasizing and lusting, took him back a few months to the cage he had been kept in for the past four years...

Othello gripped his dick with one hand and the booty flick with the other. The picture was of a porn star named Cherokee getting fucked doggy style while she looked back at the camera with a sexy-ass fuck face.

It was always the expressions that got him.

He hated the flicks where the girl was smiling like she was in a J.C. Penney catalog. He was only interested when their eyes were rolling up into the backs of their heads and they were utterly gone.

Cherokee knew how to take him over the edge.

Every time.

After four years in a cage, the edge was exactly where he wanted to go.

He came hard in the wad of tissue he had cupped around his dick, then rolled out of the bunk and dumped it in the toilet, feeling weak in the knees.

He sat back on his bunk, hands behind his head, thinking about the visit he had just had with his two partners in crime, Mac and Cash.

"I'm tellin y'all niggas, we been goin' at the game all wrong," Othello explained. *"We get down with The Commission, we eat big!"*

"Man, fuck The Commission! We gonna eat regardless!" Mac boasted.

Othello had shook his head.

"Naw yo, you always ready to see somethin' smoke. Wild niggas crash, smart niggas last, remember that. You know what's the difference between a gangsta and a thug, Mac?"

"What?" Mac had replied.

"Thugs remain pawns, because they never see the larger picture. Gangstas become dons because they always scope shit out. I do this hit for this Commission nigga, he gonna make a move on the rest of the clans. We eliminate them and get our own clan, our own seat," Othello stated.

"Seats," Mac emphasized.

"I'm wit' you, O," Cash assured him.

Othello nodded.

The three of them had been friends since they were kids. Cash was the ladies' man, Mac was the livewire and Othello was the thinker. He was also a straight killer. They were all envious of one another, each for their own reasons. Othello envied Cash because of his looks, Cash envied Othello because of his smarts. Mac was just a hateful bastard all around, but at the end of the day, they were their brothers' keepers...

Or so it seemed

2

The Commission.
Most people would tell you that it doesn't exist.
They know nothing.

It was started by Frank Matthews right before his historic disappearance. There are those among the criminal fraternity who thought it ended with Frank's disappearance, but the truth is he left it to Willie Simmons, who ran it ruthlessly until his death. Willie, in turn, left it to his son, Guy. The problem was, Guy was a lot of things, but he wasn't his old man. He lacked the acumen and insight to hold it all together.

The Commission—which was national in nature up until that point—splintered, fragmenting into factions over infighting, mutual suspicion and informants. But it lived on in those shattered pieces, with regional Commissions comprised of clans, those clans made up of families. A clan could include one family, or several, depending upon the unity of the underlining principals the clan adhered to. Some Commissions spanned whole regions, others whole states, while some owned whole cities.

Joe Hamlet was the Commissioner of a Commission whose reach and influence spanned several adjacent cities, but not quite as far as the whole state, making him a man of wealth and power. He was the top dog, the Don, the father of his clan. But his was a small Commission, relatively speaking, the whole body comprising of only five clans.

There was Rome, who ran the Southside of The Commission territories. Don ran the Westside, Malone the Eastside and Malik the Northside. Joe presided over them all like the elder statesman he was, resolving disputes between clans, providing muscle and capital when and where needed, and reinforcing the political infrastructure of police, politicians and judges when appropriate.

Joe received a tribute from every clan, in return for not conducting his own business on clan territory without their consent. It was all very civilized and ran like clockwork until...

"Who the FUCK is Othello?!" Rome barked, his Morris Chestnut-like features balled into a knot of rage.

"Fuck who he is, *where* is he? The *who* don't fuckin' matter!" Don huffed, thinking about the message Othello had the audacity to send via Benny. That took brass balls. "This muhfucka slaughtered some of my best hitters in one shot!"

"Some hitters," Rome muttered darkly.

"Nigga, I ain't see your team doing any better!" Don shot right back.

"Look," Malone, the most laid back of them all, said, "I get you're hurt. But think on this, Big L was more than my lieutenant. He was family. My friend."

"That he was," Don agreed. "No one arguing that."

"I've already put the word on the streets: ten grand to anybody that bring me this nigga dead. Fifty, alive, because then I have the pleasure of killing the goddamn fuck myself. If you put in, we can offer one hundred thousand. Then he's a dead man walking." Malone slammed his fist on the table to punctuate his point.

Malik was the only member of The Commission who made the transition to total legitimacy. With the exception of the occasional investment in illegalities through the other clans, Malik kept his hands clean.

Joe knew Malik had his eye on the top job, Commissioner, and he was making inroads in all the necessary political circles to make that happen.

So, whenever Malik spoke, Joe listened; not to the words, but to the real agenda that lay behind those smooth Islamic mannerisms of his. He may have been soft spoken, but that velvety tone, like his neatly trimmed beard, hid the truth. The man had iron fists.

"We can offer fifty. Truth be told, we can offer a million. It doesn't matter. Want me to explain it in words you can understand? We're asking the streets to handle our problems. That shows weakness. It's a mistake. Before you know it, one Othello becomes a hundred Othellos, and we're staring down the hordes at our gates. We need to be smart about this. Only one way it works, we bring the clans together and stamp the fucker out as one!"

A few murmured their agreement, but others didn't bother hiding their dissent.

"That's easy for you to say, Malik. You ain't on these streets anymore. You want us under one roof? Okay, so tell me, whose roof? And before you go getting ideas above your station, don't even begin to think you can use this to take over the clans!" Rome spat, calling out the elephant in the room. "Not while there's breath in these lungs."

Malik glared at the other men, but didn't respond.

Joe looked around the large mahogany table at the five heads of the clans. The table was round to represent the fact that there were no bosses. Like Camelot, The Commission was equal. But some folk were more equal than others, and there was no mistaking the fact that Joe Hamlet was the first amongst equals. And while he may not have sat at the head, he sat dead center, facing the door. The seat was deliberate, the meaning behind it unmistakable.

"Gentlemen," Joe began, "Have you ever stopped long enough to consider that whoever this Othello is, we are exactly what he wants? Arguing, bickering, dividing ourselves along old fault lines. All that does is weaken us so that he can conquer. It's an ancient philosophy, but it has stood the test of time. I should know," Joe chuckled, and a few of the others joined him.

"I hear you, Joe. Sincerely, I do. But you gotta face the truth, my friend. The clans have been divided for a long time," Don reminded him.

Joe nodded. "This I know. And I know the reason: some of you want to bring the heads of the gangs into The Commission and some of you don't."

"Times have changed, Joe. These gangs are getting too powerful to ignore," Malone said. "We can go to war with them, sure... But the question is, how much are we willing to lose in order to win?" Malone looked each and every one of them in the eye.

"Fuck the gangs right now, it's irrelevant to the business at hand. I want this bitch ass nigga, Othello! That's why we are gathered. That's the business we are here to discuss. Not some deeper theological issue. Othello. I want his head here on the table in front of me," Rome growled. Rome was a hot head. His temper was reflected in his clan. Joe knew it was going to be a problem. He could only hope that today wasn't the day.

"I sympathize with your loss, Rome. You know I do. Family is family. You too, Don and Malone. Big L was my friend as well. But it is important to remember a wise man never moves out of emotion. If your mother is butchered in front of you and you are covered in her blood, you never lose your head, because if you do, the cops gun you down and then the enemy has already won twice over," Joe jeweled him.

Rome reluctantly agreed.

Joe continued.

"We will not be provoked into rash action. This is what men like Othello and his backer are expecting."

"Backer?" Malik echoed, not hiding his confusion.

Joe looked over at him and smiled. "Isn't it obvious? He is not working alone. Don't you see what he's doing?" He gave them a moment to catch up. "Rome, he killed some of your best men. Don, he wiped out arguably your best hitters. Malone, you lost more than Big L in that fire. Hell, no denying we all did. Each one of us had strong pieces of our team at that club. He's taking out our armies, striking at our force. But how does he know where to strike? That's one question among many. Another is how does he know when to hit? I'll tell you, if you haven't worked it out for yourself already. It's because one of us is backing him."

Silence.

Pin drop.

Heads swiveled from face to face, studying, judging, disbelieving. They tried to wrap their minds around Joe's words. It made zero sense to them on one level. Who could commit such betrayal? But on another level, it made far too much sense. It was all about splintering power.

"What are you saying, Joe?" Malone questioned.

"Fuck me, Malone. It's not rocket science. Someone at this table, one of you, or maybe even two of you, has decided to weaken the clans. To guarantee an advantage when they make their move to take over The Commission."

"You said, 'maybe even two of you,' as if you couldn't be one of the guilty," Malik spat.

Joe laughed at that. "No offense to your genius, Malik, but riddle me this: why would I *want* to take over The Commission? Look at me. Take a good look. Want me to tell you what you see? You see the Commissioner! I don't need to take over what I already own."

"But we've all taken losses, in that club fire. You said that yourself," Don reminded him.

"Foot soldiers get sacrificed in every war," Joe countered.

"So, you think this is all about you?" Malik asked, voice dripping with derision. "Are you that arrogant? Scratch that, of course you are."

Joe rose from the table, the legs of his chair dragging back on the floor. Very slowly, and very deliberately, he buttoned his suit jacket and looked around the room. Judging them one and all.

"Othello is not the enemy. He never was. Never will be. The enemy... is one of our own... I already know who. Goodnight, gentlemen." Joe inclined his head in a subtle nod, then walked out, leaving The Commission in shocked silence.

Does he really know?

That was the question in every man's mind as Joe walked out.

Aphrodite got out of the steaming shower feeling refreshed.

Not that she'd had a particularly hard day. It was just more of the same: engagements, her luncheons and fundraisers. An outsider would have been forgiven for thinking she was the wife of a politician, not the biggest gangsta in the city.

"The Game *is* politics," her husband Joe had told her so many times, she could hear it through the shower spray. Yes, it is a game, *absofuckinlutely*, and she played it well.

She walked into the bedroom, still wet from her shower. She liked to drip dry. There was nothing quite like the feel of the chill air against her skin as it prickled into goosebumps. She stopped in front of the mirror. She posed hand on her hip, turning to see her profile from both sides. Then, because she was proud of it, her shapely ass from the back. She smiled to herself. Despite having had two grown kids, Aphrodite Hamlet was still a beautiful woman, no matter whose eye was beholding. Her body was forged from pure Columbian gold, with long jet black hair that made her look like she could've been any ethnicity or all of them. Her beauty wasn't merely timeless, it was universal. And she knew it.

"Damn, after all these years, coming home to a naked wife still makes my night," Joe said as he came through the door.

Aphrodite giggled as she turned and stepped into his embrace. She wrapped her arms around his neck.

"Your reward for still being the finest man I ever seen," she replied, tonguing him down with a wet sloppy hello.

"Even finer than Freddie Lucas?" He quipped.

"Who?" She smirked, turning away and heading over to her vanity table.

Joe slapped her hard on the ass, making her jump and laugh.

"You know exactly who Freddie is."

"*Was*," she emphasized, "Besides, you had your nose all up Rita Jackson's ass, so what was a girl to do?"

"Rita?" He laughed. "Please, that ho's pussy shoulda been a sneaker it was so ran through."

"And you were the chief track star! Don't you waste your breath lying to me. I know you better than you know yourself."

They laughed together, reminiscing about simpler times.

Aphrodite could see the concern under his laughter though.

"How did it go?"

Joe shrugged as he took off his tie and began to unbutton his shirt. "As well as could be expected. Everybody's calling for blood, but somebody is already wrist-deep in it."

Aphrodite turned around on the stool and looked at him. Her nostrils flared as she breathed in. "You still think it's someone in The Commission?"

"I know it is... I just haven't figured out who yet. But it's only a matter of time. They think I know, so whoever it is, they are going to slip... and I'll be waiting for them when they do."

"From what you tell me, this Othello seems to be a smart man."

"More like a puppet for one. I just can't get his name out of my mind. Othello Moore... Othello Moore. Doesn't it sound familiar?'

Aphrodite shrugged. She crossed the room towards him. "If it is, it'll come to you. You know what they say, stop thinking about it, and it'll come."

Joe grunted a half reply. His mind was a million miles away.

Aphrodite came over and climbed on his lap. "I must be losing my touch. Used to be, naked was all you needed."

Joe licked her whole body with a lustful gaze rougher than any tongue, then began to kiss along the side of her neck. "Baby, you haven't lost a thing, except your inhibitions."

"So true," she agreed, as she allowed his caresses to take her to that place she loved the most.

Joe laid Aphrodite down on the bed, and with hungry hands, eased her legs open for him. Her pussy was so hot and wet, as soon as he laid her down she was fingering her own clit.

"Sssssssssssshit, this pussy is on fire."

Joe pulled out his long, fat dick, gripping it at the base. It was so hard it was throbbing in his fist. He pulled Aphrodite to the edge of the bed by her ankles, cocked them over his shoulders and began to rub his dick up against her lips, teasing her clit with slow steady strokes across it. She sucked in her breath, "Don't tease me, Daddy." Only tease might have lasted a full five seconds before the serpent hiss was done.

The penetration of his enlarged bell head always made her pussy milk with the anticipation of the long, thick shaft to follow.

Always.

Joe's nails dug into her left ankle. He ran his tongue over her toes before sucking each one, lingering. He slid his dick in half-way. Waited, knowing she would press up against him, eager to take it all. Then began slow stroking her, working himself deeper and deeper into her tight pussy.

"Give me all this dick," Aphrodite purred, gripping the sheets and arching her back to meet his every thrust.

Joe didn't hesitate to oblige, even though his full length made her scream out in painful pleasure.

Her song was so sweet, Joe still had to fight the urge to cum on the spot, but he mastered the moment, savoring it as he long dicked her until he hit the creamy center and her candy rain coated his dick from head to balls. Bliss.

"Turn over," he told her.

Aphrodite bit her bottom lip, giving him a sexy smirk as she rolled onto her belly, then rising onto her knees as she buried her face down in the pillow.

"This how you want it, baby?" She asked, offering her ass up.

"Hell yeah," he grunted, sliding in from the back, gripping and spreading her cheeks and watching himself fucking her pretty pink pussy raw.

Aphrodite groaned, moaned, and finally screamed, tossing her head wildly as Joe tormented her g-spot with long strokes that made her cum back to back.

But even in the midst of her sexual abandon, she was still in control, a fact she proved the moment she had had enough. She worked her inner muscles, pulling Joe's dick and releasing it just long enough to re-grip it at the base. The move always fucked Joe, just like any of her other lovers, causing him to cum with hard, long spurts.

"Damn," one word. It was all Joe could say.

Breathing hard, he collapsed onto the bed beside her.

Aphrodite rested her head on his chest.

She smiled softly, all butter-wouldn't melt innocence. "Yep," she snickered, "I still got it."

Then they both laughed.

"Oh god, yes you do. Yes you fucking do."

"Keep your left up Joe. Your left, damn it. Up!" Dusty yelled, pounding the edge of the boxing ring with his fist.

Joe danced on his toes, watching the young Cuban boxer cautiously. He may have been a heavyweight, but Joe moved with the grace of a young Ali. Not prime Ali, raw Cassius Clay. The Cuban launched a jab. It was the kind of punch that, if it landed, would have felt like walking into a door. Joe easily dipped, rolling with the momentum. Then, on the balls of his feet, countered with a hard right hook that smashed into the Cuban's ribs.

He spat his mouthpiece out.

"Wait!" The ref barked, giving the Cuban a chance to kneel and retrieve it, then, shaking himself off, put the mouthpiece back in. He banged his gloves together, dancing around trying to sell the lie that it was nothing as he regrouped for another attack.

Joe had to give it to the man. No matter what he gave, the bastard just kept coming. He didn't know when he was beaten.

"The left, Joe! What the hell are you *doing*?" Dusty screamed his frustration loud enough that everyone in the arena could hear it.

Joe smiled to himself.

He switched to southpaw as the Cuban came in with a flurry, meeting it head on. The abrupt switch threw his opponent off balance. It was as simple as that. Joe slipped a right cross, but that was never the punch he intended to hurt him with. It was all about the combo. He sent an upper cut, crashing straight up the Cuban's chimney and rang his bell like the carnival game.

The Cuban staggered, dropped his right, dazed and trying to shake it off.

Joe capitalized.

Another big punch.

This one went straight down the pipe. Joe's glove crushed the Cuban's nose, breaking it. It knocked the guy out cold, still on his feet. The ropes were the only thing that stopped the Cuban from falling. They propped him up like a dope fiend against an alley wall. Joe went in for the kill, but before he could do any serious (and probably irreparable) damage, the ref stepped in, hugging the Cuban with one arm and waving the fight finished with the other.

Dusty quickly split the ropes and was in on the canvas, embracing Joe.

"You did it, you son of a bitch, you *did* it!" Dusty yelled joyously in his ear.

Joe couldn't do anything but smile.

He was young, fast, strong and pretty. He had a face for fame.

The next stop was Atlantic City and a shot at the belt. It was written in the stars.

Or so he thought.

Joe showered, lathering up. He was more than just the man of the hour. He was the man of *life*. Everything was fucking *good*.

He had just met the stone cold baddest bitch he'd ever laid eyes on. It was the start of something.

"My name is Aphrodite..." She'd told him, her beauty radiating like the moon at night, blinding like the shine on fool's gold.

He lathered up, singing at the top of his lungs. His voice was more like the roar of a proud lion than the timbre of an alto.

He didn't give a shit.

He dressed and walked out of there, gator shoes gleaming, toward the front of the locker room.

His trainer, Dusty waited for him.

"Frank wants to see you."

One look at Dusty's expression was enough to know something was off.

He pressed, wanting the word from his man before he went in there, but Dusty couldn't look him in the eye when he said, "Nothing," which said plenty. He was lying.

Joe exited the back of the arena. Not rushing, but walking with the swagger of someone who owned the place.

The concrete stairwell echoed with his soft shoe shuffle as he tapped his way down to the basement level. He opened the door, and walked through to the underground parking lot.

Frank Myers was waiting for him in his Lincoln Continental.

Frank was one of the founding fathers of the earliest national Commissions, working under the wing of the infamous Frank Lucas. He was a smooth Smokey Robinson dude, but it was a lethal mistake to confuse him with any pretty boy singer. The only thing pretty about Frank was his murder game when provoked. Death was poetry in motion.

Two of Frank's bodyguards stood outside the car, waiting for Joe to approach.

They opened the door for him.

The nearest inclined his head. He didn't need words to get their message across.

He got in the car.

The two bodyguards joined him in the backseat.

Frank started the engine and pulled off.

"Congratulations, youngblood. Goddamn, you're a beast in that ring, boy," Frank lauded, handing Joe a cigar.

He took it, but it didn't make sense. Frank knew he didn't smoke. "What's this?"

Frank smirked, "It's a Cuban, sonny. You smoke it the same way you smoked that Cuban in the ring."

Three of the four men in the car laughed like it was the funniest thing a man had ever said.

Joe relaxed enough to take the edge off.

"Listen, I want to tell you I'm proud of you, youngblood. I gotta be straight, when Dusty asked me to invest in you, I didn't think you had it in you. Sure, you had talent, but you were so angry, all the time filled with this rage. I didn't think you could wrap your head around the rules. Figured you'd end up on your ass more times than not. But fuck me, you proved me wrong, kiddo. No denying it, you *should* be the champ," Frank congratulated him, but Joe fixated on the *should* not *will*. There was something ominous about the compliment.

"I will be champ," Joe corrected him.

Frank just smiled that sly smile and kept his eye on the road for a beat, then said, "Tell me something, Joe, if you weren't fighting, what would you be doing? Think about it seriously for a second, then give me your honest answer."

"Don't need to think. Dead," Joe replied. Frank looked at him. "When Dusty found me, man, I was fucked up on that shit. I was shooting in any part of me still alive enough to kill. That's the truth. Cold. Bitter. But he saw something in me I didn't see in myself. So, ain't no doubt. Without fighting, without Dusty, I woulda been dead a long time ago."

"Yeah, sure, but there's more to life than just fighting."

"Life is a fight," Joe shot right back, like it was the only answer he knew.

They rode in silence for moment before Frank asked another question. "You ever heard of Fat Paulie Scarlucci?"

"Can't say that I have," Joe admitted.

"He's a lot like me, you could say... He backs fighters just like I do. Got an eye for talent. Difference is, he's backed by the Columbo crime family.... He's got a fighter named Sonny Amato..."

Joe cut him off. "Pretty Boy Amato. The fuck? That's who I'm fighting for the belt."

Frank looked at Joe, and maybe just maybe there was sadness in his eyes when he said, "But you ain't gonna win."

Joe's whole body tensed up with the threat of an explosion.

"What the hell do you mean? Pretty Boy can't beat me. I'm ten times the fighter that fuck is..."

"He don't have to beat you, youngblood. This shit's bigger

than you. It's bigger than me. The fix is in. You gotta throw the fight," Frank said grimly.

Joe launched himself across the car and grabbed Frank by the collar, hauling him back in the seat, which caused the Lincoln to veer across the road and damn near slam into a parked car, before it came to a screeching halt in the middle of the street.

Both of Frank's bodyguards had their guns to Joe's head.

Joe had Frank pinned in the driver's seat.

This wasn't ending well.

"Hey! Hey! Put the guns down! Now!" Frank bellowed, looking Joe in the eyes. He knew the kid, knew him well enough to know there wasn't any real danger here. There was zero anger in Joe's eyes, just pain, fear and betrayal.

Reluctantly, the bodyguards re-tucked their guns and sat back on their haunches, ready to explode into murderous action if their boss gave the word.

Frank stared Joe down. "Gonna give you one piece of advice kid, do with it what you will. Either kill me or get your goddamn hands off me."

Slowly, Joe uncollared Frank and sat back.

It was then he realized Frank had him the whole time. The older man had a small .32 automatic pointed at Joe's stomach. It woulda packed enough punch to put an end to any championship dreams. And then some.

"Now listen, youngblood, you might not believe me, but I understand how you feel. But that only buys so much forgiveness. You *ever* put your hands on me, I'll blow you and your mama's brains out and that's flat, got me?"

"Man, you can't do this to me... That fight is my shot! My *only* shot! You take that away... fuck... you might as well blow my goddamn brains out," Joe said, barely holding the tears in check.

"Don't be a fuckin' idiot, Joe. I'd rather cut your hands off, 'cause your brain's the best thing you got. Yeah, I'll give it to you straight, you're good, you really are, but you ain't the best. Maybe you could be a champ for a while, wear the belt for a few fights, but when the lights go out and you're old and can't stop shaking because you took too many blows to the head, then what? Who will you be then? I seen the future, kid. I can tell you. You won't wanna hear it, but it's the God's honest truth... A washed up has-been. Fame and glory is for bitches and birds and false gods inse-cure enough to *crave* worship. Now, let me school you, Joe. This is today's lesson. Men chase power. Power ain't in the fists. It's in the words of the man who can stop them."

He let his words settle in before continuing.

"I like you, youngblood, I really fuckin' do. That's why you ain't dead now. It's why I'm giving you an opportunity. Be the man powerful enough to take this shot from another kid with big dreams. Trust me, and I'm going to make you so powerful no one will be able to take another shot from you ever again. But every man needs to make his own choice, so if you ain't interested," Frank reached into his inside pocket and pulled a baggie of heroin, then tossed it onto Joe's lap, "then go find you a vein and blow your own brains out."

Joe looked down at the baggie.

He picked it up.

Part of him damn near sang out with joy at the sight of it, wanting that taste of ultimate life right before death, but that was the part of him he'd left behind. The better part of him, the stronger part of him, still wanted to look this world in the eyes and impose his will on it. He tossed the baggie out the window.

"I'm listening."

Frank smiled approvingly. "Good. You gonna be alright. But first, I gotta know if I can trust you. So, serious question: you ever killed somebody before?"

"No."

"Can you?"

"If I had to."

"What if you just want to," Frank smirked, "Or, more accurately, because I want you to? You see, I've got a problem, a problem I need you to solve. There's a guy, a bar owner. He owes me some money... actually a lot of money. The kind of money only blood can pay back. He thinks he doesn't have to pay. He's not very bright. Now, I could handle this myself, but I would appreciate if you do this little thing for me. Believe me, appreciation from a man like me will go a long way."

"Who is he?"

———

"Who is he?"

Joe woke up with a start; those three words still echoing in his head.

"Baby, what's wrong?" Aphrodite questioned, sitting up beside him. She ran her hand across his chest, like her touch could ease his tormented soul. There was no magic in her hands, not this kind of magic, at least.

"I... know who he is."

"Who is?"

"Othello." Joe looked at her, but he wasn't seeing her. He was still face to face with the past. "I killed his father."

———

Othello laid back, propped up against his headboard, reading a book by the light of the rising sun. Milk walked by, half asleep as she headed for the bathroom.

She walked by his open door and saw he was already up.

"Reading early in the morning? What are you, a towel head?" She asked.

He looked up to see her standing there, still butt ass naked, with curves so dangerous they should have warning signs.

"Naw, just a habit I picked up in prison. Good way to start any day."

She sauntered in and sat on the edge of the bed, one leg tucked under her.

She read the title.

"*The Art of War*? What is that, an urban novel?" She questioned, sounding every bit like a dumb blond from the ghetto.

Othello looked at her. He could have been a bastard, instead he replied patiently, "It's my Book of Life. It teaches you how to defeat your enemies."

"Oh," she responded, then cocked her head to the side, as though regarding him in a new light. "You're different. I've never known gangstas that read. Hell, most gangstas don't even get up this early."

He laughed.

"Most gangstas ain't gangstas."

"Ain't that the truth." Her face got serious for a moment. "Can I ask you something?"

"Yeah."

"Why did you let us come with y'all? I mean, you gave us that money and brought us back to your spot, knowing what you did. Why?"

Othello put the book down and met her gaze.

"Because real recognize real and I respect realness. Y'all bitches held it down like real bitches should, so you were due a reward. The party part, that wasn't my idea if you remember, but I let you come anyway because of what I just said."

Milk nodded.

"You know, you're like a breath of fresh air. All these so-called players and hustlers out here, a bitch would be a fool not to fuck with realness when she saw it, too."

"It's like Sun Tzu says in this book: *know yourself*. If you know yourself and you know the enemy, you need not fear the results

35

of a hundred battles. But if you only know yourself and not the enemy..."

"For every victory gained, you will suffer a defeat," Milk said, finishing the quote word for word, then smiled knowingly.

Othello barked out a deep laugh.

"Damn Ma! You fucked me up with that!"

Milk shrugged. "Most men don't want a smart bitch in their bed."

"But yet they want brains, huh?"

They laughed at the irony.

"I'm more than meets the eye."

Othello looked her up and down, his eyes fixated on the camel toe sticking out between her legs like a pout. "That you are. Shit, it's hard for a nigga to get past the eye, yo."

"A smart woman is a dangerous woman," she remarked.

"And just the type of woman I need on my team," he added.

She bit her bottom lip, then ran her fingers up his shin. "Is that *all* you need?"

She was right on time for that morning hard dick and she knew it.

Othello peeped her game from the minute she made her advance. She knew he was the leader of a crew destined for the top, and she wanted to hitch a ride. That was just fine with him. A white bitch can slide into places a black bitch can't. Plain and simple. So if she wanted to seal the deal with a mouthful of his dick, then he didn't mind giving her what she wanted.

Milk didn't hesitate once she saw the bulge growing in his boxers.

She reached in through the slit and pulled his dick out, massaging it from balls to head with skillful fingers, before running her tongue along the ridge of his dickhead.

"Damn your dick is sweet. You must drink a lot of pineapple juice," she remarked between slurps.

"Call me black fruit punch," he cracked.

She took his whole dick in her mouth, while she popped her own pussy with two fingers. The more she fucked herself, the sloppier she topped him off.

Othello grabbed a handful of her hair and face fucked her until he felt like he was about to cum.

When he did, he pulled out at the last minute and covered her face in his nut. Busting off in her face made her cum hard as hell. It was a beautiful moment.

Othello ran his dick around her mouth and smirked as he remarked, "Welcome to the team."

Adonis got out of his blue Bentley drop-top Continental, looking GQ in his Balman outfit. He had his favorite burgundy butter leather jacket on, and, doing this whole David Caruso thing, threw on his reflector Aviator shades as he looked around the street before he crossed to the cafe.

It was a quaint little spot, two cities away, well outside of the Commission's territory. A safe place for what was going to be a dangerous liaison. The cafe itself had sidewalk seating, and more interestingly, a terrace on the second floor that provided additional outside ambiance.

Devante was waiting for him up there.

As soon as he came into view, the other man's face broke into a flirtatious, *come here and fuck me* grin. Looking at Devante, there was no doubting who was the bottom in their little fuck game. The boy was just naturally feminine, as if God himself had willed this perfect androgyny. His cinnamon brown skin and piercing green eyes gave him a feline feel that was reminiscent of a more feminine Bruno Mars.

Devante stood, leaning in to give Adonis a hug, but Adonis extended his hand for a shake and a half gangsta hug instead.

Pure masculinity. The machismo of the greeting was mocked by Devante's fevered whisper in his ear as they embraced.

"I smell it on you... that cologne... you know it drives me wild. Damn I just wanna fuck you... right here, right now." Adonis chuckled self-consciously as he sat down.

"Yo chill, aiight?" He looked around, scoping out the place.

"My bad, I forgot we're gangstas, yo," Devante said, using an exaggerated street accent to make his point.

Adonis sighed. "Don't start."

"We're already running halfway across the state just to have fucking lunch, and you still wanna be on this homo-thug shit? Man, I am tired."

Adonis began to say something, but the waitress's arrival silenced him.

She was a good looking red-headed white girl. Her smile spread all over Adonis. He was used to the reaction. These pretty little things had their own code, but it always broke down to the same thing: he could get it.

"Whatever you want is on the house," she told him, acting like Devante wasn't there.

Devante wasn't gonna let it go. "Bitch breeze, that's my dick."

The waitress turned redder than her hair. "Oh my God, I didn't know. I'm so sorry," she said, then looking at Adonis one last time said, "Still, lucky you."

She took their order.

"Really?" Adonis remarked, cranked up.

"*Really*?" Devante echoed, but laced with deeper frustration. "You're just gonna flirt with some woman right in my face? And fuck me, look at your hand, you've got your fucking engagement ring on. You know what, fuck this shit," Devante got up from the table.

Adonis grabbed his wrist. "Please. Don't go."

Devante was crying. The tears ran down his cheek.

"No Adonis, this shit is crazy. You're not going to keep treating me like this. I'm not gonna let you."

"I'm sorry."

A beat.

"I am."

Devante folded his arms over his chest. He made no move to wipe the tears from his cheek.

"Take it off."

"What?"

"The ring. I'm not sitting back down until you take it off."

Adonis looked at him, seeing his resolve. Not wanting to make more of a scene, he took the ring off and slipped it in his pocket.

Devante sat down, smiling triumphantly.

Adonis chuckled.

"You're such a queen."

"And don't pretend you don't love it. It serves you right anyway. That ring is like waving red in front of a bull."

"It's just a ring. Means nothing to me. *She* means nothing to me. But my family."

"Your family? What about my family?! Uncle Malik thinks he's the gangsta Bin Laden. If he knew I was gay, he'd probably kill me himself."

The waitress returned with their orders and more heartfelt apologies before she bustled off and left them to it.

Adonis sipped his wine. It was decent. Not great.

"We have to keep up appearances, okay?"

"But I don't have to like it. You going to marry her?"

Adonis sighed.

"When my father retires, he's going to make me head of the family, which will make me head of the clan. That means Commissioner of The Commission. I'll be the most powerful man in the city. You know what that means? When that happens I'll be free to be who I want to be. Then Bianca can kiss my bright shiny ring. If she won't give me a divorce, I'll just have the bitch killed," Adonis said. It might have been a joke. It might not.

"Please Adonis, you're no killer. You faint over nose bleeds."

"I ain't no killa, but don't push me," Adonis rapped playfully, using bass in his tone like Tupac.

"And if you say the line about pussy, I'll slap your face," Devante rolled his eyes.

"Regardless, when it all plays out we will be together. Your uncle won't have a choice but to let you be with me. I'll be his boss."

It sounded so reasonable. Like it might actually work.

"You sound so gangsta when you talk like that. You know it turns me on," Devante said, leaning forward across the table top.

"Yeah?"

He nodded, giving him that look that said it all.

Adonis downed his drink. "Go to bathroom. I'll meet you there in a minute."

"You are so bad."

But that wasn't a no. Devante couldn't get up fast enough.

As soon as he was out of sight, Adonis pulled out his iPhone and made a call.

"I'll be there in an hour," he said, then killed the call and pocketed the phone. It took less than five seconds.

When Adonis entered the bathroom, he saw a white guy hunched over the sink, washing his hands like he was Pontius fucking Pilate. *Scrub scrub scrub.* They nodded polite acknowledgments, then the white guy exited.

As soon as the door closed behind him, Adonis headed straight to the one stall with its door closed.

He pushed in.

Devante was in there naked from the waist down, kneeling on the toilet, so his feet wouldn't be seen underneath the stall, waiting for him to push in.

"And what's behind door number one, contestant?"

Adonis wasted no time, dropping his pants and sliding on the condom's ridges down the length of his shaft before he slid deep inside that ass with the grunt that went so far beyond anticipation.

"Ohhh, don't... yes... fuck yes..." Devante groaned with each stroke, leaning back against Adonis' muscular chest, reaching up and around to link his fingers around the back of his neck.

Adonis gripped him by the front of his thighs and plowed, nothing tender about the jackhammer thrusts. Devante couldn't help himself. He cried out. Adonis covered his mouth, muffling his pleasure. Even so, his guttural moans echoed in the acoustics of the bathroom.

Neither one of them cared.

Right then, it was only them; their world, their own zone.

"Oh, I've missed you," Devante said, taking him deeper. His cock slapped against his stomach. Hard. Dripping.

"I've missed you, too," Adonis whispered hoarsely in his ear.

He felt Adonis bust, filling the condom inside of him.

"Fuck, that was intense. I'm seeing stars," Devante giggled, breathlessly.

"You are my star," Adonis charmed.

When they came out of the cafe, Devante was glowing like a neon sign.

He didn't give a shit about the machismo and fake masculinity as they shook hands, men saying see you around. The look on Devante's face was unmistakable. It was the look of a man in love.

It was a look that would come back to haunt Adonis.

In a car across the street someone fired off pictures at a furious rate, framing them dead center.

Mac pulled into the parking lot of the hair salon.

His wife Kandi saw him arrive.

She walked out to meet him.

Watching her strut, he couldn't help but smile. She had that Nia Long, bow-legged stride that stopped men in their tracks. And who could blame them? Sometimes you just had to admire black beauty in motion. She even favored Nia Long in her prime, except she sported the page boy style crop-cut with sideburns as sharp as daggers, frosted at the tips. Kandi was one of the realest chicks he'd ever met, which was why he hadn't hesitated to put a ring on her finger.

She got in the car and gave him a juicy kiss before he pulled off.

"I like your doobie," he remarked.

"I told that bitch I wanted platinum highlights. I don't like *these*," Kandi huffed, pulling out a blunt and lighting it up.

"You don't like *her*," he quipped.

"That, too."

They both laughed.

"The bitch just think she got all the sense. You know how it is. The only reason I still fuck with her is because she's the best in town," Kandi said, passing the blunt to Mac to take a hit. Then, adding as an afterthought, "That ballplaya called me."

He knew exactly who she was talking about.

They never used names when they discussed business.

"What he say?" Mac questioned, hitting the blunt then passing it back.

Kandi sucked her teeth dismissively.

"Nothing, really. He just be name-dropping, talking about this celeb and that celeb, NBA shit, like I'm supposed to be impressed. But I play along like, oh *forrealllllll*?" Her voice went as fake as a porn star's orgasm. They laughed at his lameness. "Anyway, he wanna get together Friday after the game."

"Friday's no good."

Kandi looked at him.

"What? Baby, I been workin' on this nigga for too long."

Mac shook his head. "Othello's got a meeting with the

Commission. We about to put the icing on these niggas' cakes."

She nodded. Understanding, but what came out of her mouth was raw. "Then I'll handle the ballplayer and you handle Othello's balls." Any other bitch and Mac would've backhanded blood from her goddamn mouth.

"Fuck you just say?"

"No, what did *you* just say? Ever since this black ass muhfucka been home it's been Othello this and Othello that, like you ain't a boss no more, Mac."

"Bitch, stay in your lane! I been a boss. When the smoke clears, we'll both have a seat on The Commission! Trust me, this shit is about to put us on top."

"You say, but the way I see it, it's about to put Othello on top," Kandi shot right back.

"Look, the nigga got a vision, and that's my man."

Kandi groaned, like she had heard it a million times before. "Here you go with that loyalty bullshit."

"Loyalty ain't bullshit!"

Kandi shook her head.

"Look babe, I love you to death, but you know like I know that no man can be totally loyal to another man, without becoming less of a man."

Mac looked at her, like, "How you figure that?"

"Because sooner or later, they're gonna want to go in separate directions. Then what? Who do you follow? His or yours?"

"Mine," Mac responded without hesitation.

"Then your loyalty is only a matter of degrees. Here's some truth: Every man wants to be king, but there's only one crown." Point made.

Mac sat back and let her words sink in, but seeing his brow still furrowed with confusion, she added, "Let me ask you something: Do you think Othello would fuck me if he had the chance?"

The mere thought was enough to spark something primal in

Mac; it wasn't what she said, but how she said it.

"What the hell are you talkin' about, Kandi?"

Kandi smirked.

"I'm just saying, if he was to try and kick it to me, and me and you was on one of our outs and shit, and I was lonely..." she let her voice trial off, knowing his mind would fill in the blanks.

Mac looked at her.

"Ay yo, Kandi, if you got somethin' to say, you best say it. You tryin' to tell me you fucked O? That it?"

She laughed, because her feminine wiles wanted to toy with him by making him seem like the silly one.

"Really? You're *really* going to ask me that? I'm being hypothetical."

"Fuck hypothetical! Did you?"

"No boy, okay? Damn!" She sighed an exaggerated huff. She knew it was time to let it go. Besides, she'd planted the seed sufficiently deep in the fertile soil of his emotional subconscious. His insecurities would do the rest.

Mac eyed her for a minute, his mind a collage of unwanted images.

She started to say something, when her attention was caught by the blur of a car driving by in the opposite direction.

"Oh hell no! Make a U, make a U!!" She damn near screamed.

"What up?" He asked, while at the same time looking for a break in traffic to turn around.

"That's that bitch Toni! I'ma kill that bitch if she ain't got my money!" Kandi barked.

Mac was always down to put in work, especially when it came to her.

The two of them together were like Bonnie and Clyde.

Finally, he saw an opening, and U'd the car like a stunt driver.

Rubber screaming, he dipped, dodged and ran a yellow light before catching up with the burgundy Honda in a McDonald's drive thru.

"Block her ass in!" Kandi hissed, as she jumped out of the car.

Mac followed her, snatching the nine off his waistline as he headed toward the passenger side of the car. He saw the head of what looked like a dude in the passenger seat.

"Yes, may I take your order?' A woman's voice crackled through the static of the order box.

"Yeah," not that she got to say much else beyond that first syllable. Kandi punched Toni dead in the mouth.

"Bitch where my goddamn money!" Kandi grabbed a fistful of Toni's hair and dragged her out of the car window, kicking and screaming.

"What the fuck?" The dude exclaimed, reaching for the car handle like he was about to be stupid and try and do something. The kiss of cold steel against his temple sent a tingle down his spine that froze his ass in his seat and saved his life. For now.

"Just chill, playa. Let them handle they biz," Mac told him calmly.

"Wait! Help! I'm sorry!" Toni screeched, when she found herself being stomped on the curb of the drive thru.

"Where the fuck is my money?"

"I'll get it, Kandi, I swear!"

"Get it means you ain't got it!" Kandi riffed, punctuating her verbs with kicks.

She grabbed the Toni by the hair and yanked her head back, forcing Toni to look into her face.

"Bitch, I don't give a fuck if you gotta sell a kidney, a kid or your stank ass pussy. If you ain't got by next week, you one dead bitch."

All Toni could do was nod, dazed, blood dripping from her nose. There was more of it smeared across her face.

The woman's voice came through the order box again. "Hello? I can't understand yelling. The speaker distorts. Can I take your order?"

"Napkins," Kandi told the speaker. "Plenty of napkins."

3

"Ready? Big smiles, and..." the photographer called out right before snapping the picture. It was going to end up in the leisure section of the newspaper.

Mona, standing between Joe and Aphrodite, cut the red ribbon in front of her new theater. Adonis was there with his fiancée, Bianca Davenport, a prissy Gabrielle Union lookalike from a very powerful political family.

Once the pictures had been taken, Mona turned to Joe, all smiles, and gave him a big hug. "Thank you, Daddy! I love it!" She gushed.

Joe chuckled, loving the feeling of his babygirl in his arms. It reminded him of much simpler times. "Thank yourself. This theater is an investment, and I believe in you enough to invest," he winked.

"I'm so proud of you," Aphrodite beamed, hugging her daughter.

It was the perfect picture of a happy, content, normal family.

"Thank you too, Mama, for helping Daddy make up his mind," Mona cracked.

They shared a laugh, heading inside hand-in-hand to join the rest of the guests.

The theater itself was a work of art. The outer facade conjured up images of ancient Roman structures, with its Doric columns and wide stone steps that narrowed as they reached a set of double doors.

Inside, there were three separate theaters, each seating over five hundred people.

In the back, there were several classrooms to teach kids dancing and acting, as well as a recording studio for music. It was a good place.

Mona basked in the spotlight, taking picture after picture, reveling in the praise and the congratulations. Everyone wanted to be a part of her initiative. It was hot, and she was loving every minute of it.

She was a beautiful woman who knew how to work a room.

She was the real jewel in her father's crown.

"Daddy, I can't tell you enough how much I appreciate this. All of it. I won't let you down," she vowed, when she got a minute to breathe between interviews.

Joe kissed her on the forehead.

"You never do, kiddo."

Mona started to say something, but saw David Bennett looking around. He was carrying an ostentatious bunch of flowers. She turned to Joe.

"Daddy..." she began, with reproach in her tone.

Joe shrugged. "It's a public event."

She narrowed her eyes.

"Okay, maybe I did mention it to him," he admitted.

"I told you, I don't want David. He's corny."

"Corny's good. Corny is pre-med. Corny is the white picket fences. Corny is..."

"Not for me," she giggled. "I want a guy with... swag."

"Yeah. Not for you. Street niggas ain't for you, babygirl. Street niggas will only break your heart and wind up getting themselves killed and you holding the baby."

"Mommy seems to have done pretty well," she parried.

Joe laughed.

"Trust me, I'm the exception," he bragged, brushing imaginary lint from his shoulder.

Mona laughed.

"Well, I'm me. Besides, I'm nothing if not Daddy's Little Girl."

"And don't forget it," he playfully scolded her.

David approached through the crowd, all smiles.

"Hello, Mr. Hamlet. Thanks for inviting me."

Mona looked at her father, who smiled, deliberately avoiding her stare as he shook David's hand. David turned to Mona. It was clear to anyone with eyes that the poor boy was totally in love. "Hi, Mona. Congratulations. You look beautiful."

"Congratulations for looking beautiful?" Mona teased, deliberately putting him on the back foot.

David stammered, "I, um, I meant the theater."

"Oh, the *theater* is beautiful," she smirked.

David held out the flowers. "I'm shutting up now."

She laughed.

"I'll leave you two alone," Joe said, and made his exit.

"I was just teasing you, David," Mona said, taking them from him. "The flowers are beautiful."

"At least I got something right, huh?"

"I'm glad you could make it."

"Anything for you."

Mona loved David's smile. It wasn't like he wasn't fine. He bore an uncanny resemblance to Boris Kodjoe. The problem was he just didn't have that edge Mona craved.

"So, what are you doing tonight?"

"I've got plans," Mona replied, looking him in the eyes with a mischievous glint, one he was too nervous to catch.

"Oh," David responded, dejectedly, "Maybe some other time."

Mona giggled. That was something else about David she liked. In the cat and mouse they played, she was the cat, not just the pussy.

"You shouldn't give up so easily, David. A girl likes to feel pursued, desired... chased."

David smiled. "Wait, let me go get my running shoes." Blank stare.

"That was a joke, by the way."

He cringed, dying a little inside.

"I know."

"Where did you have in mind?"

"This new club named Sensation. It just opened."

"Oh yeah, I heard that spot. It's supposed to be banging," Mona remarked.

"So... what do you say?'

"I say it's a date. I'll bring my girlfriend and you can bring a friend."

"Oh... a double date."

Mona gave him a smoldering look. "Don't worry, David, you'll have me to yourself soon enough."

Across the room, Joe approached Adonis. The younger man was admiring an Ernie Banks original hanging outside one of the theaters. "Bianca is a beautiful girl. You did good," Joe complimented.

"Is it her or her last name you're calling beautiful, Pops?" Adonis quipped.

"Both," Joe smirked.

They clinked their glasses in a toast.

Joe glanced around, making sure there were no extra ears, before saying, "I know you've heard about that rock in my shoe."

"Of course."

"What do you think I should do?"

"Honestly?" Adonis knew he was being tested. His life was a non-stop test. Joe liked to see how he would react in any given situation. He looked his father in the eye and replied, "Kill him." Adonis could tell by the way his father smiled that he had failed. Again.

"But then you would never know who was backing him."

"You think someone is backing him? In The Commission?"

"I don't think, son. I know. Remember, on this level of the game, there's always more than meets the eye. Always. If the guy on your left makes a move, it's probably because of the guy on your right. The ripple effect. See, a ripple may be subtle by itself, the kind of little thing you might miss if you ain't looking for it. But typhoons are made up of ripples," Joe jeweled smoothly.

Adonis nodded.

"I've got a lot to learn."

Joe patted him on the shoulder. "Don't worry, you've got a helluva teacher."

They both laughed, father and son. How many families dreamed of going into business together? The boy following the old man in the family business. It was no different when that business was criminal.

"Just pay attention," Joe continued, "I want you to take a team out there and find this Othello. But don't move in on him. Use all our resources, pull up traffic cams, run license plates, do whatever it takes to find this son of a bitch. And when you do, you wait... You watch. We need to learn everything we can, follow me?"

"I got you, Pops," Adonis assured him.

Joe nodded.

"Okay. Now, go take care of that beautiful girl of yours, eh? I expect a lot of grandkids."

Adonis watched Joe walk away, thinking: *I guess Mona better get to work....*

———

"This club is buzzing," Celeste said.

She, Mona, David and his friend Mark walked in.

The club was the size of half a football field and overloaded your senses the second you walked in, with an epileptic hell of flashing lights, pulsating rhythms and waves of heat chased by cool breezes that threw off your internal balance. It was all about opening your mind to the possibilities of the night.

The theme of the club was eroticism and bondage, and it was a feast of subversion and domination for the senses.

The club was filled end to end with topless women in hanging cages, some chained at the wrist to the cage wall, others by the throat, still free to gyrate and grind to the beats suggestively.

On the walls, images from porn flicks were projected, each pulse and flash about driving home the not-so subliminal messages meant to give impetus to everyone's inner demons.

"This place should've been called Club Orgy," Mona giggled, looking around at the people on all sides, openly engaging in all manner of sex acts. It was like nowhere she had ever been.

Had she been with anyone else, the club may have had the same effect on her, but not dear sweet David. He wasn't the type of man to push a woman to the edge of her inhibitions. He waited to be invited.

"What do you want to drink?" David asked her.

"What?!" Mona yelled over the music.

"What do you want to drink!" David repeated louder.

"Patron," she yelled back, "Make it two. One for Celeste."

David and Mark went toward the bar, while the girls took in the sights.

Mona was beginning to see she had brought sand to the beach, seeing all the delectable men. None of them moved her though, they simply tempted her....

Until she saw him.

He and his team moved like a school of sharks in a pond full of guppies. It was almost regal, as if by his mere presence, he owned the club. Hell, he looked like he owned the night itself.

It was right there she knew he was destined for great things.

A man she *needed* to know in every way.

Mona, mesmerized, hadn't realized Celeste had been trying to talk to her.

When she saw she was being ignored, the girl followed Mona's line of sight to the reason why and tutted her disdain.

"He looks like Biggie Smalls," she said with a screwface.

"Hey, I always thought Biggie was sexy," Mona replied, not taking her eyes off him as he swam with his crew into a booth in V.I.P.

Mona didn't see the faces of the other two dudes with him, but she did see the two chicks on either side of him.

"Two girls?" Celeste grunted.

Mona bit her bottom lip thinking about it. "Must have a lot to offer."

David and Mark returned with the drinks.

"Enjoying yourself?" David asked.

Mona took her drink and raised it. "The night is young and so are we."

"I have to go to the bathroom," Celeste lied, eyeing Mona. She didn't wait. She grabbed Mona's hand and led her off. "I say we leave those two lames and get our party on with Baby! Baby!" Celeste cackled as soon as they were out of earshot.

"No," Mona protested weakly, but her hormones were screaming *hell yeah* in defiance. "That would be rude."

"Shit, I'd rather be rude, than be bored," Celeste shot back. "Now let's go get at your mystery man."

Mona froze in her tracks.

"Don't get scared now. The way you were looking at him, ain't no time to be shy."

Mona couldn't deny the truth of her words. But watching and doing were very different monsters. Like the voyeur who got off on watching the killer do the deed. Not the same sickness, but she was definitely attracted to this dark as night mystery man. "I can't," she whined as Celeste dragged her towards her destiny.

"Of course you can, girl. Look, he's got his eye on you, too, see."

When Mona looked up, he was definitely beaming down on her.

"Goddamn, shortie bad," Othello grunted, relaxing in his booth, with Milk and Venus on either side of him and Mac on the outside, keeping his eyes on the crowd. King of the castle.

Cash, on the other hand, had his plate full with the Zoe Kravitz-looking hottie he had hemmed up in the corner, hands halfway up her dress and tongue down her throat.

"I know her from somewhere," Mac remarked, but the music was too loud for Othello to hear him.

"Ay yo, O, I'm out! Bitch say she gotta twin!" Cash cackled with lustful glee, as he gave O and Mac a departing dap.

"Be safe!" Othello yelled after him, his voice barely carrying over the music.

When Cash turned around to leave, Mona saw him. Her heart leapt to her throat. It wasn't because he was fine. It was deeper. Secret deep. Past deep. But Cash never saw her.

"What's wrong?" Celeste asked.

"Cash."

"Cash?"

Mona looked at Celeste, her eyes a reflection of her past. "Cash."

Celeste's eyes widened with understanding. "*That* Cash?"

"*The* Cash," Mona confirmed.

"Daaaaaaaaamn," Celeste cursed.

Othello saw the look. It was quick, and it didn't fully register with him right then as he approached Mona, drink in hand. But later, when things grew complicated and his mind was under the influence of his inner demons—whispered to and fed by an outer demon with devilish wishes and hellish conspiracies—he would remember that look and wonder how he missed it. It spoke volumes. Or it would, rather. But in that moment, all Othello saw was Mona's angelic beauty.

"Excuse me, miss," he spoke as he walked up, all smiles. "I just wanted to wish you a Happy Anniversary."

Mona, still reeling after the specter of the past had dissipated from view, turned to him with a man killer smile, and replied with a confused, "Anniversary?"

Othello smiled.

"Just getting a head start for this time next year."

That brought a smile out of her, but she had sass. "What makes you think you'll last that long?" Mona's sexy smirk was garbed in a hint of challenge.

"I'm not a man to be forgotten."

"Or to be humbled."

"Humility is overrated," he returned, reaching for her hand. " Othello."

She extended hers.

"Mona....Jefferson," she replied, giving him her mother's maiden name, instead of the one that would've changed the whole conversation just as it had done so many times in the past.

Othello kissed her hand like a gentleman.

"And they say chivalry is dead."

"A man just needs someone worth being chivalrous for. Join me?"

"I can't. Sorry."

"Don't be, we'll have our time real soon, and believe me, you're worth the wait. Enjoy your evening," Othello charmed, kissed her hand again, then slipped something into it.

His number.

As he walked away, Mona smiled at the smooth way he had given her his number. Not even Celeste had seen the move.

"Othello," she said to herself, savoring the taste of it on her tongue.

Cash...

As she lay in bed, Mona couldn't help but think of the man who had turned her out. Visions of Othello's suave and debonair style had her anticipating the future, but thoughts of Cash had her fantasizing about the past. And the past was a dangerous landscape. She lay there, in her tank top and pink panties, covers thrown off so the night breeze could caress her skin as her mind and body salivated over *that* night...

That one night when she became a woman.

It had been Mona's eighteenth birthday.

Joe had gotten her a brand new purple Lamborghini truck. She, Celeste and the twins Asia and Ashanti, had gone to Dazzle's and partied like rock stars until three in the morning. All four girls had been drinking, not enough to be wasted, but over the edge of drunk in their youthful lust. And they all looked good. Fierce. Thick and juicy. The wolves howled at their every move. No one wanted the night to end.

"Let's go to the Waffle House," Asia suggested from the back-seat, yelling over Nicki Minaj's music.

"Thugville? Oh hell no," her bougie ass twin protested.

"Hell *yeah* Mona, let's go!" Celeste seconded, in no small part because she couldn't stand Ashanti.

Mona knew if Joe caught her in the hood, he'd have an absolute shit fit, but even though she didn't make a habit of lying to him, she lived by the Golden Rule of the Girl Code: *What Daddy don't know won't hurt him.*

When they got to the Waffle House, the place was jumping with thugs, hood rats, gang bangers and hooligans. The parking lot was packed with fly whips pumping the latest thug anthem.

"I'm not going in," Ashanti huffed.

Mona shrugged. "Suit yourself, but you'll be out here by yourself."

Everyone got out, except Ashanti, but before they could reach the front door, they heard the *CLUNK!* of the car door being slammed and Ash shouting, "Wait for me!"

They laughed at her bluff.

Once inside, their sexy quartet made the men pause and the bitches suck their teeth and reveal their claws. No denying it, they were showstoppers.

At first they didn't notice Cash holding court in the corner booth, but he most definitely noticed them, especially Mona.

He liked the way her low slung hips bounced to the rhythm of her shapely ass. It wasn't overly big, but it was more than a juicy handful and his palms ached just thinking about the caress.

They ordered and even the waitress gave them attitude; it was clear these girls weren't from the hood, because all of their designer gear was top of the line, not knockoffs and none of last year's style, off the sales racks in the outlet mall.

"I'm not eating anything that bitch bring me," Celeste stated, and Mona couldn't blame her, but before she could answer, three dudes walked over to their table. They looked like nothing more than common street niggas. The first one, a Birdman-looking dude, was the leader who spoke for his two chubby partners.

"What's up, pretty girl? What's your name?"

Mona looked at him with a withering stare that said, *get out of my face*, then rolled her eyes and went back to her conversation with Celeste.

"Like I was saying," she continued, flinging a bang of hair out of her face.

"Hold up ma, you ain't gotta be like that. I was just speakin' to you," he chuckled, but his smile barely masked his mounting aggravation.

Mona glance up at him. "Hi," she said sweetly. "Bye."

Her girlfriends laughed.

That only added fuel to the fire.

"Bitch, look here..."

Before he could finish, Mona was up and in his face.

"Who the *fuck* are you calling a bitch, with your busted, run down tired-looking ass?" Half of The Waffle House laughed at the way she bassed on him.

Now, he was on fire.

"Yo, bitch! I'll break yo—" he spat, as he reared back to slap the fire out of her ass, but before he could whip his hand around, someone grabbed his wrist.

"You really wanna do that?" A voice said coldly in his ear.

He frowned up, ready to bark on the culprit, but when he saw who it was, his anger broke like an antique vase in an earthquake.

"Yo Cash, she wit' you?"

Cash had been watching the situation develop.

He liked the way she stuck up for herself, but she knew the nigga wasn't going to let it go until he straightened his face. Cash wasn't going to let that happen.

"My bad, my nigga! Goddamn, I'm sorry. I ain't know."

The dude broke down like a shotgun, like a jackal chest to chest with a lion.

"Yo ma, sit down. I got this," Cash assured Mona.

"No, I got this," she shot right back, chest heaving with indignation.

Cash looked at her.

"I said sit down. I got it," he reiterated, more firmly this time, a hint of a smirk.

Mona liked the way he took charge, but she still wanted to show the lame nigga she wasn't a scared little girl. Even so, she sat.

"My word Cash, I ain't know!"

The dude was damn near in tears.

"Don't apologize to me, nigga, apologize to *her*." Cash said.

If he would've been wearing a hat, he would've been wringing it in his hands, pure supplication. He was the bitch here, and no mistake. "My bad shorty, I mean ma, I mean... Miss. I didn't mean no disrespect."

"You accept?" Cash asked.

She took one look in Cash's eyes and had this flash of understanding: the dude's life was riding on what she said. She felt protected and powerful all at the same time, just like when she was with her father.

"I guess," she replied.

Cash looked at the nigga.

"Why don't you pay for these ladies' meals. It's the least you could do, don't you think?"

Dude wasted no time digging into his pocket like he was breaking himself. The few dollars he had barely covered the bill, but he would've given Cash his cheap 10 karat gold chain if he had to. Anything to pay off the bill. He slithered away.

Cash turned to Mona.

"I know you could've handled it, but you didn't have to," he said, adding, "I'm Cash."

"Cash?" She echoed, skeptically, and folded her arms over her chest.

She looked him up and down.

His appearance lived up to his name.

In his Red Monkey jeans and Coogi hoodie, he was definitely looking good, but she knew that wasn't his real name.

He read her tone and chuckled.

"Cassio, but that's what everybody calls me."

"I'm not everybody."

"Then you can call me what you want, ma, when you want and where you want," he charmed.

She blushed. "I'm Mona."

"Hmmm, I think I like the sound of that," he winked.

She couldn't stop smiling. She was feeling his style, his game, his swag. Before she knew it, she and her girlfriends were following him and his man, Mac, back to his apartment. Ashanti wanted to go home, but she was out voted.

The night felt young again, the possibilities endless.

Cash's apartment was a stylish condo, his choice of decor fell under the manly but tasteful umbrella. His bar was stocked with the best, his bedroom, dark and cozy, the music, soft and warm. It wasn't such a bad place to be.

Even so, "I shouldn't be here," she demurred, as Cash enveloped her in an embrace that led to a sensual slow drag.

"Why? You got a man?"

"No."

"Are *you* a man?" He cracked.

She playfully hit him.

"Do I feel like one?" Mona flirted, grinding her body up against his.

"Hell no."

"But I'm saying, we just met."

"You wanna leave?"

"No."

"Then you stay right where you are."

Laying in bed, Mona remembered the moment their lips first touched, and she couldn't help but push the elastic of her panties aside and touch herself. Her pussy was soaked as she began to massage her own clit, remembering as Cash ran his tongue down the curve of her spine, tracing the path of the chill he caused to course through her flesh like the rawest electricity.

He licked along the crack of her ass, pushing her leg forward and cocking it up on the bed.

"Damn that feels good..." she groaned, deliciously.

"I want to taste every inch of you," Cash whispered.

When his tongue entered her pussy, she thought she would pass out, the feeling was so intense. He bent her over the bed and tongue fucked her until her pussy juices ran down her trembling thighs.

Mona cocked open her legs as widely as they would go, and finger fucked herself with two fingers to the knuckle. She was on fire with the memory of how Cash had made her feel.

"Oh Cash, I can't take it...all," she barely managed the words, clawing at the sheets as she tried to scoot away from the big black dick threatening to drive her out of her mind.

"Ssshhhhh, take it like a big girl," he urged her, slowly penetrating deeper and deeper until he had his whole shaft, balls deep inside of her and it was bliss.

"I can... I can feel it... in my stomach." Then, "Don't *stop*," she whispered to herself.

She was so gone, her room felt like it was spinning.

In her mind, she was back in Cash's condo, her legs wrapped around his waist, her arms around his neck, nails dug deep into his back while he dug deep into her.

"You feel so good..."

"Say it again?" He crooned, vigorously long dicking her and loving the way her tight little pussy gripped his dick.

"You feel so good," she repeated, sucking on his bottom lip.

When he came, the force of his ejaculation sent her over the top. She coated his dick with her creamy milk center.

"Damn lil' mama, one more shot like that and I'll be asking you for your ring size."

She giggled.

"Seven."

They looked into each other's eyes and in that moment both wanted time to stand still, freezing them in that space and time just a little bit longer.

But by the time she got home, the future she'd been imagining was blown apart, never to be put together again. She crept through the door, barely beating the rising of the sun. Shoes in hand, she tried to tip-toe up the stairs to her room. The house was quiet, and for a moment she thought everyone was still sleeping until she heard, "You're late."

The study was still dark.

It took a minute for her eyes to adjust. When they did, she saw her father sitting in the chair, the tip of his cigar reddening as he inhaled, the fire lighting his face.

"I didn't know I had a curfew."

Joe rose and walked out of the shadows, his face a scowling mask. "Don't play with me, Ramona," he seethed. She knew he was more than just angry because he used her whole name.

"Daddy, I wasn't trying to be smart. I just lost track of-"

"Who were you with."

She frowned with subtle confusion. "Celeste!"

"No. You know who the hell I'm talking about, Ramona. I'm only going to ask this one more time, so I seriously encourage you to tell the truth. Who were you with?"

"I-I-I... I met a guy..."

Joe glared at his babygirl.

"I own this city, do you understand? There's *nothing* I don't know, especially when it comes to my family. I do this to protect you, even if it's from yourself. His name is Cash, right?'

A beat, then Mona nodded.

"He's a gangsta, Mona, a common thug. A nobody, a fucking nigga not long for the grave, do you hear me?"

"But Daddy!"

"Don't *but Daddy* me. You stay away from him. End of discussion. You do not fuck with him, are we clear?"

Mona loved her father, but her spirit wouldn't let her just back down. "I'm not a little girl anymore, I'm eighteen. You may not like every decision I make, but they're *mine* to make, mistakes and all. You can't control who I see."

Joe knew his little girl had his heart, his fire, and understood full well she wasn't about to let him dictate her life. But she was still a woman, a woman with feelings and emotions. Something he didn't have.

"Okay... you're right, Ramona, it's your life. I may not be able to control who you see, but I can control who sees you. I'm making you a promise, babygirl... As of this day, right now, hand on my heart, if you ever see that nigga again, I'll have him cut into little pieces and scattered around this city like the seeds of the dead. Do I make myself clear?"

Mona's heart seized in her chest. "You... you can't."

Joe chose to avert his eyes, not wanting to see her cry, but this was an important lesson in power. His mind was made up, his resolve resolute.

"You're wrong, I can. But what that means is ultimately it's on you. Only you can make the decision whether he lives or dies. You want to be grown up, make grown up decisions. You are more than welcome to go fuck him again. You know the consequences of your actions. You decide. Not me."

"That's not fair!"

"Life isn't fair, babygirl," Joe responded, then walked out.

Mona laid in the bed, feeling the hurt and pain of her father's ultimatum all over again.

She remembered how badly it had hurt to send Cash's calls to voicemail until he finally stopped calling.

Fortunately for him, she didn't run in any of the circles he did, so she never saw again.

Until she did.

Now her stomach knotted knowing he was back in her life.

And knowing that her Daddy was a man of his word.

Benny walked out of the corner store and headed toward his burgundy Range Rover, sitting on 22's. His eyes widened with curiosity when he saw the beautiful Latina chick leaning against his driver's door.

She wore a pair of coochie cutter shorts that hugged her camel toe and made him want to suck that sweet pussy through her shorts.

Her toes looked delectable in the wraparound Roman sandals she was wearing.

He stepped to her, smiling from ear to ear.

"Benny, right?" She asked, her accent sharp as Cardi B's.

"Wifey, right?"

She smiled, then extended the cellphone in her hand to him. "Venus. Someone wants to speak to you."

His street instincts kicked in and the smile dried up on his face. "Who?"

"Only one way to find out."

He paused for a moment, then took the phone and said, "Hello?"

"Remember me?" The raspy voice on the other end answered.

"Naw," Benny said, "And I ain't got time for games."

"Let me help jog your memory then. Othello."

As soon as he heard the name, he snatched the gun off his waistline and aimed it at Venus. She smiled to herself, thinking how slow he'd been with the draw, how close he was when he drew down and how she could've spit the razor out of her mouth and slit his throat before he even gripped the handle.

But since she wasn't there to take his life, she amused herself with his weak bravado.

"Fuck you want, man?" Benny growled, trying to sound tough, but too scared to do a good job.

Othello chuckled down the line at him.

"Naw Duke, I don't want no smoke, and if I remember correctly, neither do you. I'm not looking for enemies brah, I got enough of them. I'm looking for friends. I thought you and I got along pretty good the other night."

"Yeah, 'cause you had the gun. Now I do. I suggest you get this bitch out my face, or—"

"Mami can take care of herself," Othello cut him off before he could say something he wouldn't live to regret. "Bottom line is this: shit is going down and I'm coming up. The only question is, which team you on? Take a beat. Think about it. I like you, Benny. You a real nigga. You held water under pressure the other night. You ain't panic. But your man Don, he's finished," Othello explained.

Benny thought about what Othello said.

He had been hearing how hard Othello was going, and it did seem like The Commission was shook, maybe even going to war with him. Besides, since he was Don's last man standing, he could come up himself if he played his cards right. "What you have in mind?"

"Mami's got something for you. Ten grand. I need a favor."

"Like what?'

"I want you to take her out, chill, maybe you might even get lucky. But I need you to introduce her to Don. That's it."

An indecent proposal?

"That it?'

"No more, no less."

Benny looked at Venus. She winked at him, then pulled an envelope out of her back pocket. He didn't know what looked better, all those big faces on the green or her thick, shapely body.

He held out his hand.

"Good choice. I knew you were a smart man," Othello commented, as Benny reached for the money.

Benny's brow furled.

He looked around.

That was when he noticed Othello sitting across the street in a black on black Benz G-wagon.

Benny figured right then, had he made the wrong decision, he would've been a dead man.

Othello's slight nod of the head confirmed his mental theory.

"We about to do big things," Othello told him.

***

Benny didn't get lucky, but he did find Don, which was not exactly the next best thing, but it was something.

They pulled up driver's door to driver's door in a darkened parking lot. It was late, and the sky was black. Venus was in the passenger's seat.

"I got somebody here who wanna meet you," Benny introduced.

Don took one look at her and said, "Damn mami, Butter Pecan Rican is my favorite flavor."

"I'm Cuban," Venus corrected

"Then make it Butter Cuban Rican," Don joked, "Come holler at a nigga."

Venus got out and walked around to the driver's side of Don's two-seater Porsche 918 Spyder. In the passenger's seat was a big black bodyguard. Venus leaned on the door, her pretty, perfectly round titties sitting up like cantaloupes in her cleavage. Don was mesmerized. He never saw her drop the penny-sized GPS tracker down inside the car.

"Damn baby, unfortunately I ain't got room for you right now."

"There's always room for me. I could just sit on your lap."

"Yeah, and I'd end up killing us all, you'd get me so distracted. Just give your number to Benny and we'll get together soon," Don suggested, thinking he was being extra cautious. He was well aware of the tactics niggas might use to get at him. He was no fool, so he wasn't about to bring the bitch with him so she could set him up.

But, he had already been set up.

Othello could have had him gunned down on the spot easily,

but he wanted to make a point with the way he killed Don—a point The Commission would never forget.

"Okay papi, just call my name and I'll come running."

"And what's that?"

"Venus," she smiled.

He chuckled, but his eyes told a different story.

"Venus huh? Like the flytrap?"

"Nah," she lied, smiled and added, "Like the goddess on a mountain top."

As Don pulled away, she thought to herself: *and goddess of war.*

———

Mona glanced in her rearview mirror and smiled to herself as she noticed the car following her. It was only a few car lengths back. Amateurs. She wasn't worried about it. Over the years, she'd gotten used to her father's overprotective ways. Sometimes she even welcomed them, like the time she'd been seconds away from getting car-jacked, but the jackers got a deadly surprise. Most of the time, she allowed them to think they were being discreet, because it was in her best interest for them to report to Joe Hamlet how good his babygirl was behaving.

But there were times, times like right now, when she wanted to be alone because she was gearing up to do what Daddy's Little Girls do when Daddy ain't around to stop 'em. And as the situation demanded, she already had a plan.

Mona picked up her phone and speed-dialed Celeste.

"What?" Celeste answered, with playful aggression.

"Please bitch, you are not busy, so don't even stunt."

Celeste laughed. "How you know I ain't about to get my groove on?"

"You wouldn't have answered the phone."

"Forreal."

"I need you."

"To make a move?" Celeste asked, using their code word for the strategy.

"Yep."

"Let me guess, Othello?"

"Bitch stop being nosy and put on a red skirt and white tank top."

"Bye, bitch."

Several minutes later, Mona pulled up outside Celeste's apartment and started the switch. It wasn't all that complicated. She was out of the car and in the foyer as the tail pulled up, side by side with Celeste as they waited out a few minutes. Then Celeste emerged, as if she were Mona, got into her car and pulled off, taking the tail with her. Mona watched them follow Celeste to the corner and away.

Too easy.

She got into Celeste's car and hurried toward her first date with Othello.

Ironically, she didn't know it at the time, but she had saved Othello's life with that little subterfuge, because had they tailed her all the way to the restaurant and seen him, they would've pulled the trigger on the spot. Such was the war she'd stumbled into.

Death was never more than a breath away…

Mona fancied she was fast becoming a master of disguise.

By the time she had reached the restaurant, she changed from her skirt and tank top into a purple silk wraparound Donna Karan dress that hugged her shapely frame tastefully, without being crass or sluttish.

It was a cozy little Italian spot that Mona had never been to.

Othello had offered to pick her up, but not wanting him to know who her family truly was, or her family to know who he was, she told him that she'd meet him at the restaurant.

When she walked in, Othello was already there, sitting at a

table with his seat facing the door. She didn't flatter herself into thinking it was so he didn't miss one sexy stride of her entrance. It was all about not showing your enemies your back. She got that from her old man. Always be watching. She walked in, the ambiance of the restaurant becoming the backdrop for her beauty. Everything else blurred while her radiance stood out in full blaze to Othello's every sense. He had never met a woman so beautiful, so graceful and oozing so much class all at the same time.

It was as if she had been born a Queen.

He was a man on the way up, with sexy women all through the game ready to give him whatever he asked, but this was different. The minute he laid eyes on Mona right up until the day she was killed, she would be the only woman for him.

Othello stood to greet her.

"Hello, Mona. Looking beautiful as always," Othello charmed, kissing her hand.

Mona smiled that slow sweet smile that was nowhere near as innocent as it pretended, taking him all in. For a big man he moved gracefully. He looked good in his Steve Harvey burgundy suit and cocked Stetson Ace-Deuce hat.

"Thank you. You don't look so bad yourself."

They sat, they ate, they drank, they laughed.

It was easy.

Their conversation flowed smoothly, naturally.

They had similar interests and perspectives.

By the end of the night, they were at that finishing each other's sentences stage, so in tune. It was a new experience for both of them. They ended the night in a small jazz club, slow dragging and enjoying the music.

"I had a real good time tonight," Mona told him.

"Me, too. So, million dollar question, ma, when will I see you again?"

"When do you *want* to see me again?"

"Now, tomorrow and forever," he said, smoothly.

"Just three more times?"

Othello couldn't help but kiss her. It was the type of kiss that most nights ended in a hotel room, up against the railing of the balcony, and the shadow of the beast with two backs. And Mona was perfectly willing to let it go where it led, but Othello wanted more. He had his queen and he wanted everything about their new relationship to be special, so he broke the kiss, looked into her eyes and said, "Until tomorrow, sweetness. It's getting late. Let me walk you to your car."

Mona wasn't used to the gentleman in the 'hood.

She really liked the feeling.

It didn't take long for Othello and Mona's relationship to grow its wings, taking both of their feelings and emotions to new, dizzying heights. They spent hours on the phone and sneaking away to secret rendezvouses, just the two of them and to hell with the world.

It was their own heaven, a place between their two worlds.

And tragically, neither of them were remotely aware of how close the other's world really was.

Because in their heaven, Othello was the loving, gentle and considerate man she always wanted, but in the real world, he was the beast the streets feared.

The Commission pulled out all the stops, but it didn't matter.

Othello seemed to have their every moved figured out. Truth was, he did, and it was all because of his own secret weapon.

Things came to a head when Othello made his move on Don.

It was always going to happen.

Written in the stars, like fated lovers or whatever the mortal enemy equivalent was.

Don, unaware of the GPS under his driver's seat, laid out a pattern of his most secretive moves for Othello to map. Othello knew where he laid his head, where his baby mothers laid their heads, even where his stash houses were and where his connect would meet him. His whole empire was laid in the palm of Othello's hand.

All Othello had to do was make a fist...

"Tonight, we crush that nigga Don," Othello began, looking around the room at the inner circle of his trusted souls.

Mac, Cash, Venus, Milk and Benny sat around, some smoking blunts, some with drinks, all focused on the task at hand.

"Mac, you take his safe house. Get every fuckin dime," Mac nodded with a crazy grin.

Mac kicks in the door of the safe house with his five-man team of stragglers and expendables rushing in behind him. They pound the place. Three dudes inside return fire, killing one of Mac's goons as soon as his first foot crosses the threshold. It ain't enough to save them. Three more of Mac's men kick in the backdoor and end the three dudes in a barrage of bullets. Mac looks around at the dead bodies twitching on the floor, tucks his gun away as he steps over them and heads towards the back room. Inside, sitting on a long table are stacks and stacks of money, a money machine ready to count and several kilos of cocaine. Mac smiles.

Mission accomplished...

"Cash, you and Benny take a team and go take care of his connect. Murder everything moving," Cash smiled demonically.

It's a birthday party. A child's birthday party. Ten little kids, boys and girls, jump and play merrily, screeching and hollering, and it's just fucking beautiful, like the Salma Hayek-esque piece carrying out the cake, six little candles dancing on the sugar icing.

Miguel, Don's connect, a man who looks more like a pitbull terrier than a human sits back proudly, enjoying the sheer joy on his daughter's face.

This is what he works for.

Sure, he kills, but this is why he kills. These moments are why he is so ruthless in everything else he does... It is all so he can show his family mercy.

"Daddy, Daddy! Look at me! I'm a ballerina!" his daughter calls

out in heavily-accented English. He'll have to pay to get that straightened out. He doesn't want her sounding like a dumb immigrant.

Miguel watches her spin like an unbalanced top.

"Hello boys and girls!" A big, pink bunny rabbit calls out happily, as it hops in alongside a big red tiger.

Miguel sees his daughter's face light up with glee.

She loves this type of shit.

The bunny and the tiger begin to dance around. It isn't long before the kids join them, living inside their innocent imagination... until reality screams a wake-up call they will never wake up from.

BBBBBRRRRRRRRAAAAAAPPPPP!

The bunny and the tiger ain't cute little fury party guests. They are murderous marauders bearing automatic weapons concealed inside their costumes. They let loose a swarm of bullets, worse than Biblical locusts, that eat through the flesh of any and all in their way.

Miguel never has a chance to react. He's frozen. A failure.

He watches helplessly as his children, nephews, nieces and the children of close friends are torn to shreds like living piñatas, only they aren't alive as their blood sprays across the yard.

When death finds him, he thanks God.

It is a mercy-killing.

The bunny and the tiger survey their handiwork.

The only thing moving in the absolute still of the yard are the flames flickering on the short candles, all six, still burning down on the birthday cake with no birthday girl to blow them out and make a wish...

"Milk and Venus, you two go get his baby mother and daughter," Othello told them.

"Kill them, too?" Milk asked, with all the enthusiasm of someone asked to swat a fly.

"No. Bring them to the rendezvous spot."

Milk and Venus, carrying Bibles and wearing dresses fit for church revival, cover their voluptuousness as they ring the doorbell of a brownstone at dusk, all holy roller smiles plastered on their peachy fine faces.

"Who is it?"

"Jehovah's Witnesses."

Vanessa opens the door, wearing only a robe wrapped tightly around her.

"Can I ask, have you made your peace with God and accepted the Lord into your life? Because if you haven't you are going to hell," Venus asked and answered. She might have been going for the Oscar, she was that convincing in the role of holy-roller.

"Look, I got no beef with your God, but he ain't mine, and I don't got time to jaw, so why don't you run along?" Vanessa replies.

From under the bibles, Milk and Venus pull out twin chrome 9mm pistols.

"Hell it is, then," Venus snickers devilishly.

"Oh Jesus!" Vanessa cries out, praying to the very God she just denied.

He isn't listening.

"I'm going to take the rest of the team and see to Don myself. The next time we see each other, we'll be in a position to take over this city," Othello vowed. "Go make some noise."

7.

Don sat back in his brand new Porsche, top down, allowing the worries of the city to wisp away in the wind as he raced toward the countryside. There was a metaphor for life in these seconds, rubber burning away on the road, wind battering his face, music pounding out beats only he could hear.

He lived twenty miles outside of the city, deep in seclusion, isolated. No one knew the exact location. A man like him needed a retreat, a fortress away from the grind of the streets. It was a safe house.

Or so he thought.

Don took every precaution. Fuck, he was paranoid when it came to protecting his family from his street life. He took the whole *two worlds must never collide* idea to heart. He never drove straight home, never took exactly the same route. Some nights he'd go the opposite direction for several miles, switching lanes, taking detours through half a dozen slices of pastoral America, before finally making the turn that would send him in the right direction.

He was beyond cautious.

But he still made mistakes, because he was human, and every fucker makes mistakes. It's the unwritten law. His was not vacuuming his Porsche. The GPS still pulsed out its signal that pinned his whereabouts on Google Maps for all to see, so it really didn't matter how many twists and turns he took. Big Brother was still watching.

Don pulled into his sprawling estate, following the driveway as it wound its way up to the six-car garage. He parked and got out.

He slammed the door behind him.

First thing hit him—not oil, not garage smells—the whiff of a man's cologne. It wasn't his smell.

But just like that, it was gone again, and maybe he hadn't smelled it after all. Maybe it was his imagination. It wasn't like his girl would step out on him.

Had he been in his other life, he would've been more alert, but the problem with building your fortress of solitude is that right along with it you build complacency. Those walls of ice will rock you to sleep.

Don learned this the moment he set foot inside the kitchen.

Six dudes stood around his kitchen island, eating sandwiches, cooking, drinking and laughing, their guns on the counter as if they didn't have a care in the world. It took a split second for the scene to register in Don's mind.

"What the *fuck*?" He spazzed, reaching for his gun.

The men eating just stopped and looked at him.

None even went for their guns.

That should have triggered a thousand alarms, but he was off his game.

CLICK!

He felt the steel against his temple a second before he heard the silky smooth words tell him, "I wouldn't do that if I were you."

Don stopped, his hand on the butt of his .45.

"Okay, you got it. Easy, man. This don't have to go to Hell," Don said, compliant, calm, and conciliatory.

The gunman took his pistol. "I got somebody here who wants to meet you," he said, pushing Don into the living room.

When he entered the living room, his world fell away from him, the ground opening up beneath his feet.

He saw his wife, Angela, sitting on the couch. She looked a mess. Tear stains on her cheeks, skin pink and puffy.

Across from her, in his own armchair, was the man he had been looking for. The man sat cross-legged, his gun resting on his thigh.

"I'm Othello. I heard you were looking for me," he smirked, as if to say: *Well, here I am.*

Seeing the terror in his wife's eyes, impotent rage washed over him.

"Have a seat. We need to talk. Best we do it like men, eh?" Othello said, keeping his tone light. He didn't need to waste swagger, the gun on his lap did all that for him.

Don sat next to his wife.

He took her hand.

"The safe's in the bedroom. There's money in there. Take it. I won't stop you. It's a lot of money. It's yours, but you better use it to get you to the other side of the world," Don said, still thinking he had some sort of power in this negotiation.

Othello chuckled, like he really didn't have a care in the world and wasn't about to waste good money running when he'd just made himself at home. He said to one of his goons, "Take the wife up there, open the safe. Bring all that lovely money out here."

Don squeezed his wife's hand. "You're not taking her anywhere."

"Donny, Donny, Donny, I know you're used to giving the orders, but tonight, you're the bitch, comprende?" Othello growled, looking Don dead in the eyes. "Now, there's something you should know about me. I'm a man of my word. If you don't have that, you got nothin', right? So, believe me when I tell you, you have my word. You play fair, we'll play fair. Nothing's going to happen to her. Nobody will touch her. But we're going to do this my way. Understood?"

Don glared at Othello. He had never hated another living being with such immediate intensity, but he knew people. You didn't get to where he was in this life without knowing people. Looking the big man in the eye he knew he could be trusted.

Slowly, and still reluctantly, he let go off his wife's hand.

She got up and led the goons into the bedroom.

Once they were out of the room, Don rasped, "You know you fucked up coming here, right? You kill me, The Commission will hunt you down like a fuckin' dog and put you down. So fuckin' stupid, man. How you think you can come into my home, threaten my wife, and just walk away? If it ain't me coming after you my connect Miguel will, and believe me, ain't nowhere in the world you can hide if he's looking to hunt you down."

Othello yawned.

"Donny, you need to read the more than just the headlines. The world's changed, and nigga, it's changed fast. Let me do the whole CNN thing for you: Miguel's dead. His whole family, from the kids to the grandmothers, dead. That's tonight's headlines read for you by O."

Don stared in disbelief at Othello.

Miguel's dead? His whole fucking family wiped out?

"You feel me, Donny? This shit, me being here, it ain't no

mistake. It's a respect thing. I have Vanessa, I have your daughter, I have your money. I have every fuckin' thing. I wanted you to be able to look me in the face when you finally understood life was over. We both men of the world, Donny. We know."

"I'm next," Don said flatly. He was ready to face death. He wasn't about to beg. No piss running down the inside of his leg. None of that shit. If it was his time, it was his time. He wouldn't give the rat bastard the satisfaction of seeing him as anything less than a man.

The goons came back into the room with Angela and a large duffel stuffed with money.

"Goddamn big brah, it must be a million dollars in here, easy," The goon marveled.

Othello looked at the money with disdain.

"Chump change. Y'all niggas split it up."

Don and his wife sat on the couch. She was crying, but Don was hard as stone, staring into the abyss where his future should have been.

"Do what you came to do," Don said, bracing himself for the bullet.

Othello shook his head. "It's already done." He stood up, walked over to where Don sat, and put two bullets in him, one in each knee. No way he was walking out of this place. "Burn it down."

His people did their job.

As the house burned, Don sat on the couch, feeling the heat rise. It wouldn't be long before the fancy fabric Angela had taken weeks to pick out began to fuse to his skin. He couldn't walk away, but he was fuckin' damned if he was gonna drop onto his belly and try and drag himself out of Hell by the fingernails. Fuck that. His blood boiled like the heat of the flames gathered around him.

He took a deep breath, then closed his eyes and waited.

Don sat back in his brand new Porsche, top down, allowing the worries of the city to wisp away in the wind as he raced toward the countryside. There was a metaphor for life in these seconds, rubber burning away on the road, wind battering his face, music pounding out beats only he could hear.

He lived twenty miles outside of the city, deep in seclusion, isolated. No one knew the exact location. A man like him needed a retreat, a fortress away from the grind of the streets. It was a safe house.

Or so he thought.

Don took every precaution. Fuck, he was paranoid when it came to protecting his family from his street life. He took the whole *two worlds must never collide* idea to heart. He never drove straight home, never took exactly the same route. Some nights he'd go the opposite direction for several miles, switching lanes, taking detours through half a dozen slices of pastoral America, before finally making the turn that would send him in the right direction.

He was beyond cautious.

But he still made mistakes, because he was human, and every fucker makes mistakes. It's the unwritten law. His was not vacuuming his Porsche. The GPS still pulsed out its signal that pinned his whereabouts on Google Maps for all to see, so it really didn't matter how many twists and turns he took. Big Brother was still watching.

Don pulled into his sprawling estate, following the driveway as it wound its way up to the six-car garage. He parked and got out.

He slammed the door behind him.

First thing hit him—not oil, not garage smells—the whiff of a man's cologne. It wasn't his smell.

But just like that, it was gone again, and maybe he hadn't smelled it after all. Maybe it was his imagination. It wasn't like his girl would step out on him.

Had he been in his other life, he would've been more alert, but the problem with building your fortress of solitude is that right along with it you build complacency. Those walls of ice will rock you to sleep.

Don learned this the moment he set foot inside the kitchen.

Six dudes stood around his kitchen island, eating sandwiches, cooking, drinking and laughing, their guns on the counter as if they didn't have a care in the world. It took a split second for the scene to register in Don's mind.

"What the *fuck*?" He spazzed, reaching for his gun.

The men eating just stopped and looked at him.

None even went for their guns.

That should have triggered a thousand alarms, but he was off his game.

CLICK!

He felt the steel against his temple a second before he heard the silky smooth words tell him, "I wouldn't do that if I were you."

Don stopped, his hand on the butt of his .45.

"Okay, you got it. Easy, man. This don't have to go to Hell," Don said, compliant, calm, and conciliatory.

The gunman took his pistol. "I got somebody here who wants to meet you," he said, pushing Don into the living room.

When he entered the living room, his world fell away from him, the ground opening up beneath his feet.

He saw his wife, Angela, sitting on the couch. She looked a mess. Tear stains on her cheeks, skin pink and puffy.

Across from her, in his own armchair, was the man he had been looking for. The man sat cross-legged, his gun resting on his thigh.

"I'm Othello. I heard you were looking for me," he smirked, as if to say: *Well, here I am.*

Seeing the terror in his wife's eyes, impotent rage washed over him.

"Have a seat. We need to talk. Best we do it like men, eh?"

Othello said, keeping his tone light. He didn't need to waste swagger, the gun on his lap did all that for him.

Don sat next to his wife.

He took her hand.

"The safe's in the bedroom. There's money in there. Take it. I won't stop you. It's a lot of money. It's yours, but you better use it to get you to the other side of the world," Don said, still thinking he had some sort of power in this negotiation.

Othello chuckled, like he really didn't have a care in the world and wasn't about to waste good money running when he'd just made himself at home. He said to one of his goons, "Take the wife up there, open the safe. Bring all that lovely money out here."

Don squeezed his wife's hand. "You're not taking her anywhere."

"Donny, Donny, Donny, I know you're used to giving the orders, but tonight, you're the bitch, comprende?" Othello growled, looking Don dead in the eyes. "Now, there's something you should know about me. I'm a man of my word. If you don't have that, you got nothin', right? So, believe me when I tell you, you have my word. You play fair, we'll play fair. Nothing's going to happen to her. Nobody will touch her. But we're going to do this my way. Understood?"

Don glared at Othello. He had never hated another living being with such immediate intensity, but he knew people. You didn't get to where he was in this life without knowing people. Looking the big man in the eye he knew he could be trusted.

Slowly, and still reluctantly, he let go off his wife's hand.

She got up and led the goons into the bedroom.

Once they were out of the room, Don rasped, "You know you fucked up coming here, right? You kill me, The Commission will hunt you down like a fuckin' dog and put you down. So fuckin' stupid, man. How you think you can come into my home, threaten my wife, and just walk away? If it ain't me coming after you my connect Miguel will, and believe me, ain't nowhere in the world you can hide if he's looking to hunt you down."

Othello yawned.

"Donny, you need to read the more than just the headlines. The world's changed, and nigga, it's changed fast. Let me do the whole CNN thing for you: Miguel's dead. His whole family, from the kids to the grandmothers, dead. That's tonight's headlines read for you by O."

Don stared in disbelief at Othello.

Miguel's dead? His whole fucking family wiped out?

"You feel me, Donny? This shit, me being here, it ain't no mistake. It's a respect thing. I have Vanessa, I have your daughter, I have your money. I have every fuckin' thing. I wanted you to be able to look me in the face when you finally understood life was over. We both men of the world, Donny. We know."

"I'm next," Don said flatly. He was ready to face death. He wasn't about to beg. No piss running down the inside of his leg. None of that shit. If it was his time, it was his time. He wouldn't give the rat bastard the satisfaction of seeing him as anything less than a man.

The goons came back into the room with Angela and a large duffel stuffed with money.

"Goddamn big brah, it must be a million dollars in here, easy," The goon marveled.

Othello looked at the money with disdain.

"Chump change. Y'all niggas split it up."

Don and his wife sat on the couch. She was crying, but Don was hard as stone, staring into the abyss where his future should have been.

"Do what you came to do," Don said, bracing himself for the bullet.

Othello shook his head. "It's already done." He stood up, walked over to where Don sat, and put two bullets in him, one in each knee. No way he was walking out of this place. "Burn it down."

His people did their job.

As the house burned, Don sat on the couch, feeling the heat rise. It wouldn't be long before the fancy fabric Angela had taken weeks to pick out began to fuse to his skin. He couldn't walk away, but he was fuckin' damned if he was gonna drop onto his belly and try and drag himself out of Hell by the fingernails. Fuck that. His blood boiled like the heat of the flames gathered around him.

He took a deep breath, then closed his eyes and waited.

Everyone around the table wore the same somber expressions, like they were at a wake.

They couldn't help themselves, eyes went toward the empty chair where Don used to sit. Every one of them experienced a different tide of emotions brought on by his absence and what it meant for The Commission.

Malone was the first to speak.

"They killed the fuckin' children. Ten little kids. Fucking animals. That little girl didn't even get to blow out the candles on her fuckin' cake. What kind of man does that?"

"Truth time? This is the life we signed up for," Joe reminded them. "Everyone at this table knows the risk, knows the kind of people whot would take out ten little kids, and probably fuckin' well calls them a friend. That's the grim reality."

It was a truth none of them could deny.

"The question is, what are we going to do about it? Malik questioned, ever practical, guided by his own warped sense of justice.

"Murder every fuckin' body we find in the streets, torture the fucks until somebody gives Othello up!" Rome barked.

"And spark a war?" Joe said, coldly, still trying to be the voice of reason.

"Fuck the streets, man. Look out the window. They're already at war with us!" Rome raged, and he wasn't wrong.

Anger fumed the room like the fragrance of that bitch named Revenge.

"The way I see it, us and the streets have the same enemy. If we bring in the street leaders and incorporate them, we can isolate this fucking piece of shit. We still got the power here. We can destroy him," Malone reasoned.

Joe shook his head. "You never give up, do you? You won't be happy until we expand The Commission."

"This ain't about what *I* want, it's about what we need," Malone shot back.

Joe sat back, taking it all in.

He thought about his own dilemma and inner guilt. He had killed Othello's father and in doing so had created this problem long ago. He wasn't about to tell the others at the table these were his chickens coming home to roost.

"We can at least arrange a sit down," Malik seconded.

Joe was a lot of things, and one of them was smart enough to know when the tides were turning against him. With Don gone, the vote to expand The Commission was tilting to his disadvantage. The irony, which he appreciated right now, was the fact that it was only Rome's rage that kept it from being three to one. He needed to keep Rome simmering without letting him boil over. As long as he did, it was deadlocked.

"Okay," Joe conceded. "Set it up."

And with that concession, the meeting adjourned.

Joe was out of there without a word to anyone, headed to his car and on the road before he put a call through to his lieutenant, Black Sam.

"How'd it go?" Sam wanted to know.

"As expected. They're all scared they may be next," Joe replied.

"They may be."

"The tide is turning," Joe agreed.

"Maybe it's time we turned with it," Black Sam suggested.

Joe sighed.

"Not you too, Sammy."

"Hear me out, boss. I may be off base, but we both know this is Malik's desire. He wants to expand in order to dilute your control of The Commission. He wants more than just a seat at the table, but the fact is he doesn't have the connections we do. If we don't steal his thunder, then he might be the one who strike lightning," Black Sam surmised.

Joe still wasn't convinced.

"Just sit tight. The traitor thinks he's winning. He will be looking at what just went down and see the boulder rolling down the hill, gaining momentum all the time. It's now he makes a mistake." Joe responded.

"We'll see," Black Sam answered, skepticism coloring his voice, then he hung up on the boss.

He tossed the phone in the passenger's seat just as he turned into the parking lot of the motel. It was a shithole, chosen for a reason. Even the roaches turned their nose up at the place.

He drove around back, where Room 136 was located, concealed behind the motel pool.

Black Sam killed the engine and clambered out. He was on edge. He looked around half a dozen times as he approached the room. Anyone watching would think he was a spinning fuckin' top. He skipped up the three concrete steps, stepping into the shade of the overhang from the walkway above. There was a half-deflated pink flamingo up against the wall. He couldn't imagine anyone actually using it to paddle in the pool.

Before he could knock, the door opened.

"I take it everything went according to plan?" Black Sam asked, as Milk closed the door behind him. She crawled back up on the bed, making herself more than at home in this shithole. Maybe he'd gotten it wrong. *Maybe the roaches did make this place their home after all*, he thought.

Othello sat in the corner. He was at the small table that looked like a children's furniture set next to his hulking frame.

"Of course."

Milk was laying across the bed clad only in a tank top, her nipples perked and protruding, pressed provocatively against the silken fabric. Her boy shorts fit more like a thong on her dangerous curves. She would've been sexy if she didn't have that AR-15 between her thighs like a big, black dick ready to bust a nut all over Black Sam.

She stared him down coldly.

She was one fucked up bitch.

"And the money?" he asked, not looking at her.

"You'll get your cut," Othello assured him.

Black Sam smirked.

"You mean, I'll get what you want me to have. No matter what, when it's all said and done, we'll be sitting on a fucking goldmine! You killed 'em all, right?"

"Why? You writin' a book?" Othello shook his head. "It's on a need to know, nigga, and you don't need to know."

"No, I just... nevermind."

Black Sam glanced over at Milk.

She was still staring him down.

"Bitch, you know me? Fuck you keep starin' for?" Black Sam gritted, more out of nervousness than bravado.

Milk didn't say a word. She just stared him down, expressionless. The atmosphere was way beyond tense.

Black Sam turned to Othello.

"Why the guns, O? I thought we were friends?"

"No, we're closer than friends, Sam. We're allies. But, you know it's a dog eat fuckin' dog world outside this door. Can't be too careful, huh?" Othello replied, blatantly disrespecting Sam. The thing he didn't realize was, the only thing you keep closer than friends are enemies.

"Well, just don't forget who found you rotting in that prison cell... *old friend*," Black Sam spat, offering a sour smile.

Othello returned the expression, just as sour. "I won't. Anything else?"

"I'll be in touch for the final phase. Until then, lay low," Black Sam instructed him.

Milk slithered off the bed, ass jiggling as she went to the door and held it open for Black Sam.

As soon as he left and she watched him walk off, she turned to Othello, "We've got a problem."

"You think?"

"I know, baby. That dude, he's the police."

4

———

When Mac got home, Kandi was on the couch watching *Love & Hip Hop*. "You handle that?" he asked her, heading for the kitchen.

No response.

He didn't think anything of her silence. He knew her well. She was always wrapped up in these shows, properly losing herself to the false reality of it all, buying it hook, line and sinker. He went in the kitchen and came out with a bottled water and a cold drumstick straight out of the refrigerator.

Chewing, he asked again, "You handle that?"

Kandi just sucked her teeth and ignored him.

When he heard her suck her teeth, he got the message: *I hear you, but fuck you,* and grew instantly heated. He stayed calm. He finished his drumstick, threw the bone away, then stepped between her and the TV and said, "You heard what I said?"

"Move," she hissed with attitude.

Mac smirked. It wasn't a pretty look.

"Ain't shit funny, boy. Move."

Mac downed his bottle of water, sat the empty plastic bottle on the table, and with the quickness of a ninja snatched Kandi off the couch by her arm and hauled her to her feet.

"Bitch, come here!"

She didn't go limp like a rag doll or fold like some timid bitch, she swung on his ass with a right cross that connected hard.

The impact barely fazed him.

"Get off me, Mac!" She huffed, realizing her protestations were futile.

Mac slammed her against the wall, hand around the throat, and snatched her skirt up around her waist with his free hand. She clawed at his wrist, but he had an iron grip on her, and wasn't about to give, no matter how deep she dug her nails in.

He snatched skirt down and panties aside at the same time.

Nothing but ass and pussy fell out.

"Stop, damn you," Kandi whined, her pussy heating up to the point of fiery passion.

"Shut the fuck up," Mac roared, as he snatched her off her feet.

He pinned her to the wall.

She didn't struggle. Not no more. It was different when she clawed in a sexual frenzy, not in defense.

Mac pushed deep inside with all the force of his fight, taking her breath away and punishing her with stroke after stroke of pure power.

"Oh fuck baby, fuuuuck," Kandi moaned, protest broken. Her body banged up against the wall to his rhythm, her will totally subjugated.

Mac didn't loosen his grip around her throat. His fingers tightened, choking her as he grudge-fucked the bitch until she came so hard, her pussy squirted.

"No more, please, no," she begged, but she had started it and now he was damn sure going to finish it.

Mac spun her around and bent her over the couch.

Smack!

She cried out in pure pain.

He beat her again.

"I'm sorry!" She screamed, the pain cutting so deep.

There was no forgiveness in Mac. He grabbed her by the hair, yanked her head back until it touched the ridges of her spine, and plowed into her, beating her back out until tears of pain ran down her face.

"Bitch, when I speak you listen!" he roared. "You hear me?"

"Yes!"

He punched her this time, no open handed slap, a proper back of the skull punch.

Mac felt the rumble of the cumming train inside, like a locomotive about to run off the track. He released an explosion inside her as she collapsed over the arm of the couch, snot and tears streaming down her face.

"I needed that!" Mac sat on the floor, back to the couch, breathing hard.

They had been together for so long, he knew her inside and out, including the one where she needed that thug loving shit to get her head right.

Kandi slid down beside him.

"You want a sandwich, Daddy?" she asked, spirit broken.

"Yeah," Mac replied.

He watched her get up and head for the kitchen.

He loved to watch her walk.

She knew how to move. It was like sex, made flesh. Her bow legs had a gap that he could see clean through, and her pussy lips, fat and juicy, pouted out like a monkey paw between her thick ass and shapely thighs.

She came back with a tuna melt on wheat bread. His favorite. It was a peace offering.

As he ate, she laid her head on his lap.

"So what happened?" Mac questioned, wiping tuna off his mouth, then licking it off his hand.

"What you think happened? I took that lame nigga for everything he had. I slipped that shit in his drink, and by the time I jive-flirted with him, did my little dance, I ain't even get to my panties before he was out like a light. Jewelry, brand new Bentley and about twenty five hundred in cash. Not a bad night's work."

"You get pics?"

Whenever she ran game on a celebrity, she always got compromising photos. That was the money shot.

"Did I? Check this shit out!" She grabbed her phone off the coffee table, unlocking it with her thumb before she handed it to Mac. Looking at the pictures, he knew she'd hit a power move.

"Goddamn, this nigga gonna pay big for this shit!"

She had taken pictures of the dude with a long ass dildo sticking out of his ass, but the way she took the picture, you couldn't tell if it was a dildo or a real dick. The thing was that life-like. She'd taken the same type of picture with the dildo in his mouth and what looked like cum all over his face.

"You hit him up yet?"

"Naw. I'ma let him sweat for a minute."

"I want the Bentley," Mac chuckled.

She kissed him passionately. When they broke, she looked up at him, smiling, all those tears forgotten now, and told him, "Then it's yours."

Mac took the last bite of his sandwich.

"I had a dream," Kandi told him after a minute.

"What about?"

Mac always paid attention to her dreams—it wasn't like she had no sixth sense or any of that shit—but there was no getting away from the fact they had a tendency of coming true. Even when she was wrong, something in the dream would still play out. She'd joke that she was from New Orleans, the home of Voodoo, and that shit flowed through her veins. She was told she had been born with her eyes open, which, she reckoned was a sure sign of the gift of vision. So he paid attention.

"I dreamed you were trying to climb this like... pyramid of gold. The shit was ill. All shiny and shit. I was standin' at the top, calling your name. That's when all this blood started coming out of the pyramid, like gushing hard, and all these hands started reaching out too. You were climbing, kicking, punching, fighting your way to the top, and no matter how hard they tried to drag you down you kept on climbin'. Then once you got to the top, all the blood disappeared and the gold was shiny and pure again," Kandi said, and looking at the shine in her eyes he was sure she was seeing it at that moment.

Mac saw the significance of the dream right away. "A pyramid?"

She nodded. "I'm tellin' you bae, you gonna be the king of these streets! Watch!" she emphasized.

"Kings fall," he dipped his head, like he was being humble.

"We all fall sooner or later, but not everybody rises, bae. That's the magic. So when you get that chance, you take it, you don't fuckin' wait. For what? For who? You talk about loyalty and shit, but the first person you need to be loyal to is you," Kandi told him, putting her hand on his heart for emphasis.

"When the time is right, if it happens, I'll be ready," Mac vowed.

"My dreams come true. You know that, bae. Don't matter what you think, it *will* happen. It's your destiny."

Hearing her say the word *destiny*, sparked something deeper in Mac; a sense of purpose that he had never felt before.

The seed she had planted was beginning to take root.

His phone chimed with a text.

It was from Othello.

We got a problem.

"Yeah, we do," Mac mumbled to himself.

Othello, Mac and Cash, Venus and Milk had their cars parked in a makeshift circle.

They all leaned on their respective hoods.

They were in a park, in the dead of night, the only light was the full Blood Moon above them.

"You sure about this, ma?" Cash pressed. He didn't like it. He needed it dead set, locked in, pure 100% proof.

"Absolutely. I would never put that label on someone if I didn't know, like for sure know, with my own two eyes. I live on the outskirts of the city, near the docks. There's a diner there, an out of the way greasy spoon. Anyway, that's where I saw him, several times, with this white guy. His whole being screamed Fed, you know?"

"You see a badge or a uniform? Anything more than you interpreting, ma? Gotta be sure."

"I'm sure. Waitress kept callin' him Officer when she refilled his coffee."

"Fuck!" Mac cursed, then looked at Othello. "I thought you said this nigga was fuckin' solid? Who the fuck you got us in bed wit?"

Othello, not used to being questioned, felt Mac's frustration. He was burning up inside. It was a struggle to keep his calm. He squared up to Mac. "First of all, who the *fuck* you bassin at, Mac? Second, and this is real important to remember, shit happens. I'm in just as deep as you are. Deeper, because I'm the face he met with, you feel me?"

Mac snorted like a thwarted bull, all steaming head ready to charge, but was smart enough not to say anything.

"We gotta do something," Cash stated.

Othello looked at him. "Well, what do you suggest? We can't turn back, that's for sure. We in too deep. Blood been shed and lines have been drawn," Othello pointed out. "So I'm all fuckin' ears, Cash."

"Sam got us where he wants us," Mac remarked snidely.

Mac and Othello glared at one another.

There was gonna be a moment, real soon, when this got ugly.

"Ay yo Mac, you got a lot to say tonight. You think you can handle this thing better than me?" Othello spat.

"Better? I thought we was handling it together, remember? Team? Or is it all about you now, O?" Mac fired back.

Othello smirked, but his eyes remained cold.

"By all means, the floor is yours, brah."

"Like you said, you been the one he met with, so like, I don't know all the ins and outs of this shit. I'm simply asking you to keep us all in the loop, brah," Mac replied, fronting him.

Milk, seeing the tension growing out of the mutual frustration, sighed and moved to put it right, "Bottom line, we know something nobody else does. That's got to be worth something, right?"

It was a different perspective.

Othello nodded.

"Exactly. So like I was sayin' before Mac hot-headed on his bullshit, we still got the ace we ain't played yet. We sitting on a flush, so there's nothing to worry about. Milk, you sit in your goddamn window night and day. You see them meet, you get in that diner and record everything, you got me? I want it all. Go online and get some of that spyware shit off the Dark Internet. We need proof. Hard proof, got me?"

"I got you," Milk assured him.

Othello scratched at his jaw, thinking for a moment, then said, "The game has changed. So we have to change with it. Lay low, everybody. Time to play these niggas against one another."

Venus and Milk left. When it was just the men, Othello turned to Mac and put his hand out. "Yo brah, I apologize. I know we a team. No question. We tight. It's just, I formulated the plan, so I guess I got little caught up in being the one to execute. We go back too far to beef over petty shit."

"I agree," Mac said.

"On the real, you always kept it a hunnid wit me, no matter what. I can always depend on my man Mac to keep it real."

They shook hands.

"You still my nigga, you ugly Yaphet Kotto lookin' muhfucka," Mac cracked.

They all laughed, tension broken.

"Oh, you got jokes huh? You shitty midget eatin' ass nigga! Breath smell like you shit out your mouth!" Othello hollered back, smile wider than the Holland Tunnel. The three of them laughed like the old friends they were, releasing the tension of the situation. "But yo, on some real shit. I got somebody I want y'all to meet," Othello announced.

"Who?" Cash asked.

"You'll know soon enough. Little shortie I met and, keepin' it one hunnid, I'm really feelin' her, yo," Othello admitted.

"Aw man, not you, too. First Mac got pussy-whipped, now you gonna join the club?" Cash groaned in mock despair.

Othello grinned at him. "Ay, Black Love is a beautiful thing."

"Man, fuck that. The only time I love 'em is when my dick hard," Cash cackled, grabbing his crouch.

"So when we gonna meet her?" Mac asked.

"Friday, yo. Bring Kandi. Cash, you just bring any bitch you can dig up," Othello chuckled.

"I'll be there. Gonna be good to meet the chick who locked that ass down," Cash said.

Be careful what you wish for...

Milk did as she was told.

She knew there was a lot riding on catching Black Sam with the federal agent, and putting solid proof on the table that went beyond a word, so she stayed in her window damn near 24 hours a day, watching.

She went online and bought these long-range listening devices the size of a dime, as well as recorders to keep the information on.

She felt like a fuckin' spy herself.

Maybe today she'd strike gold?

Black Sam pulled up and looked around. The same cautious triple check. Maybe he figured the 5am truckers would conceal him in the traffic?

Milk was onto him.

She watched him get out of the car, cross the hardstand and enter the diner.

She watched him take a seat at a booth. Watched him order. It was a well-rehearsed routine.

She waited.

Several minutes later, the federal agent pulled up and parked side by side with his vehicle.

She watched him talk into his cellphone before hanging up. Watched him pocket it. Watched him clamber out of the car, lock up and go inside to join Black Sam.

Milk took picture after picture of both of them, then the two of them together in the booth. She knew beforehand that she couldn't just go down and enter the diner. Black Sam knew her now, and knew who she was with. But money had a way of getting around shit like that. She'd paid one of the waitresses a thousand dollars to plant the listening device in the base of a salt shaker. It wasn't her fault these fuckers were creatures of habit, always the same time, always the same place. She hadn't told the girl exactly who she was after, so she picked up her cell and called the waitress on the spot.

"Hello?" She answered.

"That's them, The white guy in the blue suit and the older black guy in the trench coat. You see them, table by the window?"

"Table 5. Yeah, I got them."

"Handle your business."

Click.

A few moments later, she watched the waitress approach the table and take the Fed's order.

When she returned with the food, the salt shaker was on the tray.

They never noticed a thing. Milk turned on the recorder, and heard Black Sam's voice "...to get the rest of them?"

The other man said, "All of them."

"That's going to take some time," Black Sam objected. "Joe Hamlet is a very powerful man. He won't just talk about this type of shit on the phone."

"Far be it from me to tell you your business, but you're his right hand man, right? Make him talk."

"I'm tellin' you, it's not that simple. Look, I can deliver Malik Muhammad, Tony Malone and Jerome Peters. That's some serious hitters. Ain't that enough?"

"We want Hamlet. The rest are fucking gnats, irritating but barely worth slapping down. It's all about Hamlet."

The conversation went on like that for another twenty minutes with Black Sam trying to convince the Fed it was going to be just about impossible to get hard evidence on Joe Hamlet and his political manipulations and kickbacks. The harder he blustered the more insistent the Fed became. The message was obvious: *either get Joe or we send you away for a long time.*

Milk smiled to herself. Maybe he wasn't a cop after all, but this was better.

"O is going to love this."

Othello held the get together in his apartment.

Mona arrived first.

When he opened the door and saw her come striding in dressed in a pink cat suit, cleavage popping, her hair done up with shocking pink highlights, he could barely control himself. She was a mighty fine sight. He grinned from ear to ear.

"Damn ma, you making that suit look good," he complimented, as he pulled her into his arms and tongued her down.

"Don't start something you know we don't have time to finish," she told him, walking in and dropping her clutch on the table.

"I see you cleaned up."

"Some," he chuckled.

He couldn't believe how nervous she made him feel. He wasn't used to it. She got under his skin. He was a man who prided himself on handling any situation, and not just handling it, handling it well. But not around her. She left him feeling like a little schoolboy.

"Patron?" he offered.

"But of course," she replied, giving him a wink.

He poured her the drink, clinking the bottle on the rim of the glass.

His doorbell rang again.

"Get that for me ma," he told Mona.

She opened the door to Kandi and Mac.

Kandi and Mona assessed one another. Eyes up, eyes down, judgment passed. Mona was looking good, but Kandi was no slouch. Her dress hugged her curves, showing off that bow legged stance that drove men crazy.

"You must be the woman that has our Othello wrapped around her little finger, huh?" Kandi smirked.

Mona smiled.

"I wouldn't say all that, but... Hi, I'm Mona."

They shook hands.

Othello approached, wrapping his arms protectively around Mona from the back.

"Mo, this is Kandi, and my man Mac Bethel. The Bethels, Mona," Othello playfully introduced with mock flourish.

Mac looked at Mona strangely, she caught the look, but he quickly smiled to cover whatever had him twisted up.

"It's nice to meet you," he told her.

"Same here," Mona said.

It was all very normal for the next few minutes—the four of them getting acquainted, a few stories about how they'd come up together, war stories, inside jokes and all that shit she wasn't really part of—right up until the doorbell rang again.

Othello went and opened it.

Cash walked in with this gorgeous little Asian chick with a body like a black girl, all tits, ass and hips.

"Sushi anyone?" Cash quipped, the girl at his side giggling. There was no doubt what Cash had been eating before they rolled up.

Othello embraced Cash with a gangsta hug. "Come on in my nigga, everybody already here."

He walked Cash into the living room, arm around his shoulder.

Mona had her back to them as they approached, still chatting away with Kandi when Othello said, "Mo. Meet my man..."

She turned around, deer in the headlights, and froze.

"Cash."

Cash was every bit as surprised, but he kept his game face on. Inside, though, his nerves were twanging like electric guitar strings, his brain wiring lit up like a Vegas casino.

He couldn't believe his eyes.

Hers said: *You?*

His screamed: *What the hell are you doing here?*

But outwardly, both just about kept it together, even if they weren't exactly composed.

Mona's voice was a little shaky when she said, "It's nice... to meet you."

Cash wasn't his smooth self. The best he could muster was, "Yeah."

Othello put his arm around Mona, proudly.

"Yeah yo, didn't I tell you she was somethin', my nigga? Mo, Cash and Mac, these two niggas go back with me to my Underoos days," he laughed, truly content and happy to be surrounded by his family. Right here, in this room, were the only people in the world he could trust.

Mona and Cash stole glances while Othello beamed.

As the night wore on, they played a subtle game of eye tag.

The glances were real quick, real furtive, and they thought no one saw them.

They were wrong.

Someone did.

Kandi.

She was watching Mac at first, trying to figure out why he kept side-eyeing Mona. She was about to get in her feelings, when she noticed that Mona wasn't looking at Mac, she was steadily stealing glances at Cash, and that nigga was returning them.

It didn't take her long to figure out what was going on.

"That bitch fucked Cash before," she told Mac after they walked out of the party.

She said it with absolute confidence.

That was when Mac's brain dinged like he'd just hit three in a row on a slot machine, bells going off everywhere.

"I knew I knew that bitch! That's how I know her! We snatched up her and her girlfriend one night at the Waffle House...*fuck*."

"What you mean snatched up?" Kandi snapped with attitude, but Mac disregarded her petty jealous flare up.

"What the fuck?" He shook his head. It didn't make sense. "Why Cash don't just tell that nigga?"

Kandi laid her hand on his arm. "Just make sure *you* don't tell him. Not yet," she warned.

"What you mean, *not yet*?"

"Trust me on this. A woman's intuition never lies."

Kandi slipped her arm into his and leaned into Mac as they walked to the car, knowing the information would come in handy one day.

Meanwhile, Cash was thinking along similar lines.

He wasn't even paying attention to the Asian girl as she sucked his dick on the drive home. He was normally all for the speed thrill, powering through the streets, lips wrapped around his hard dick. But nothing about this night had been normal. All he could focus on was Mona's beautiful face.

After their one night stand, he couldn't get her out of his mind.

It was like she'd taken up residence in his fantasies.

He tried to act like she was just another fuck, but that smile, her style, her presence, the whole fuckin' thing that was Mona, it just blew him better than an army of Asian chicks. He'd tried to call her several times, but every time she sent him to voicemail. That just made his obsession worse. He couldn't believe a woman was blowing *him* off. He was the one who didn't return phone calls; he was the one who left bitches cold and lonely without as much as a kiss goodbye. That shit didn't happen to him. He didn't like the way she'd flipped the script on him. He couldn't trust the way he was feeling. But fuck, the universe was a stone cold bitch. Black fuckin' heart and all. It was like she had just dropped off the map only to reappear on the arm of his man, his best friend.

"Baby, are you okay?" the Asian girl asked, looking up at him, precum glossy on her lips.

Cash pushed her back down as he made a left onto the highway.

'You're doing fine, yo," he replied absentmindedly.

Mona was back in his life and he knew shit would never be the same again.

Aphrodite lay poolside.

She wore a two-piece bikini practically made of dental floss.

The woman was an exhibitionist. She got off showing her mature, shapely frame. From head to toe, she was definitely a dime. Adonis walked out in a pair of swim shorts that bulged with his healthy package.

Aphrodite took the time to admire his chiseled frame as he walked to the board, and climbed the ladder. He stood there for a moment, golden sun streaming down, master of his domain, then took three fast steps, bounced on the board and dove into the pool.

He swam the length twice, powerful arms cutting through the blue before he came over and rested his elbows on the edge of the pool.

"Adonis, come have a drink with your loving mother," Aphrodite called out playfully.

Adonis rose out of the pool, water dripping down his cut muscles. Aphrodite didn't turn away. "Don't you mean, Adonis bring your loving mother a drink?"

"That, too," she laughed.

Adonis's bare feet slapped on the wet stone as he walked over to the poolside bar and poured them both a stiff one.

Glasses in hand, he walked it back, handed Aphrodite her drink, then sat sideways on the deck chair facing her.

"Have you seen your sister?"

Adonis shrugged and sipped. "Not today."

"Hmmm, she's been *very* secretive lately. I figured, if anybody knew why, it would be you," Aphrodite watched his expression.

He knew his mother was on a fishing expedition, so he kept his face straight. There was no way he was going to breathe the fact that Mona was literally sleeping with the enemy. She had sworn him to secrecy.

"You're just being your usual paranoid self, mommy dearest,"

Adonis chuckled, trying to deflect and change the subject with humor.

Aphrodite allowed him to lead her where she wanted to go anyway. "Well, what about *you*? You haven't exactly been an open book. You ready for this wedding?"

"As ready as I'll ever be," he mumbled, downing his drink.

That wasn't the enthusiastic response she'd hoped for, given the amount of money they were putting into the whole show. "Is there something wrong, baby?"

"Should there be?"

Aphrodite sat up, crossing her long, sexy legs.

"I know you, son. It's written all over your face." She asked the question she didn't really want an answer to. "You do love her, don't you?"

Adonis looked off in the distance, thinking, *it depends on which her you're referring to*, but he said, "I'm marrying her, ain't I?"

Aphrodite laughed. "Marriage doesn't love, boy."

"You sound like you know that firsthand."

"If you're asking if I love your father, the answer is yes, very much. Can we speak honestly? As adults?" Aphrodite asked, a curious expression on her face.

"I thought we were."

She smiled.

"No, baby, you were telling me what I wanted to hear."

"What are we going to talk about?"

"Your...preferences," Aphrodite said, flatly.

He looked at her.

"Meaning?"

"Adults, remember? Baby, I'm your mother. We are blood. You think I don't know my own children? Believe me, a mother knows, a mother *always* knows, even if she pretends she doesn't.

"What are you trying to say?"

"I know that Bianca isn't who you really want," Aphrodite told him straight out.

Adonis wanted to fix his mouth to deny it, deny himself, but he made a conscious decision to be bold for once in his life. To be himself.

He nodded.

"How long have you known?" he questioned.

"All your life. Haven't you been listening? I remember that little boy you went to school with, what was his name? Oliver?"

Adonis couldn't help but smile to himself.

He definitely remembered Oliver.

They were both thirteen.

Oliver was flaming even in grade school.

Unapologetically gay, with all of that fabulousness and flair to match.

Oliver had enticed what was deep in his adolescent mind, bringing that latent desire to the surface.

Oliver had set him free.

"Yes. Oliver."

"You think I didn't know what you two were doing in the attic? In your playhouse?"

"Why didn't you tell Daddy?"

"Why do you think? Your father would've killed you and killed me for having you. Besides, I knew there would come a time he would leave this family and all our business in your hands. Without you, it would've gone to Black Sam and his son."

He looked at her, not following. "But Uncle Sam's son is dead. Didn't he drown in our pool?"

Aphrodite laid back on the chair, put her shades back on, very deliberately covering her eyes before she replied, "Of course he did."

It wasn't *what* she said, it was *how* she said it that sent a chill up his spine.

"What do you mean, of course, ma?"

He couldn't tell if she was looking at him or not.

Her stone expression said it all.

"You think your father is the only gangster in this family? We do what we have to do to protect ourselves, no? Black Sam is your father's next in line. Had your father found out about you, then he would have given the crown to Kenny. So, I made sure that when Kenny came to spend the summer with us, the only crown he'd be wearing was seaweed," Aphrodite explained flatly.

My mother is a murderer? Adonis thought to himself, trying to wrap his mind around what it took to kill a child, a friend's son...

He'd always known she was a diva, a social creature, who delighted in entertaining some of the most powerful people in the city and made damn sure she looked beautiful while doing it. But how the hell was he supposed to reconcile that his mother was capable of killing a 12-year-old child in cold blood just to preserve her son's birthright?

"When you run this family, you will have to do a lot more. That's just the truth of the life you are inheriting. Tell me the truth, baby, are you ready for that?" Aphrodite asked him.

Adonis dropped his head.

"I don't know."

Aphrodite sat up and took her shades off again.

She leaned forward, her legs were between his.

She caressed his cheek, lovingly, almost sensually and Adonis responded, looking up at her.

He hated to admit it, even to himself, but his mother was the only woman that had any effect on his flesh. She turned him on.

Her smile said she knew it.

"Dearest Adonis, this world is about sacrifices. Do you know what a sacrifice asks of us?" Before he could answer she said, "It asks, how badly do you want what you want? How far will you go to get where you want to go? Dearest Adonis, life isn't worth living if you don't desire something you're willing to give up everything for," she explained.

She was the very voice of desire.

He didn't know what to say. He didn't know how to react, not only to her words, but to the fact that he felt so.... aroused. He felt his dick getting hard in his swim shorts.

Aphrodite laid back again.

"Think about what I said, sweetheart. And when you see your sister, tell her I need to see her."

He had been dismissed.

---

oe Hamlet was a man of appetites. Big appetites. To satisfy some of them, he kept a mistress laid up in a skyrise apartment. The building was like something a stoned Trump had designed. She was a bad bitch in all the best ways; an ex-porn star that fucked like Mia Khalifa and looked like some Egyptian goddess stepped out of mythology. She'd played Isis in some fantasy TV show on HBO a few years back and starred in her own porn parody which generated serious bank. The bitch had a business head on her. She knew her looks were money, and by holding onto some shit back then, down the line she'd make a killing by getting into some real perverted shit that had the freaks lining up around the block, wallets and cocks in hand. She'd just done some German shit, real depraved stuff. He'd bust a nut to it more than once. That was the thing about their relationship, it was transactional. He wasn't into ownership, walking down the street with this honey on his arm and turning heads. And he could give a fuck who else was in there doing her, that was her business. When they were together, they were together. She kept him young. Watching her riding his dick, the way her body moved beat any fucking belly dancer. And it didn't matter how much dick she'd had, her pussy still gripped his dick and always fucked his head up and sent him over the edge.

After they finished fucking, Joe sat on the side of the bed, strapping on his watch, fully dressed while she was still naked. She slung her naked body over him, kissing at his ear.

"Do you have to go?"

"I told you, shit is hectic right now. I got a lot on my plate. But I promise, after this, we'll get away and go somewhere nice. I know a place: black sand, azure sea, proper paradise."

Her face lit up. "You promise?"

"I just did."

She covered his face with kisses.

"I love you, Joe, more than you know." She thought about it for a second. "I want to go to Bali. I saw a commercial about it and I want to go there."

"Then Bali it is," Joe said, standing up.

On her knees, she looked up at him. He couldn't begin to understand how a woman like her could always look so fuckin' innocent. It was like a magic spell that always made his dick hard.

He pulled out his black card and threw it on the bed.

"There you go. Burn it up, okay? Get a whole new wardrobe for the trip. I'll see you next week." She kissed him so passionately he had to pull himself away before he got lost in her lips and needed to lose himself in her body all over again.

"I love you, Daddy," she sang as he opened the door.

"I know you do," he winked, then walked out.

Outside the door, his bodyguard leaned against the wall, waiting.

"Ready, Mr. Hamlet?"

"Yeah, let's go."

They got on the elevator. The damned thing was gold and diamond. He hadn't seen anything like it in his life. It cost more than a Third World Country. The bodyguard pressed for the underground parking level. He wasn't a great talker, but silence in elevators was always uncomfortable, so they made small talk— the usual did you see the game stuff as the elevator descended.

The thing about elevators is most people feel safe.

They think there is no way in, flying past floor after floor, staring at the only entrance to the elevator.

They forget to look up.

Joe didn't hear the emergency hatch above his head slide open slowly, well-greased and silent.

"Move and you're dead."

There was a moment of confusion, Joe looking at his bodyguard, bodyguard looking for the threat and not seeing it. Then both men looked up staring down the barrel of an AR-15 fully automatic machine gun that was being pointed at them by a sexy Latina chick. It was Venus.

"Don't play with me, gentlemen. Hands up. Down on your knees," she ordered.

They hesitated.

BBBBBRRRRRRRRAAAAAAPPPPP!

She let a few rounds loose, the sound ricocheting inside the small space as the bullets pierced the outer shell. That got their fullest attention.

"On your knees. Now. Or lay on your back in a church some goddamn where! Do it!"

They did what they were told.

Joe was calm.

It wasn't a hit. If it had been, he would have been dead already.

"What's this all about?" he asked, his hands laced behind his head, on his knees.

Venus dropped down through the hatch, landing lightly on her feet. Moving quickly, she relieved both men of their guns. "You'll find out soon enough." She promised.

The elevator door opened up to the underground parking area.

Middle of the day, pitch dark. All the lights in the underground were out save one on the ceiling, bright like a spotlight. They stepped out of the elevator.

Joe's Phantom was surrounded by two black SUV's.

His driver was face-down on the cement.

Finally, Joe looked into the face of his enemy's foot soldier.

"Othello, I presume?"

Othello smiled.

"In the flesh."

"Come to kill me?"

"You know if I had, you'd be dead already. No, I've come to talk and I really think you'll be feeling what I have to say."

Joe looked around at the other faces, people he would later come to know as Mac, Cash and Milk.

He glanced at his bodyguard, then at his watch, like he really didn't have time for this shit, so be done with it. He said as much. "So talk."

"Just me and you. We'll take your car. No guns. You drive," Othello laid down the terms.

The two men eyed one another. Joe was slightly shorter, but bulkier. He'd been a boxer. He was good with his fists. He could handle the young upstart if shit got hectic.

"Okay," Joe agreed, then turned to his bodyguard, "You wait here."

"After you," Othello handed his piece to Mac, then turned around so Joe could see he didn't have another one concealed.

Joe reached down and pulled his ankle holster off, tossing the snub-nosed .380 to Venus with a wink.

"You would've never got your hands near it," Venus told him.

Joe shrugged.

"We'll never know."

Othello patted him down, then offered Joe the chance to pat him down. "Like you said, I'd be dead already, right?" Joe repeated. O nodded.

Joe got in under the wheel while Othello joined on the passenger's side.

They drove off. Nothing fancy. No burning rubber. Off for a nice afternoon drive. "Any particular destination?"

"Take the scenic route to understanding," Othello quipped.

Joe chuckled.

"I must admit I've wanted to kill you for quite some time, but I can say that you make a decent first impression."

"Likewise," Othello returned. "I'm sure you're wondering what I have to say."

"Mildly curious."

"Well, it's not me that has something to say, really. Listen." Othello lifted his phone up and hit play.

He heard Black Sam say, "...to get the rest of them?"

Another man said, "All of them."

"That's going to take some time," Black Sam objected. "Joe Hamlet is a very powerful man. He won't just talk about this type of shit on the phone."

"Far be it from me to tell you your business, but you're his right hand man, right? Make him talk."

"I'm tellin' you, it's not that simple. Look, I can deliver Malik Muhammad, Tony Malone and Jerome Peters. That's some serious hitters. Ain't that enough?"

"We want Hamlet. The rest are fucking gnats, irritating but barely worth slapping down. It's all about Hamlet."

Othello killed the playback. He said, "He's talking to the Feds."

Joe's expression said it all. His brow darkened with volcanic rage that could take the roof off the car if it exploded, but Joe maintained his composure and finally chuckled.

"Son of a bitch..."

"Among other things," Othello added. "Like I promised, enlightenment. I guess now you know who was behind all of this." By this, he meant the war.

Joe looked at Othello, studying his expression.

Up until that moment, he had taken him for a two-bit thug, the puppet for some real gangsta puppeteer pulling his strings. He'd read that wrong. Othello was pulling the strings. Black Sam just thought he was.

"Why are you telling me this?"

"Because he's a problem for both of us."

"I didn't hear your name mentioned on the tape."

"You didn't hear the whole tape," Othello said.

Joe nodded.

"Where is he?"

Othello smiled. "First the deal."

"Deal?" Joe echoed.

"You give me Black Sam and you and your people get to live, that's the deal."

"I think me and my people have proven we can take care of ourselves. We're looking for a little more."

"Like?"

"Like, I give you Black Sam and you get me a seat on The Commission," Othello proposed.

Joe chuckled, it was worse than mocking laughter. It was patronizing.

"A seat? Are you serious? After the shit you've pulled, you'll be lucky to have still have an ass you try if to confront The Commission!"

"I know your Golden Rule, if I'm a member of The Commission, no other made member can touch me, right?"

"Yeah, but to get made, I can't just *give* you a seat. It's a vote, and the vote has to be unanimous," Joe explained.

"So, if I give you Sam, do I have *your* vote?" Othello looked Joe in the eyes.

Joe pulled over.

"Let me tell you straight, you've killed men that I admired, respected, even loved. How do you suppose I forget about that?"

"I've lost men too, men that I loved. No one can bring them back, but this is the life we chose, you and I. Tomorrow.... that's something you tell children and women to give them something to look forward to, but us, all we have is today," Othello replied, like he was dropping some serious wisdom.

In Othello's mind, thoughts of his father filled him like the bellows filled the flame with the power to grow, leap and devour.

Joe's heart flinched when Othello mentioned losing loved ones. He could see the father he had killed in the son sitting before him. His demeanor softened and sighed.

"I agree. But you're asking a lot."

"I have a lot to offer."

A beat.

"And out of curiosity, if I say no?" Joe asked.

"Then I let Black Sam hear his own tape. What do you reckon he's going to do then? Can you say, witness protection? You're the whale they're after."

Joe looked away for a moment, then responded with, "You have my vote if you pull it off. But it doesn't matter, you'll never get the other votes."

"Let me worry about that. All I ask is that you guarantee my safety during the sit down," Othello held out his hand.

Joe paused, looked at his hand, then in his eyes, then finally nodded and shook his enemy's hand.

"Now... where's Sam?" Joe's eyes flashed with the color of hell.

Othello smiled. "Let's go."

Black Sam loved to play cards.

His favorite game was Georgia Skin.

Over the years, he'd won and taken many a man's life savings by the turn of a single card.

It was an old gangsta's game, a lesson that Benny was learning the hard way.

"Goddamn! Fuckin' eight!" Benny spat, watching Sam rake in another four thousand dollars of his money with calm assurance.

Sam very methodically pulled the cash toward him like one of those fairground grabber hands reaching out to scoop it all up.

"I told you youngbuck, I was skinnin' wit' the best of them when your Daddy was a pup," he grinned.

"That's aight old timer, just shuffle them shits up," Benny replied, upping the ante to an even thousand to start the betting on the next hand.

"Big boy money, excellent, let's—" Black Sam began, but stopped when he heard the front door bang open.

He didn't push up from the table.

He didn't reach for his piece.

He waited for shit to materialize.

He didn't have long to wait.

Two seconds.

Othello entered, followed by Mac, Cash, Venus and Milk.

The old dawg smiled, ready to offer a welcome to his palace. Not even half a heartbeat later, he saw Joe walk in behind the others.

He closed the door.

"How you doin', Sam?" Joe greeted, his voice calm. Underneath, a cauldron bubbled.

Black Sam's eyes instinctively looked down, a twitch. A tell. His mind pictured the gun strapped to his ankle.

Joe inclined his head, "That'd be uniquely dumb, Sam," Joe said. "Besides, it's too late for all that."

"Too late?" Black Sam echoed, a nervous smile spreading across his face. "You got me all wrong, Joe."

Joe couldn't stand the sound of his voice. He smacked him with such savagery blood flew from his mouth. His knuckle loosened a couple of teeth. Sam toppled to the floor.

He made a move, nothing to lose, grabbing for his ankle holster. But before he'd gotten his trouser leg up, he felt cold steel against his forehead.

"I wish the fuck you would," Benny sneered.

Black Sam, defeated, relaxed his reach and leaned back on his elbows.

Joe pulled up a chair and sat inches from Sam's fallen body.

"You never told me you knew Othello, Sam? All the times we talked, and you never told me. When I found out, it damn near broke my heart to know the man trying to overthrow me was none other than my best fuckin' friend. Scratch that, my fuckin' BROTHER!" Joe remained ice calm, right up until the word brother broke his composure. He took a deep breath to center himself.

"J-J-Joe please, listen, just... hear me out," Black Sam begged.

"What could you *possibly* say, Sam? What could possibly make this right?"

"Right? Nigga, right? What do you know about right?" Black Sam roared, tears of betrayal filling his eyes. Not the betrayal he had committed, the betrayal he felt he was the victim of. Nothing left, knowing he was going to die, he removed the mask. "You the last muhfucka in here who need to be talking about right. You forget the wrong you done? You think time has forgiven you? You think *I* have forgiven you? Do you?"

Joe glared at him.

"What the hell are you talking about?"

"KENNY! That's what I'm talking about, Joe. My dead son!" Black Sam shot back, with the force of years of grief, pain and rage.

Joe looked at him like he was crazy.

"Sam, what the fuckin' fuck do I have to do with Kenny's death?"

Black Sam shook his head, unable to stop the tears he'd been holding back for so long.

"Everything... Kenny's death was no accident. He didn't just drown in your pool and you know it... Or fuck maybe you don't, or just don't wanna admit to it... But the blood is on your hands; yours and Aphrodite's."

Joe grabbed him by his collar, yanking him forward, lips inches from eyes so his anger spat into them. "Don't you *ever* speak my wife's name like that. She didn't have anything to do with Kenny's death!"

Black Sam laughed bitterly.

"Fuck you, Joe. Fuck you. You married to the devil herself."

Joe smacked fire from Black Sam.

He let his body fall back limp and dazed on the carpet.

Joe paced the floor, his mind balled like a piece of discarded paper, crinkling, and folded back, wrestling with Black Sam's words. He had *never* suspected Aphrodite's involvement in Kenny's death. It had been a tragic accident. A fuckin' horrible thing. But maybe he wasn't the man he'd always thought he was and didn't know the secrets of his own family?

He slammed his fist into the wall so hard he was sure he broke something in there.

The pain was nothing compared to the hurt inside.

Finally, he stopped. He knelt beside Black Sam. It was almost tender. Like friendship remembered, right until he opened his mouth. "If you felt like that, why didn't you come to me like a man, Sam? We got history. Instead, you sneak and connive behind my back like some lil' bitch? I thought you were better than that, man. I thought you were better."

"Better? You wouldn't expand The Commission. No seat at the table for Black Sam. You wouldn't let me out of your shadow. I wanted my own seat, goddammit, not carry your nutsack my whole goddamn life. But you wouldn't open the door, would you? It was all about Joe Hamlet. So I blew a fuckin' door open wide enough for an army to walk through. So kill me, I been dead for years. I don't give a fuck anymore, Joe. I'd rather be dead than a nutsack carryin' ass nigga."

Joe put a hand on his shoulder. Again, it could have been mistaken for friendship. "So it was never about your dead kid, eh, Sammy? Kenny was just your justification. Truth is what truth always is, greed. You're hungry to be number one. You wanna be on top? Well, nigga, is that what you want? Okay, fine, a seat at the table, sure, you got it. You shoulda just talked to me, nigga," Joe shrugged, then turned to Othello and added, "Bring him with us."

Othello frowned in confusion as Joe rose from the crouch and walked out the door.

Othello didn't understand until he saw Joe head for the stairs that led up to the roof.

He followed Joe as Benny and Cash held Black Sam between them, dragging him up to the seventeenth floor. The rest of the crew followed behind. They came out onto the roof in time to catch the setting sun. Below, the city buzzed with activity, people going home for the night, but for Black Sam, he was going home in another way...

Sam had known his fate from the first step on the concrete stairs.

"At least let me do it myself," he requested.

Joe looked at his old friend, a man he would've walked into Hell for, died for and was now about to kill.

"Okay, Sammy, I'll give you that."

Joe nodded at the men pinning Black Sam's arms. Following his lead, they released their hold on him. Black Sam straightened his clothes, determined to take his last breath with dignity.

He turned and looked at the setting sun.

"So this is how it ends, huh? I always thought it would be a bullet in the back of the head. So I guess I ought to be kinda grateful, Joe. I get to walk into the sunset."

Joe held the tears in. "That you do, and if I read the stars right, I'm not far behind you... old friend."

Black Sam nodded, then turned to Othello.

"You a sharp young cat, O. One of the sharpest I've ever seen. Too bad your blindness will always blur your sight." Othello didn't understand, but he wasn't about to give Black Sam the satisfaction of knowing that.

Black Sam walked to the edge of the roof.

He looked down, then he looked up, directly into the sun, blinding himself with its searing glare, and then he did what he came to do...

He walked in to the sunset.

No screams. No last words. No fear.

They watched as he went down, arms spread to embrace death with the bravery of a soul at peace.

When he burst across the blacktop seventeen floors below, the only ones flinching were the living.

Joe looked at Othello.

"Three days from today. I'll let you know the time and place. I've done my part, the rest is up to you."

Joe turned and walked away.

"Joe, I can't thank you enough for your support. Without you, I don't think I would've been re-elected," Mayor Jameson gushed, shaking Joe's hand firmly with that practiced grip politicos did so well, hand over hand, power and supplication.

Joe smiled knowingly.

The Mayor, a real Cuomo of a man, was destined for the top. He was a smoother politician than Clinton and more crooked than Boss Tweed.

"I bet you say that to all your donors," Joe laughed.

"Just the whales, Joe," the Mayor winked, "and it doesn't hurt when their wives are as beautiful or as supportive of my initiatives."

"When it comes to Aphrodite, anything for the children," Joe replied.

The Mayor had no clue just how much of a double-edged sentiment that was.

They shook hands and the Mayor moved on to work the crowd. The man was a master when it came to the schmooze. He pressed the flesh, offered the smiles, just the right chuckles. Joe sipped his drink and scanned the crowd, moving from face to face until he saw his wife, surrounded by sycophants. She was a bright star amid the wives and ambitious women that made up the elite of the city. He thought of Black Sam's admonishment, that he'd married the devil, so maybe that bright star was more than a little apropos. These were the women who sat on boards, all politically powerful, rich women, and they bowed down to Aphrodite's alpha femininity.

Joe watched his wife without her knowing.

To his eye, her emerald green dress had her outshining every woman in the place, her smile sparkling brighter than her jewelry.

You're married to the devil herself!

Joe moved through the crowd, stopping occasionally when decorum and acquaintances bid him to, picking a flute of champagne off a passing waiter's tray, and brought it to his wife.

"You're beautiful, you know that?" Joe whispered in her ear.

"So my husband tells me," she quipped.

"Trust me. In this, as all things, he has exquisite taste."

"How much have you raised for the Mayor's Youth Initiative?"

"Four hundred thousand," Aphrodite shrugged, "but the night is still young."

Joe raised his glass. "To the children..."

Clink...

"I.. have some bad news," he said, tone somber, voice pitched low. The words weren't meant to carry.

"Oh?"

"It's Sam. He's dead."

Aphrodite looked at him, shock behind her eyes. "Dead? How? I don't understand."

"Suicide. He jumped off the roof of his apartment building yesterday."

"Jesus... Why would he do such a thing?"

"Who knows, the mind of a desperate man? Last time we spoke, he was really down. Like blacker than black. I've never seen him like that. He was all wrapped up in Kenny's death," Joe replied, watching her expression.

"One more tragedy," Aphrodite sipped her champagne.

"What do you remember about that day, baby?"

"Some. It's been so long. Some though, images, feelings... the kinda stuff you never forget."

"Just try. For me."

Aphrodite took a deep breath.

"I remember being in the kitchen. I heard the splash in the pool, but the kids were always jumping around out there. But, this was different. It wasn't the kids messing around. I heard more splashing. It was... frantic. I looked out through the window. That's when I saw him... flailing. Oh Joe, I wish I could turn back time to that day, do it all again, differently. React quicker. I would give anything to have the chance to save him... I ran out of there, by the time I reached him, it was too late."

Joe snorted softly.

"Joe, what's the matter?"

"Nothing. I just remember you telling me you were asleep when it happened. That was why you didn't get there. Not in the kitchen. But hey, it was a long time ago, and the memory is a fickle thing. Dead is dead, right?" He smiled, but not with his eyes, and leaned in to kiss her forehead. "It's late, and I've got an important meeting in the morning. I should go."

He walked away leaving Aphrodite watching him with a curious, but amused expression.

Mona fell into Othello's arms as soon as he walked into the hotel suite.

Her face was molten with tears.

"What's wrong? What happened? Why are you crying?" The questions tumbled out of Othello in rapid succession, all kinds of bad thoughts crossing his mind.

He was ready to murder anything or anyone that had brought tears to Mona's eyes, anyone except one.

"It's... it's my uncle, baby. He's dead..." Mona cried.

Othello scowled.

"My God baby, I'm so sorry... What happened?"

He sat with her on the edge of the bed.

"It was a few days ago," she sobbed, "I can't believe he's gone. I loved him so much. He was just... so... he was always so..." she couldn't get the words out. "Why would he kill himself?"

Othello held her tightly in his arms, stroking her back, slowly and comfortingly.

"Baby, sometimes we don't know people as well as we think we do. No matter how close. There's a darkness in a lot of people we can't see on the surface. We don't know what demons they are wrestling. Sometimes they just can't take living under those conditions."

"It still hurts," she sniffled, resting her weight against his big, strong frame.

Othello sighed.

"That's crazy, because I lost someone in my circle recently."

"Really?"

"He's was murdered," Othello answered, leaving out the part that it was his hand that was behind the metaphorical push.

"Life is so crazy," Mona ran her hands back and forth across his chest.

"Yeah, it is," he agreed.

They both faded into their separate thoughts for a moment, finding a different kind of peace in each other's company, until Othello said, "Hey, how about we get away for a while? Just me and you? Go somewhere and just enjoy black love."

Mona looked at him, a big smile breaking through the clouds of her grief.

"Forreal, babe?"

"Yolo, right?"

"Right Yolo!" She smiled through the tears.

Othello folded her into his embrace and held her tightly.

She forgot her tears as she began covering his face with what started as butterfly kisses but quickly became more and more passionate until her tongue was down his throat and his hands were up her skirt, pulling her panties off. Sex and death. Powerful aphrodisiacs. Mona was frantic, grabbing his pants and fumbling with the belt and buckle until she got them open and he slid his pants down around his ankles. No foreplay. No seduction. She mounted him, gripping his dick and pushing him inside of her.

"Yes baby, stroke your pussy good," she purred, her hips winding like a dancehall queen from down yard.

Her pussy was so creamy, every stroke sounded like macaroni and cheese being stirred, the smack of her juices making him pump even harder. The spontaneity of the moment had them ready to bust quick. Othello gripped her ass cheeks, spreading to get deeper. Mona rode him, head thrown back, biting her bottom lip, her moans and cries urging him on until they both came simultaneously, shaking and shivering with orgasmic delight as the rush of release coursed through them.

"Damn, that was love," Mona giggled.

"The best is yet to come," he promised.

"Oh yeah? Don't let your mouth go making promises your dick can't keep," she smirked.

Othello stroked her cheek, his expression solemn and vowed, "I'll never break a promise to you, babygirl. Word is bond." They kissed, this time slower and more sensually as they took their time with round two.

After Mona had dozed off, Othello found himself thinking about Black Sam.

He laid there beside her, eyes closed, and remembered how it had all begun...

running... harder... faster...

The sound of his own breath loud in his ears, his legs cramping and the blare of police sirens and K-9's pushing him forward. Chasing. Muscles burning. Sweat poured down Othello's face as he leaped, making a grab for the gate, halfway up, and was damn near over until his pants got snagged on the old barbed wire spiraled on top.

The gate separated one abandoned factory from another, and the snag was all it took.

"Freeze!" The officer yelled, gun aimed, trembling with murderous anticipation.

But Othello feared a cage more than he feared death.

He hit the ground hard, jarring his senses, but he was back on his feet and moving off pure adrenaline.

Buck! Buck! Buck!

Three shots rang out, the blaze of the barrel bringing light to the pitch black alleyway. But it wasn't no kind of god. The only way the officer knew he had hit Othello was because of the grunts when the bullets found their target.

The next sound he heard was several trash cans being knocked over.

"I'm shot!" Othello bellowed in the darkness, the smell of his fresh blood driving the dogs into a frenzy.

"Don't move!" The young, nervous officer screamed, as several more officers ran up behind him. More came from both sides of the gate.

Othello laid on his back, the pain of the leg and hip wound burning like a branding iron stamping his black ass, the pain of being caught, the thought of prison and the loss of his freedom.

"Cuff him!"

"I'm fucking bleeding!"

"Next time don't run!" a smart-mouthed Irish cop shot back.

It took twenty minutes for them to call an ambulance and ten more before it arrived. The fuckers were hoping he'd die, or at least put him through so much pain he would have preferred it.

Othello went to trial and kept his mouth shut about Mac and Cash's involvement. It was the code. They were brothers.

He took his five-year sentence with a smile.

Once he hit the yard, he hit the ground running.

There were no thoughts of redemption or discovering God. He wasn't into that shit. His only regret was getting caught, so his only thoughts revolved around getting out and doing it all again. Better the second time around.

His time was spent hustling and working out, and when the situation called for it, bustin' niggas' heads for bread.

If you wanted the job done right, you called Othello.

They saw him as this big, black dumb ugly motherfucker that you didn't want to cross, but he was a lot more than that, and one old timer saw the truth. His name was Rudy. Rudy had been banged up so long, no one alive knew he was still there. Confined to a wheelchair and being eaten away by cancer, Rudy spent his time playing chess and reading. "Say young buck, let me rap a taste with you," Rudy asked him one day.

Othello had never said two words to the man before, but had a natural respect for the old timers, so he stopped working out long enough to walk over.

"What up, Unk?" Othello asked, chest heaving.

"Push me a couple of laps, I need some exercise," Rudy told him.

Othello chuckled.

"I'm the one doing the pushing."

Rudy pulled out one of his trademark cigars, ones that they didn't sell in the prison commissary. "Unk, better not let the police see you smoking that."

Rudy snorted.

"Fuck the *po-lice*, I'm dyin," Rudy retorted between puffs, then added, "Othello, right?"

"Yeah."

"I been keepin' my eye on you, watchin' how you move. You a smart nigga, dumb... but smart."

Anybody else would've called Othello dumb would've been swallowing teeth, but he respected the bluntness of the old timer. "Dumb?"

"You run around here chasin' this short ass penitentiary money, for what?"

"Just doin' time."

"Naw nephew, you lettin' the time do *you*. That different. You could be a force in this game, if you get your head together," Rudy jeweled him.

Othello nodded, letting the wisdom of the older man soak into his brain. "Get my head together how?"

Rudy pointed to the bleachers set off away from the rest of the yard.

Othello steered him over.

He sat on the bleachers.

"When you get out, what do you plan on doing?" Rudy questioned.

"Hit them streets and eat," Othello answered, his focus lasered in on the vision of freedom.

Rudy shook his head. "No neph, what's your *plan*? Any dumb muhfucka with a gun and a dick can get money. I'm askin' you how you gonna *make* it?"

"I don't know what you mean," Othello admitted.

"You ever heard of Frank Matthews?"

"Naw."

"Frank Matthews was the baddest hustla in the game. He the only nigga to do it and get away with it. To this day, muhfuckas don't know the real story, but I'ma pour you a drink. See Frank set up this organization called The Commission. It was to bring all the biggest hustlers around the country together. Sort of like the Black Man's mafia, you got me?"

"I hear you."

"Okay, but Frank disappeared right after he put it together and left it to a man named Willie Simmons. Now Willie put it down, but it wasn't the same and soon, shit started going south. But The Commission is still around: here, there, everywhere, ya dig? Now, a man named Frank Myers wanted a particular area in The Commission territory, but it was already going to another man. You ever heard of Joe Hamlet?"

"Yeah, Big Joe. That's the most powerful muhfucka in the city," Othello replied.

Rudy puffed and nodded.

"Yeah, but he wasn't always. Frank put him on. He gave him a seat on The Commission in exchange for killing the man who was supposed to get Frank's territory. You know who that was?"

"Who?"

Rudy smiled. "Your father."

Othello's whole world tilted hearing the world *father*. That was a word he had never known in his life, never held in his arms, never threw him a football in the falling leaves of autumn. No such man in his world.

"My... *what*?"

Rudy eyed his expression and nodded.

"Raymond Moore. He ran a bar on the Southside, but that was just a front. Ray was a cold blooded killer. He was Willie Simmons' blood kinfolk."

"You're telling me I'm some sort of nigga mafia royalty and Joe Hamlet killed my father, Unk?" Othello repeated, his anger begin to rise.

"That's *exactly* what I'm telling you. Everything Joe has is because he killed your father and set Frank Myers up to be top dog in The Commission."

Othello stopped, stood up and paced a few feet to the edge of the grass bordering the concrete track. He looked across at all the inmates playing basketball and working out, but his mind was a million miles away, thinking of the man he would never know, all because of a man he knew all too well.

He turned back to Rudy.

"Why are you telling me this?"

Rudy smiled. "Because you needed to know, boy. But listen more, I ain't done. Joe's right hand, is a man named Black Sam. He's been with Joe since damn near the beginning. But Joe won't let Sam be his own man. Sam is ready to make a move, but he needs a team, a young team a team he can trust."

"With a shared enemy, so that team doesn't turn on him," Othello surmised.

Rudy smiled.

"See? I knew you were smart."

"When do I talk to this Black Sam?"

"You talkin' to him now. Sam is my brother. He needs you to handle something for him, to prove your loyalty."

"What's that?"

Rudy unlocked his wheelchair wheels.

"I'll let you know," he said, then slowly rolled away.

Two days later, Othello got the call...

Othello gripped the sharpened toothbrush like a grudge. He pushed it down inside his waistline as he got in line to go to chow. The smell of the kill was in the air. Looking at the passing faces, he enjoyed their obliviousness. It made him feel special. He was he only one who knew what was going to happen. He eyed the metal detector as he got near it. It was a useless precaution in a shithole like this. No one had to carry metal shanks anymore, making metal detectors redundant.

He passed through the detector, the guard on duty eyeing him hard.

Othello dipped his head, not deferential, but knowing.

Most correctional officers were pussies and punks. Dudes that used to get picked on in school by dudes they now lorded their authority over. The world had come full circle. Revenge of the nerds, forreal.

Othello entered the chow hall, taking a beat to look around.

His prey was sitting in the corner. An older man, maybe a child molester, he had that look, but Othello had already been given the rundown on the joker. He had snitched on a bunch of old timers to the Feds. Because he had such a long sentence for embezzlement, the Feds couldn't just let him walk, so they transferred him to a state facility and cut his time in half.

He thought he only had six months left in prison.

The good news for him: it was less than that.

The bad news, it was less than ten more minutes.

Othello moved like a tiger in full stalk, using the other inmates as camouflage, from other snitching inmates, police observation and surveillance cameras. He knew how to move. This wasn't his first prison hit, but it was the most important when it came to determining his future.

He allowed his prey to finish his meal. It was only right. The man got up and made his way toward the tray disposal window. Othello smiled to himself. The man thought he had it made. Othello hated snitches with a passion. He would've killed this bitch for free, but this was a paid hit, so business *and* pleasure.

Othello slid in smoothly behind the prey, keeping a few inmates between them in line.

He waited until the prey turned the corner to go up the stairs to his dorm to make his move.

The stairwell was built at an angle, that included a landing that turned a corner, before rising up another flight. The landing was a blind spot. The camera on the second floor didn't start focusing until you reached the steps and the camera on the first floor only picked up your back right before you disappeared around the corner.

In that sweet spot for violence, Othello made his move.

"This is for The Commission, nigga!" Othello hissed like a cobra right before he struck, seven times in the neck, kidneys and chest. Fast, brutal, savage, hard. The plastic shank was sharp, but it still needed serious strength to penetrate, which only made it that much more satisfying for him and agonizing for his victim.

The man cried out, dropping to his knees, then flat on his face.

Othello dropped to one knee and hit him ten more times, driving the shank home, then jetted up the stairs, taking off his shirt and heading straight to the shower.

He dropped the shank in the common area toilet as he got in the shower.

Two other guys were under the spray, but when they saw this big, black cock diesel motherfucker get in, covered in blood, even the realest niggas knew to give a man space. They backed the fuck out of there.

Othello showered alone.

While he was under the water, he heard the *whoop whoop!* of the prison alarm, signaling Lockdown.

"Hurry up, Moore, lockdown!" The officer bellowed, when he stuck his head around the corner and saw Othello.

"Word? What up?"

"Somebody got stabbed."

"Stabbed?'

"Killed! You need me to use smaller words?"

Mission accomplished.

Othello went back to his room to find his cellmate laying on the top bunk, reading an urban novel. They called him Rihanna because he was a faggot. He'd been dead set against having Rihanna as a cellmate, until one day, he saw a dude trying to push up on him in the yard, playing him like a straight punk. Rihanna spit a razor so swiftly, the dude never seen it coming, sliced the cocksucker literally blind in the right eye and criss-crossed his face with so many buck fifties, the dude needed reconstructive surgery and came out of it looking like Frankenstein.

"I ain't gay cause I'm scared, nigga. I'm gay by choice!" Rihanna screeched.

Ever since then, the two killers respected one another's space.

They even came to have a mutual respect for one another, if not a gangtsa friendship.

"You good?" Rihanna asked, without taking his eyes out of the book.

"You already know," Othello assured him.

The hit solidified Sam and Othello's relationship.

When Othello stepped out through those prison gates, he definitely had a plan...

Kill Joe Hamlet and take back what was his by birthright.

Othello looked over at Mona. He kissed her gently on the forehead. His heart ached because he knew he had taken someone away from her that was precious. He knew what that felt like.

His guilt wouldn't let him sleep.

———

"Marry her?" Cash exclaimed, echoing Othello's words. "Are you forreal?"

He had rode with Othello to the jewelry store, thinking Othello was just going to pick up some new shine, but Othello had brought him, because, "You know women, brah. I need you to help me pick out the right engagement ring."

Cash couldn't believe his ears.

Not in a million years had he expected his man to get married, and not in a million more to the woman he was in love with.

The universe was a bastard.

"You hardly know this chick," Cash sputtered, his indignation mocked by the sparkle and bling of the promises of forever on full display all around him.

"Brah, she's *the one*. Believe me, I never believed that Hollywood shit, but it is what it is. When you find the special someone, you hold onto them with all you got," Othello replied.

The saleswoman's approach stopped Cash from saying more.

"How are you gentlemen doing today?"

"Good. And your fine self?"

"I'm well thanks. Can I help you with something?"

"I sure hope so. I'm here for an engagement ring," Othello told her.

"Oh, congratulations to you. We've got a lovely selection of pieces, if you'd step down to this next display case, I can show what we have. And if there's nothing that strikes your fancy, we also offer a few specialty pieces."

"Specialty?"

"Yes, you can design your own ring and we'll make it for you," she smiled.

"Interesting. Can you give us a minute, please?'

"Certainly, sir."

The saleswoman walked away. Othello eyed all of the different style rings. Cash's mind was in a whirl. He still hadn't had a chance to talk to Mona. Every time they were around each other, Othello was there, too. He had caught her looking at him several times, so he knew there were things on her mind as well.

"Cash."

I have to talk to her. I know she doesn't want to marry O. She can't, not after what we shared. How can she do this to me?

"Cash."

Why should he be happy while I suffer the pain? Women love me, they would never pick this black, ugly muhfucka over me! But he is my man, I don't know...

"CASH!" Othello half-shouted, snapping him out of it.

Cash looked up at Othello.

"Nigga, you gonna help me pick out something, or what?"

"My bad brah, my head is killing me. I'ma wait in the car," Cash explained. He wasn't lying, because he was dying, but it wasn't a headache. It was the pounding of his own broken heart tearing him apart.

He had to get out of the store.

Cash went out to the car and slammed the door.

"I'm..... I'm just gonna holler at her next time she around," he said out loud to himself. "Just pull her to the side. But what will I tell O? I'll tell him I'm feeling her girlfriend. No, no, that won't work. Fuck it, I'm just going to start a fake Facebook page and friend her! Then when she hits back, I'll tell her who I am..."

It wasn't exactly a genius plan, but it was something, and he had to be doing *something*. Cash snatched his phone out of his pocket and began to create the page. He didn't even have to think about a name for it...

Black Love Hurts.

When he was done, he sat back and smiled to himself.

He had cast his hook in the waters.

"Black Love Hurts?" Mona remarked, her face screwed up with confusion. She didn't recognize it, or the icon, and they had zero friends.

"What?" Celeste asked, disinterestedly, as she tried on a pair of stiletto boots in her mirror. "How do these look?"

"Fine," Mona answered, just as disinterestedly.

They were both in their own world.

Mona accepted the friend request.

A private message came almost instantly.

Thank you for accepting my friend request

She fired back an answer. *No problem. Why do you call your page Black Love Hurts?*

Because it does. My heart was broken by a woman I loved and I thought she felt the same way.

I'm sorry to hear that. There's always other fish in the sea.

Not for me.

"Nigga, you like a broad with that social media shit," Othello chuckled, as they drove. Cash put up his phone and glanced over at his man.

"What can I say, I'm in love," Cash told him with a straight face.

"Yeah," Othello laughed, "With yourself."

5

J oe looked around the table at the rest of The Commission.
Every eye was on him.

He had called this emergency meeting, something he rarely did, which meant it had to be big. The smoke from his cigar curled in a lazy corkscrew up in front of his face, then caught a light breeze and wafted around the light fixture, lending the room a hot, smoky feel.

"I called this meeting for two reasons, but primarily because we have an outsider that wants to address us," Joe began.

"Who?" Malik wanted to know, not giving him time to finish.

"In due time, Malik. But know this: I have vouchsafed this meeting. Nothing is to happen to him. No retribution. No violence shall be perpetrated, do I make myself clear?" He waited for each one of them to make some sort of acknowledgment. It took a while for the lights to come on. "All hostilities must be held in abeyance. That is my word."

Rome spat, "Othello?" contemptuously.

"Yes," Joe confirmed.

Malone shook his head.

"You expect me to sit on my hands when the murderer of my

family stands before me? What sort of bullshit is this safe passage, Joe?"

Joe looked at the man. There were so many things he could have said in that moment. "With all due respect to you and yours, Malone—and believe me I grieve with you— but we are running a business here. He asked to speak, and for that reason alone, I think we need to hear what he has to say. It will be enlightening," Joe promised. "Especially when he gives up the name of his backer," Joe explained.

"This is bullshit, Joe," Malik said.

"Maybe, but you want that name as much as I do, and only one man is going to give it up, so what are you gonna do?" Joe replied.

He rose and opened the door.

The heat in the room boiled up from the rage radiating in the hearts of the men around the table at the sight of Othello walking into their haven like some sort of conquering general, a black Caesar expecting to be crowned.

He did not look like a man one vote away from his execution.

"Peace," Othello spoke, adding a subtle bow, a little more than an inclination of his head that barely broke his erect stance.

He looked around the table, face to face.

No man returning his greeting.

"You asked for this opportunity... Don't waste it with petty bullshit," Joe remarked.

"Or pleas," Rome hissed.

Othello looked at Rome and smiled.

"I never make excuses for my actions. That's not what I came for. When we first heard of each other, we did so as enemies. I take the blame for that. But the stench you sought to attribute to me, that was coming from one of your own."

"Give us a name," Malik demanded.

"With pleasure. Black Sam," Othello told them.

The men looked one to the other. There were murmurs. Disbelief.

It was Malik who broke the silence.

"You mean to tell me, after all your accusations and shit you slung around the place, the traitor to this body was in *your* house, Joe?"

Joe Hamlet looked at his soldier. "He was, but hear me, I was the first to be betrayed, Malik. But when you have a rotten limb on a tree, you cut it off, when you have a rotten limb on your body you cut it off or wind up a corpse. I have cut the limb off. Black Sam's death wasn't a suicide. He... fell on his sword."

"What's that supposed to mean?" Malone translated.

"He took the last honorable step and jumped, but make no mistake he would have been pushed if he lacked the fortitude," Joe responded.

"Black Sam was conspiring with the gangs to take over The Commission and execute each and every one of you," Othello said.

"The fact remains, Sam may have been the ends, but you were the means. The blood on his tongue is on your hands," Rome bassed.

Othello nodded. "This is true, no denying it. But let me ask you, Rome, do you remember Bobitto?"

Rome's face clouded over with the guilt of recognition.

"Bobitto was a friend of mine, a friend that you decided was no longer useful, and so he is no more."

"Bobitto was greedy. He wanted what wasn't his," Rome deflected.

Othello laughed out loud.

"On stolen lands, everything we get isn't ours! Greed is good, greed gives us a reason to get up in the morning. It's treachery that changes greed from a virtue to a vice, and to kill Bobitto in front of his own mother..." Othello allowed his voice to trial off, the silence making his point better than any words could.

He turned to Malone.

"Malone, I've heard several times over how you want to see me bleed for the death of Big L. You do know I did time with L, don't you?"

"And?" Malone growled.

"L had a nurse bringing him coke packages. He was eating hard, until the bitch started supplying another dude. L caught feelings, and he had the dude transferred, giving a known rat the information to dime on him and the nurse."

Malone jumped to his feet. "Muhfucka, you don't know that!" He spat, lunging away from the table, but Joe was quicker, moving to restrain him before it could turn ugly. He wasn't about to let this be the spark.

"Everything I say can be confirmed. Talk to your own connects on the inside," Othello countered.

"It's true, Malone. I was told the same thing by my boy in there," Malik seconded.

Malone sat, chest heaving and glaring at Othello. "Bullshit."

"But it isn't. Believe me, I take no joy speaking ill of the dead, but that don't mean I won't repeat that the dead bespoke ill with their actions towards me and the sanctity of this thing of ours, this sacred game that so many take lightly. I've brought you the head of your traitor, the man who was working with the Feds to end The Commission... I moved to save you. In return, I ask for one thing. I do not believe it is an unreasonable request."

"What do you want?"

"A seat at the table," Othello proposed.

"A seat? I'll give you a fuckin' seat, in hell!" Rome barked.

Othello took his rage in stride, waiting it out.

"Outside of your walls, outside of the places you think belong to you, the wolves are waiting. They are stronger, and have less to lose and more to gain. These gangs that you think can't unite, *will* unite. I can promise you this, because I stand in a position to do just that, courtesy of Black Sam. His treachery stands to be your gain. See, Sam's plan was to unite the gangs, promising each flag portions of your territories, while he eliminated you. Unlike Sam, I don't need the Feds, I've never been a rat and that's confirmed by the streets and my pedigree. They trust me out there, they know me as the face of the very conspiracy Sam failed to complete. But I will, and when I do, I won't ask for a seat. I'll take the whole table," Othello warned, with steel in his words. "Seems to me you got an easy choice to make, gentlemen."

Rome laughed in his face.

"We got guns, too. We got money. We got the power of the city behind us."

"But for how long? What happens when the city burns and the people cry for peace? What I offer is a chance to remain on top, unmolested. I feed the streets and you can continue growing old, fat and rich," Othello offered.

Despite their hatred, they saw the seeds of truth in his words. The gangs were getting more organized. That had long been a bone of contention. So, if they didn't bring them inside the house, sooner or later, they would tear it down. It was only a matter of time, and that was exactly the point Malone had been making for months. Thanks to Othello, he was confronted with the face of his own truth.

"What makes you think we can't make our own deals. Our own alliances?" Malone countered.

"They don't trust you. Plain and simple. The power you wield makes the streets think you're too cozy with the city, with those very same judges you claim are in your pocket. They see it as the other way around," Othello laid it out boldly.

They listened, but they didn't like what they were hearing.

"And you expect us to just trust you? And even if we did, a seat at this table means you can't harm another Commission member, it's got to be straight. The peace depends upon it. And the problem is you clearly hurt Don," Rome pointed out.

Othello nodded.

"This is true. By killing Don, that would shut me out forever. But, suppose I hadn't?"

"We don't deal in hypotheticals here, or are you trying to pin this one on Black Sam, too? Mighty convenient, since he's not here to defend himself. Nah, you're gonna have to wear it," Malik chuckled.

Othello's smile looked like a checkmate.

"You are right, Malik, Black Sam isn't here. But I'm not asking you to take my word for it, I have a more reliable witness," Othello answered.

He turned to the door and opened it.

Don walked in, leaning heavily on the crutches he used to support his weight. He looked pained from the exertion but remarkably healthy for a dead guy.

"Don? What the actual fuck!" Rome exclaimed.

"Alive and in the flesh."

"Someone better fuckin' explain it to me, real slow," Malone said.

"When Othello first came to my home, unwelcome, I felt nothing short of hatred for him. Believe me," Don said. "I would've loved for nothing more than to put a bullet in his head every day for a thousand years... but I listened and once he explained why he was at my door, well, I have to admit, gentlemen, Othello here saved my life."

"Explain more," Malone pressed.

"Sam wanted me dead, plain and simple. He saw it as a way to open up my territory for the gangs. Othello was smart. He knew it had to look real, and a couple of fucked up knees were a small price to pay for my life and my family's lives. So, he came back and dragged me out of that burning house and stashed us out of harm's way. It cost me my stash, and I won't be running any fucking marathon's for a while, but it was a decent price, because with that stash, he bought the respect of the gangs," Don explained, then looked at Othello, adding, "This is why I come before you and propose his joining The Commission. He has my vote."

Joe couldn't believe his eyes.

It didn't make a lick of sense. Don was dead, dead as dead can ever be. To see him walk in, to hear that Othello spared him, it changed things. It told Joe that Othello was a force to be reckoned with. He was not only ruthless, but ruthlessly deceptive and cunning.

"I second his induction," Joe voiced.

"He has my vote," Malone said. For him it was a no brainer. The pair shared the same goals.

Malik didn't speak but inclined his head. Another yes.

Rome looked around, realizing that he was the lone holdout.

He was no fool. He knew that if it stayed that way, the only thing standing in the way of the future, he would be sacrificed in the past.

Reluctantly, as though he were lifting the weight of the world with that one hand, he raised his hand, and said, "I ratify."

It was done.

Othello looked at Don.

"One more thing, my friends. I promised you I'd give you a gift. It's a simple gift, but it's the gift that men of our stature value in times like these. The gift of revenge."

The door opened and Venus walked Benny in, hands tied behind his back and blindfolded.

He was naked but for his boxers. His dick, half-hard, peeked out of the slit in them.

"We almost there, baby?" Benny asked, voice full of lustful greed.

The men around the table said nothing. It was plain that Benny thought Venus was taking him somewhere for some seriously fucked up kink game. She said, "Oh, we're definitely here. You ready to be fucked like you never been fucked before?"

"Hell yeah!" Benny cackled.

Venus moved around behind him, fingers working the knot of his blindfold, and took the cover away from his eyes.

The first face Benny saw was Don's.

"Surprise!" Don spat, punching him dead in the face with some serious brutality behind it.

Benny hit the floor. His blood spat across the table top.

He looked up, dazed, at Othello. Trying to understand. To grasp salvation. "O, what's up? I did what you said."

Othello shrugged.

"You're a cockroach, Benny. You can't be trusted. Look at it from where I am, if you gave Don up, then one day you'll give me up, too. That ain't loyalty. I demand loyalty."

Venus laughed, then leaned down and kissed Benny on the cheek. "Consider yourself royally fucked, puta."

Othello looked at Joe.

Joe simply nodded, seeing that the young man had more than proven himself. He had done the impossible, earned himself a seat at the table. From that moment on Othello would be both an ally and an adversary.

―――――

Mac came in and slammed the door, full of rage.

Kandi came out of the back, alert, her gun in her hand, tucked in beside her thigh as she approached the living room. Ready. When she saw who it was, she breathed out a sigh of relief and set the gun on the coffee table.

Mac was already across the room at the bar, but instead of pouring himself a shot he knocked back a healthy swig straight from the Henny bottle.

"I take it things didn't go well?"

"Oh no, it went well," Mac said, taking another swig before adding , "For O."

"Meaning?"

"Like you gotta ask."

She didn't.

She understood her man as well as any woman. She had an instinct for his rhythm.

"You didn't get a seat," she stated. Cold. Hard. Fact.

Mac sat down, balancing the bottle on his thigh.

"Fuck no. He gave me that bullshit, talkin' about how they were only willing to give up one more seat, but that ain't even close to true. Fuck outta here, he didn't ask but for one!"

He hit the bottle harder.

"You were right. Loyalty is only loyal to itself."

"Being right doesn't make it just," she quipped.

"Naw it doesn't, but now that I know, I know. Means I simply have to wait for my opportunity to move," Mac planned.

Kandi nodded, taking the bottle from him. She took a deep swig of her own.

"You know what O's weakness is?" She asked.

"What?"

Kandi handed him the bottle back.

"His ego. Yeah, he's a beast when it comes to puttin' in work and puttin' a plan together, but when it comes to who he is, his looks, true fact is his self-esteem is rock bottom. Always has been."

Mac nodded, taking in her womanly wisdom.

She was not wrong.

"True. Around women he gets tongue tied, less sure of himself.'

"Exactly. You ask me, that's where he can be attacked. When the time is right... you won't need no gun... only a mirror."

How r u? Remember me?

141

Cash typed the message into his phone, laying back on his bed.

He had been thinking about Mona 24/7.

Every time Othello disappeared, he knew where he was going, who he was with, and the thought burned him up.

If he could just get Mona alone he could convince her to...

To what?

His better half, the loyal Cash, chided his desirous side, reminding him what was right. Othello was his childhood friend. Sure, Mona was beautiful, but how many beautiful women threw themselves at Cash on a daily basis? He was young, fine, gangsta and paid. With that combination, he knew he could have any woman he wanted...*every* woman he wanted, except the one he truly burned for.

Hey u! Of course I remember u. I hope u are well.

I haven't heard from u in a while. R u ok?

Pinged back.

Cash thought of the irony of her words.

Remember him? Not even close. If she knew the real man behind the messages on the screen, how would she react then?

The worst thing she could do was reject him. So instead of owning up to who he was, he hid in anonymity and tried to just enjoy sharing these few words every now and then.

Just trying to get my head together.

I can't stop thinking about her

He had almost typed the word you, instead of her, which would have been bad. True, but so, so bad.

I can't stop thinking about you, he thought to himself wistfully.

Let her go, Black Love. If it's meant to be, u will have her. B patient.

He smile, and messaged back.

I'm not the most attractive guy in the world. No one wants to love a loser.

The three dots told him she was thinking about her answer.

He watched the screen for what felt like ages before her message finally appeared.

U seem like a nice guy 2 me. Love over looks. Looks fade, true love doesn't.

God, if only she knew...

I hope u r right.

Her answer came back faster this time.

I'm always right! LOL I have to go. On my way 2 Vegas.

Vegas? Cash thought, Othello hadn't said anything about Vegas.

Regardless, he was determined to go on that trip.

If only to be close to Mona, and maybe get a chance to talk to her...

Get lucky...

———

"Look, I'ma need you to stay here and finalize everything with Joe," Othello told Mac, as he drove toward the Eastside of town.

Cash sat in the back seat, puffing a blunt.

"No problem. Unless you're expectin' one," Mac answered.

"Naw, everything's a go. I'm just going to go out to Vegas to relax, and when the moment's right, love is in the air and all that shit, I'll give Mona this," Othello smirked, holding out the ring box.

Mac took the box and laughed as he opened it.

"Get the fuck outta here! You gonna marry shortie?" Mac asked.

Othello shrugged.

"Yeah, well, she still has to say yes."

"Of course she gonna say yes, brah, especially with all these karats making her feel like a fuckin' rabbit! Cash, you hear this ol' sucka for love ass nigga? How sweet it is, eh?"

"Yeah," Cash deadpanned, unenthusiastically.

Othello chuckled.

"Call it what you want, but when you got that good shit, you don't let it go."

Mac gave him dap.

"Congratulations, big brah," Mac said, but words were cheap, like loyalty. In his heart he was thinking of a master plan.

"Thanks. Just keep Joe on ice for me. When I get back, we move into the driver's seat."

They dropped Mac off on the corner. They were three streets away before Othello told Cash, "I need you to go with me, okay?"

Cash perked up. "No doubt."

"I've got somethings on bubble, so I'ma need you around to watch my back. Mac don't need to know about this until we get back. Ain't nothin' assured, got me?" Othello explained.

"Say no mo' brah, I got you," Cash replied, smiling from ear to ear.

———

Mona looked out the window at The Vegas Strip.

It was something.

Like an alien world.

She and Othello rode in the back of the limo.

She eyed her own Chanel-shaded reflection in the window, watching the dilemma pass over her like the city over her reflection. When Othello had told her Cash was coming with them, her heart leapt with anticipation, but her soul made it abate. Her attraction for Cash fought constantly with her love for Othello. There was only ever gonna be one loser in that fight: her.

"You okay, babygirl?" Othello questioned.

She glanced back at him, offering a little smile, and gave his hand a squeeze. "I'm fine. Jet lag," she demurred.

Othello ran his fingers over her cheek, eyeing her with that look. Any other time, she adored that look, like a devout soul at worship. "You sure? You look like you have a lot on your mind."

"I was just thinking about my uncle. He used to love Vegas," she lied. It was an easy lie. The secret was to keep it close to true. Even so, her answer was like a slap in the face to Othello, because it brought him back to the reality of what he had done to her like a truck slamming into roadkill.

Othello pulled her close to him.

"Well, babe, I hope this trip helps you relax. Who knows, maybe a surprise or two might even put a smile on your face."

She wrapped her arms around his frame and nuzzled up against his chest.

"Oh yeah? Like what?"

"Baby, the word was *surprise*. Ain't no surprise if you already know."

She giggled, climbing up into his lap.

"Oh, believe me, I have ways of making you talk if I want you to," she said, leaning in to share a delicious kiss.

She was right, he would talk if she played him right, but she was happy to be surprised.

The limo pulled up out the bright lights of the Bellagio hotel. It was a horseshoe of elegance and ostentation with its dancing fountains and faux-Italian lake out front. To Othello, it looked exactly like what it was: a place of worship.

Cash was already waiting for them, leaning back against the fountain wall, the light show making him look like some sort of Disney character, larger than life.

They climbed out of the car.

Cash and Mona's eyes met for a fleeting, painful second.

She looked away—like she'd looked through him, like he wasn't even there—then turned and gave the smile he wanted so badly to Othello. Othello greeted it with a kiss. The whole thing turned Cash's stomach.

The bellhop took their luggage, transferring the cases to the golden trolley.

Cash gave Othello dap.

"See? I told you flying ain't shit!" Cash chuckled, barely able to keep his eyes off Mona.

"Yeah well, if I ain't had babygirl to hold onto, I mighta not made it," he grinned back at his man, giving Mona a squeeze for emphasis.

"What's up, Mona?" Cash greeted, keep his voice as neutral as possible.

"Hi," she replied, blandly.

"Soon as we check in, I'ma take a nap. I promised Mona I'd teach her how to shoot dice."

"You mean lose money," Cash cracked.

Othello threw a playful punch.

"Oh you got jokes. But yo, tomorrow we need to talk, okay?"

"No doubt. I'm just gonna cruise the strip, bag about three broads and see about making something to stay in Vegas, if you feel me," Cash bragged.

Mona shook her head, just slightly, then rolled her eyes.

"You ready, baby?" she asked Othello.

Cash smirked to himself, knowing he'd gotten under her skin. Too easy.

"Yeah yeah. Yo, Cash. Enjoy, man. Show 'em the legend of Brooklyn in the flesh."

He watched Othello and Mona walk inside through the huge portico. He couldn't help but follow her sashaying stride, thinking she was putting a little something extra in it because she knew he was watching. Who couldn't love a bitch like that?

He spent the day in a haze of drinking, gambling and playing the bad boy for the bad bitches of all races, all swagger and style, trying to drown the one thought on his mind.

Meanwhile, Othello and Mona were doing much of the same, but focused on one another's company and enjoying the intimacy this shared time brought. There was no such thing as time in this place. No windows. Pumped-in oxygen to keep the mind sharp. All sorts of tricks to part a fool and his money. Othello didn't mind. He'd come to make memories, whatever the cost. They'd been alone a while when she saw the craps table.

"You wanna learn?"

"Is it hard?"

"Not yet, baby."

"Funny boy. The game?

"None of the games in here are hard, if they were people wouldn't be so willing and eager to part with the green. The idea is you think they're easy, but you know the saying, *the house always wins.*"

"Aye."

"Well, that's the truth. If it didn't they wouldn't be here. They hate losin' money.

"So why play?"

"Fun. And because it ain't about the individual, it's about the day, see. If you got one hundred players and 50 lose some, 40 win some, 5 lose big and 5 win big, the house is still up. The trick is bein' one of the five who win big. Do you feel lucky?"

She nodded.

Watching a player at the table, he taught her the game, and when a space freed up, she picked up the dice.

She was a natural.

Roll after roll, her hot hand ending up winning close to fifty thousand dollars amid cheers, giggles, deep kisses and congratulations. It was a movie moment. Perfect.

"I can't believe it," Mona said, throwing the cash on the bed. "Look at it! I want to go back right now!"

Othello laughed. "Like the K-man said, you got to know when to fold em', too. Remember, the house *always* wins."

Mona came up and got on her tippy toes to wrap her arms around his neck.

"How about we fuck in it then? Roll around on that cash while you deep dick me, honey?"

They kissed, and it was everything; her taste, his need, coming together, long and passionate.

When they broke it, Othello stared into her eyes for so long, Mona asked, "Baby, are you okay?"

"More than okay," Othello sighed then sat down. "You know, I never knew my father. I barely knew my mom, too, because she spent all her life chasing that next high. So growing up, I didn't know what love was. Fuck, I didn't even *believe* in love. It was shit peddled by TV. I wasn't the best looking dude in school, so when I was growing up, I grew up hard. I learned to stop the teasing with these," he said, holding up his fists. "I was never a bully, not my scene, but niggas knew I would bring the smoke to they ass, so they respected me. Anyway, I gotta be real. I had planned on living my life inside of that pain, that anger, and I was okay with that. Until I met you. You showed me so much love and sensitivity, that since I've had you in my life, everything I thought I was has changed, everything I expected to be is changing. I truly know what love means, and it ain't TV shit. Babygirl, you mean the world to me, more, you *are* the world, the moon, the sun, all of those stars in the sky. And if I had to I would trade my whole life just for the chance to love you totally for five minutes. Bottom line, I ain't no Shakespeare," he chuckled, "but I love you and I want to spend the rest of my life with you as my wife." He pulled out the ring box, and slipped off the edge of the bed and got down on one knee.

He opened the box.

"Will you?"

He looked up into Mona's face. There were tears on her cheek, and for a moment he thought he'd done something wrong.

She looked at him through the prism of the tears.

"Yes, Othello, yes, yes, yes," she gasped, her voice clipped with the exhilarating rush of love taking flight.

She crouched down beside him, into his arms, and covered his face with kisses. He lifted her. She wrapped her legs around his waist. Othello palmed her ass with his hands, kissing her neck, cleavage and the top of her breasts until he laid her back on the bed and the scattered bank notes, and kissed down the length of her body.

Her dress was so tight, she didn't want to wear panties or a bra underneath because the line would show, so as he pushed the material up her thighs her chocolate goodness spread before him like a feast fit for a king.

He put her legs on his shoulder and sucked on her clit, until she her back arched so deeply she damn near bent doubly with pleasure, gasping and moaning, toes curling and cumming. Othello devoured her pussy until she begged him to enter her sloppy wetness.

He turned her over and slid inside of her tight, wet center, stroking her.

"Damn, you fuck me so *good*," she creamed, groaning as deep as a growl, as her hands clenched around the money.

She threw it up in the air, over his naked back.

Cash.

"Damn nigga, you look like you been drinkin' all night," Othello commented the next morning. "Drinkin' and fuckin'." He was with Cash, having breakfast on the balcony of Cash's suite. Mona was back in their room, beautifying.

Cash sipped on his Bloody Mary. His head was on fire. "Don't remind me, yo. Shit was crazy last night."

"Yeah, it was," Othello grinned, "I asked Mona to marry me."

Cash looked at him. "What she say?"

"Nigga, what you *think* she said? Look at me, of course she said yes. I'm gonna be a married man." Othello held up his orange juice for a toast.

Cash's hangover doubled in the thump, but he held his glass up and met the toast.

"Congratulations, brah."

"Thank you. Truthfully, life is good, brah, better than good," Othello replied, sipping his juice, then digging into steak and eggs. "We almost there. Everything we ever worked for, murdered, hustled and bled for, baby. It's in touchin' distance. So close I can taste it like pussy juice on my tongue. It's about to be ours. Yours and mine."

Cash mustered a smile. None of that mattered anymore. Everything they had hustled for, every risk they had taken, all the bloodshed, none of it mattered. "No doubt," he answered.

"But look, I have a meeting this afternoon."

"What up?"

"I'll let you know when I get back. But Mona won her a grip last night, and it's burning a hole in her pocket. Do me a solid, brah, take her out, show her the delights this place has to offer." Othello had no idea he was sending the fox to guard the henhouse.

Cash's heart thumped in his chest. "Yeah. Sure. I'll take her shopping. No problem."

"You sure? I know all that pocketbook holding shit ain't you," Othello chuckled.

Cash grinned. "Call it your weddin' gift."

Othello wiped his mouth, then stood up.

"Cool. Ay yo, once I put this thing in place, the sky's the limit," Othello winked.

He left Cash, taking his hangover with him.

"This brandy is older than you, Mac," Joe chuckled as he poured himself and Mac two fingers full. It clung to the sides of the glass as it went down, forming a little lake of fire.

He handed the glass to Mac.

"You guys pulled off one helluva a strategy. I raise my glass to you," Joe toasted.

Clink!

Mac took a sip and nodded. "Tastes like success."

They both laughed, warmly and friendly. It sounded like victory.

They were in the study of Joe Hamlet's mansion, reclining in leather chesterfield armchairs that cost more than the tenement Mac had grown up in. Three of the walls were covered with bookshelves, leather spines, gilt lettering, proper expensive books, first editions, rare and probably in some cases as expensive as the original Monet gracing the wall behind Joe's desk.

Out through the windows, the view of the sprawling estate's acreage served as a panorama.

"Othello surprised me with the appearance of Don. I've got to admit, I thought for sure he was already dead," Joe remarked.

"I told O that Don was worth more to us alive than dead," Mac lied. There was an advantage in the lie. It made him look like the long-thinker.

Joe's eyebrows arched. "Oh, that was your idea?"

Mac shrugged.

"We're a team."

Joe nodded.

The two men sat back enjoying the taste of the ancient grapes and savoring the sweet smoke of their thick Cuban cigars. Joe always joked the richer he got, the thicker his Cubans became. Mac believed him. Right now, he was sucking on a fuckin' dick of a cigar, thicker than most white boys. The only word he could think of to describe the room was opulent. Well, not the only word. It was ostentatious, too. He marked the painting on the wall, Mona and Adonis, and almost spat out his drink. It took every ounce of his composure not to.

Joe didn't even notice that Mac had scoped the picture.

Mona? Goddamn, he realized she must be his daughter. *What the fuck!* The gears ground in his mind. *Wait a minute... Why didn't Othello ever mention that Mona was Joe Hamlet's daughter? And when Joe was going at us, why didn't he come at us through his girl?* The second realization hit him like a freight train. *They don't know!*

Everything became clear to him, right then and there.

The whole time Othello was fucking with Mona, he never knew she was the daughter of the man they were gunning for. And Joe never knew they were right under his nose, balls deep in his daughter.

Mac couldn't help but chuckle.

"Amuse me," Joe said.

"I'm sorry, I just... I gotta be real. Never expected this to happen. Life definitely comes full circle," Mac replied, enjoying the double meaning of his words.

Joe chuckled.

"Very true, I—" Joe began, but a light knock on the door interrupted his flow. "Come on in, sweetheart," the Commissioner called out.

When the door opened, Mac couldn't believe his eyes. She wasn't a cougar, she was a fuckin' panther. Pure blood. Her whole body growled through the sensually styled silk dress. She moved with the grace of a Nubian Queen, firmly in command of her Queendom. He had never been into older chicks, but Aphrodite was pure sex and he couldn't help but fight back an erection watching her move and imagining her riding his dick into slavery.

Aphrodite knew the power of her sexuality. How could she not? She smiled to herself, pretending as if she hadn't noticed Mac's presence, and told Joe, "Honey, you have an urgent call in the living room."

"I'm a little tied up here," he answered, nodding his head towards Mac. Aphrodite turned, faking her surprise as well as she faked an orgasm.

"Oh, I'm sorry, hon. I didn't even see you. Aphrodite Hamlet," she held her hand out for Mac to take.

He shook it, loving the silky softness of her smooth skin.

"I know. My mother died of cancer several years ago, but you were a part of the non-profit that helped her get back and forth from chemo. I never got a chance to thank you before now. I'm Macklin Bethel," Mac said.

Aphrodite touched her hand to her chest.

"I'm so sorry to hear that, but I am glad we were able to help in some small way."

Joe stood up. "Aye, can you keep Mac entertained? I'll be right back."

"Of course, love. Go, take care of business."

Joe stepped out of the room.

Aphrodite looked at the brandy in Mac's glass.

"I see Joe broke out the expensive stuff. He must really like you, or you must be somebody important," she smirked.

Mac smiled. "One or the other."

Aphrodite sang him a silent lullaby with her eyes. It was a subtle song, one that allowed the man to read into what they willed as she remarked, "May I assume you're a part of the Othello gang?"

Mac's expression twitched with subtle irritation he failed to keep out of his tone. "We're not a gang, or a crew, or anything that basic. And even if we were, it wouldn't be named Othello."

"I'm sorry if I offended you," Aphrodite apologized, but the truth was in one sting she'd pulled his card and learned all she needed to know about him.

Joe walked back in. She knew her man. She knew that look. He was concerned about something.

"Is everything okay, honey?"

"I'll talk to you in a minute, can we have the room?" She nodded and left them to it. He turned to Mac. "Listen, I'm going to have to cut this short. Tell Othello we will be getting together later on tonight."

"Tonight? Naw, O ain't even in town. He went to Vegas and took this bad little bitch named Mona," Mac making sure to keep that undertone of innuendo in his chuckle, letting it torture Joe's parental imagination.

Joe stopped and looked at Mac hard.

There was a moment.

A beat.

Then:

"*What* did you say?"

Mac acted as if he was surprised by Joe's reaction. "I was just sayin' O is wit some bitch..."

Joe snatched him up by the collar and with force belying his age, had him off his feet and slammed Mac up against the expensive books. He was already hot because of the phone call, but now Mona slipped away from her tail. They'd been following the wrong girl. Celeste came out of the motel too early. Joe was sick with worry, and now Mac was telling him Othello had some bitch named Mona in Vegas? It wasn't fuckin' funny. It was like some nigga had just cornholed his heart with a giant dildo.

"Joe, man, what the fuck?" Mac asked, fronting like he didn't know exactly what had the other man riled.

"Nigga, that's my *daughter*!" Joe roared.

Mac's eyes got big.

He could've gotten an Oscar for his performance.

"Shit, man. I didn't know, Joe! I swear!"

Joe grilled him hard, damn near nose to nose for a moment, breathing in his grill tasting like he was about to spew fire. "Joe, be reasonable, man, there are a lot of bitches...I mean *women* named Mona. What's the odds?"

"Does she look like that?" Joe spat, pointing at the painting Mac had already scoped.

He acted as if that was the first time he'd noticed it, looking at it for a beat, then turned back to Joe and dropped his eyes.

"Yeah, man, sorry, that's her."

Joe let him go with a shove and began to pace the floor. He couldn't believe his ears.

"I'm going to kill that nigga...You said they went to Vegas?"

"Joe listen, I'm sure Othello didn't know."

"Muhfucka answer me!"

A beat.

"Yeah. Vegas."

"Out of my sight. Now. Go." Joe seethed.

Mac didn't waste any time getting out of the lion's den.

Damage done.

"I hear congratulations are in order," Cash remarked sourly, as he and Mona got situated in the back of the limo.

"Thanks," she replied, without looking in his direction.

Her cool attitude, heated him like boiling lava.

"That's all you can say? Thanks?" He spat.

She continued to ignore him, making out like the view through the window was the most fascinating thing in the world.

Cash sighed hard.

"Look ma, I ain't tryin' to be on no bullshit, okay? I just wanna know what the fuck happened? I called you, I texted, I did *every-thing* I could to reach you and you ignored me."

The desperation, pain and frustration in his voice, broke her veneer of ice. Finally, she looked in his direction.

"I wasn't looking for anything serious, Cassio," she lied.

She had to be lying.

The truth was, she was still deathly afraid her father would do something awful to Cash if he knew the truth. She knew Joe Hamlet wasn't one to threaten lightly, even if he had tried to shield her from his world for most of her life.

"You're lyin'," he replied, calling her bluff.

Mona shrugged nonchalantly. On the inside she was trembling.

"Believe what you want."

A beat.

"Do you love him?"

"Honestly? Yes. I do."

Her words broke his hurt all over again.

He couldn't answer with words, so instead he answered her with his phone.

He went to his fake Facebook profile and tapped out a two word message.

She watched him, hating the ignorance of it.

Her phone rang in her clutch.

She glanced down at it, opened the clutch, then took out her phone.

She saw the message from Black Love Hurts.

Congratulations... Mona

She looked at him, penny dropping. "Black Love Hurts is you?"

"It does," he answered.

She didn't know what to say to that.

"The girl I was talking about was you, Mona. The one woman in the world that could break my heart, was you, and you did. But hey, I guess I deserved it, huh? As many hearts as I have broken... Now I know how it feels," he admitted.

Seeing Cash on the verge of tears, softened her heart even more.

Her spirit reached out to him as tenderly as an Al Green song.

"Cassio, I..." she began, but her phone rang in her hand. She almost dropped it in surprise.

It was Othello.

She glanced up, and Cash knew who it was from the look in her eyes.

She answered.

"Hey baby.... yes, I'm good. Of course he's taking good care of me," she replied, forcing a smile, glancing up at Cash.

He looked away.

"Okay... I love you, too."

She hung up, then started to speak. "Cash..."

"Don't speak, ma. We both know ain't nothin' to say."

They sat back, both lost in the regret of possibilities.

They went about the rest of their time together bubbled off from their own inner emotions as Mona burned through fifteen thousand dollars like she was spending nickels and dimes on Broadway. From time to time, they'd share a laugh or some wise-ass comment, but even that was dangerous. It was too close to being normal, and they could be anything but that.

By the time they were through, they had found a sort of closure through shared silences.

Once they got back to the hotel, they went straight to the suite. Othello was already there, sipping a drink and watching a game on TV.

Weighed down with bags, Cash waddled through the front door. Othello cracked up. "Damn ma, you bought half of Vegas, huh?"

"Yeah, and I'm a buying the other half tomorrow when *you* come with me," she shot back playfully.

Othello shook his head, chuckling as she took her bags into the bedroom.

He turned to Cash.

"Ay, I appreciate that brah. I hope it wasn't too painful."

Cash shrugged.

"Torture, actually," he replied, but the irony was lost on Othello. "How was the meeting?"

Othello smiled.

"We got a green light. Shit about to pop off big! Our connect just gave us a blank check on consignment!"

Now Cash understood why Othello was being so secretive. He had arranged a meeting with a cocaine connect to ensure a steady flow of coke moved through them. It was the next step up. Logical. Now that they were getting their own territory, they were going to need it. He who controlled the coke controlled the streets.

"That's what's up," Cash replied and gave him a gangsta hug.

The two men drank to their new found success. And for a few seconds at least, everything was right with the world.

A little while later, there was a knock on the door.

"Who the fuck is that?" Othello questioned.

"You order room service?" Cash asked.

"Naw."

Cash moved towards the door and peeped through the peephole.

Joe Hamlet glowered back at him.

"It's Joe."

"Joe?" Othello echoed. "What the fuck is Joe doing here?"

"You tell him you were going to Vegas?'

"Naw."

"Let him in?"

"Why not?'

Cash opened the door, but before he could greet Joe, the man barreled past him, shoving him into the wall so hard his body cracked the plaster.

Behind Joe were three immense black goons.

"What the *fuck*!" Cash spat, trying to get his balance, but before he had even half-straightened up one of the goons uppercut him so hard he spat blood.

"*Muhfucka!*" Joe thundered, raging as he roared at Othello, both fists balled into steel.

Othello had a split-second to react to Joe's aggression.

He didn't know what was going on, but he wasn't about to wait around and find out.

As soon as Joe stepped into striking distance, Othello caught him with a nice two-piece that would've knocked any other man flat on his ass.

But Joe ate them both like pieces of gummy bears.

"Nigga, that's all you got?" Joe sneered, his eyes seething like molten lava. He crouched in his boxer's stance, faked a jab that Othello leaned away from easily, moving straight into a kidney crushing left hook that lifted him off his feet.

Othello grunted beneath the impact, his ribs feeling broken, but refused to go down. Not that easily.

Joe launched two more head shots that would've sent Othello out over the balcony rail had he connected properly, but Othello weaved one, and caught the glancing end of the second before tying Joe up.

"What in the actual fuck is going on, Joe?!" Othello huffed, wrestling with the larger and stronger older man.

"My daughter, nigga!"

"Daughter? What the fuck you talking about?"

The answer came from an unexpected source.

"Daddy!" Mona cried.

Joe slung Othello into the bar, knocking drinks, glasses and with another brutal jab, Othello onto the floor.

Joe pounced on him, knee on chest, and drew back to knock his head through the floor. And he would have, had Mona not grabbed his arm, slowing the momentum enough to ruin the punch. But that wasn't what saved Othello from the beating. He ended up flinging her across the room as she lost her grip on his arm. She hit the floor. Hard.

His babygirl crying was the only thing that calmed Joe's wrath and saved Othello's life.

He got up and went to comfort Mona.

"Daddy, why are you doing this?" She managed through snot and tears.

The three goons had Cash hemmed up in the corner, working him over like a punching bag.

Joe held up a hand to say enough, and they stopped.

Cash fell to the floor, dazed and bruised.

"What the hell are you doing in Vegas, child?" Joe barked.

"I'm with Othello, Daddy. I love him!" Mona screamed.

"Love him!" Joe exclaimed. "You don't fuckin' love him, girl. You don't have a clue what fuckin' love is." He spat out his distaste, eyes going from her to Othello, to Mona then back to Othello. In Joe Hamlet's world, there were no coincidences. Maybe Othello didn't know and just fell for the wrong girl, maybe not. The bigger question was, did Mona know who Othello was and that he was working in Joe's world?

Joe came back over to Othello who had struggled back up onto the couch.

"How long have you been boning my daughter?"

"I didn't know she was your little girl," Othello said, his mind ablaze with vengeful rage.

"Not what I asked. How long?"

"A few months."

Joe shook his head, but he read the man. Othello was telling the truth. Had he been using her to get to him, he would've made his move by now. Meaning, if he did know, it wasn't about the game. That was something.

Joe sighed hard and looked at Mona.

"Okay... Booker, get that other nigga out of here. Get him cleaned up. Treat him with respect," Joe begrudgingly added on the end.

Booker reached down to help cash up, but Cash snatched away and stormed out. The three goons left out after him.

Alone, Joe looked at Othello.

"I'm going to forget this happened. I'm going to forget you

were here, and in return you are going to forget my daughter," Joe warned.

"What?" Othello bassed.

"You heard me."

"But Daddy, we're getting married!" Mona sobbed, holding up her ring finger for Joe to see.

"Married?" Joe echoed. "Ain't no fuckin' way short of hell freezin' over! This is done."

Othello stood up, his face bruised, spirit unbroken, and looked Joe in the eye. He said, "Ain't *nobody* gonna stop me from marrying Mona. Not you. Not no one. She's the woman I love. And before you get beat up, I respect you as her father, and as a man, Joe, but that's the way it's going to be."

Joe stood toe to toe with Othello.

The other man had him by a few inches, but Joe was a warrior.

"Oh, is it now? This ain't about The Commission, this is about my family!"

"I love Mona."

The two men looked at each other, knowing the other would never be moved from their position. It was a standoff that would only end when someone on one side or other was dead.

Mona stepped up and stood beside Othello.

"Daddy, Othello is the man I love. I will always be your baby-girl, but I'm not a child. I have a mind of my own. I'm marrying Othello," she stated firmly, fronting up to her father.

Joe looked into his daughter's eyes.

He saw his own determination reflected back at him.

She wouldn't back down, same as he wouldn't.

Joe sighed hard and went over to the wrecked bar.

Everything was on the floor, including the ice.

He picked through the broken glass until he found three unbroken glasses and a bottle of Johnny Walker Black.

Without a word, he poured the three of them a drink.

Finally, he sat down, ready to lay down more home truths, starting with the most obvious. "If I hadn't come in here and found a ring on your finger babygirl, there would have been nothing you could've said to keep me from dragging you out and putting a bullet through this nigga's skull. You burned me. But marriage, that's something I have to respect."

She nodded.

Joe turned to Othello.

"And as for you... You need to understand this: my daughter is my heart, my world. I only have one. You say you love her. Fine, you love her, but I am old enough and ugly enough to know words are only wind. If you want to marry my daughter, you have to give up the game, plain and simple."

Othello sipped his drink. "Is that an ultimatum?"

"You can call it what you want, but you need to understand I will not allow my daughter to be subject to the dangers that go along with being a gangsta's wife. You can keep your seat on The Commission because the power will benefit you in the civilian world. Fine, I'm good with that, but all ties to the underworld, they need to be cut. Period, non-negotiable."

Mona looked at him.

Love of her or love of the game?

She appreciated her father's wisdom.

Othello thought about the move he had just made.

The game laid before him wide open. It was *the* dream. Everything he had been trying to realize from those first hours as a small-time hustler. But looking at Mona, there was no comparison. He would never give her up in a thousand years.

"That's no choice, Joe. Mona, always. Every time." Othello answered with pride.

Mona smiled through her tears.

Joe nodded, happy with an answer that at least guaranteed his daughter a safer life.

The two men shook on it, deal brokered and sealed.

They were joined now in ways more important than the thug life.

"I guess congratulations are in order, O. Welcome to the family."

In a private gentleman's club later on that evening, Joe and Othello could at least laugh about it.

"Yeah, I ain't gonna lie, when you gave me that kidney shot, I thought I was gonna piss blood for a goddamn week," Othello admitted.

"Yeah, I'm sorry O, but all I thought about was you and my daughter. No fuckin' father wants to think about some big dick nigga breakin' up his little girl, and frankly, I still don't wanna," Joe chuckled, sipping his drink.

"You still could be a heavyweight, fuck the age factor, man you still got a fuckin' punch on you man," Othello complimented him.

"How you know I used to box?" Joe asked.

Othello shrugged. "Sam told me."

What else did Sam tell you? Joe thought, but he said, "Yeah, I think about those times a lot. What could've been, what should've been. I have no doubt, I could've been a contender," Joe reminisced, doing a lousy impression of Brando.

"You ever regret it?"

"Every day, man, every day. But what's done is done. I got into this game with one thing in mind: to get out of this game. It's been a long time, but I'm almost there."

Othello nodded, thinking: *Not before you get what's coming to you.*

"But I'll tell you what's really fucking me up. I can't believe babygirl has been giving me the slip all this time. I can't lie, she slick as muhfucka, but the way she had me following her girl-friend instead of her..." Joe let his voice trail off, as he sipped and his smile disappeared. He shook his head. "I never thought my babygirl would lie to me."

"I know what you mean," Othello commented.

"Do you?" Joe looked at him over the rim of his glass. "Because I'm going to tell you some real shit. That's my daughter and I love her to death, but if she'll lie to me, and I'm her father what makes you think she won't lie to you when it suits?"

Those words would echo in Othello's head until...

6

"I'm sorry babe, just got a *lot* on my mind," Adonis said.

He and Bianca lay in her bed, naked. Her chocolate spread all over him, teasingly.

Problem was, he couldn't perform with women. Even though he called himself bi-sexual, that was just a word, not an identity. At least not for him. In reality, only men turned him on, with a singular exception.

Aphrodite.

Adonis didn't know what the fuck was going on inside his own skull. The thought of it made him sick. It was disgusting. How could he look at his own mother like *that*? But he couldn't help himself. What was that shit he'd used to explain Devante? The heart wants what the heart wants? But his heart? How could it be so utterly fucked up? It tore him up inside. It went beyond torment. The problem was, whenever he thought about Aphrodite, it turned erotic and his dick hardened. Every single time. Nothing he could do about it but go and bust a nut. Thinking about his own mother. That was some degenerate bullshit.

"It's okay, baby," Bianca soothed. "I know with everything

going on, and on top of that, the wedding getting closer, you've been stressed lately. It's only natural. But I can help you with that," she cooed in his ear, rubbing his dick with the palm of her hand, before lowering herself and taking him into her mouth.

It was deliciously warm.

It should have been heaven, but it wasn't. Not until he did something about it.

He imagined it was Aphrodite wrapping her sexy ass lips around his shaft, Aphrodite moaning that passionate pleasure as she ran her tongue around his engorged bell head, and his dick grew and grew, harder, as she ran her tongue down the length of his fat shaft.

His toes curled as Bianca bobbed harder, sucking, licking, focused. A groan escaped his lips. He barely held out from calling out his own mother's name. And like some sick twisted fuck, his revulsion just turned him on all the more.

He used it.

Adonis grabbed the back of her head and began to grind his dick all in her mouth, picturing Aphrodite on all fours, seeing her ruby red lips sucking his dick harder, those manicured fingernails scratching across his nuts then slipping a finger into his ass as she urging him on with her throat muscles, willing him to cum in her mouth.

He couldn't hold it back anymore.

He exploded in Bianca's mouth, the powerful shivers of his orgasm sending a current coursing up and down his spine as his body bucked uncontrollably against them.

Bianca came off his dick, wiping the cum off her lips with the back of her hand as she smiled proudly up at it, foolishly thinking it was her head game, not that it was his head game that fucked him up.

"See? I told you I could help," she said, cuddled up beside him.

Adonis kissed her on the forehead.

"Just what the doctor ordered," he told her, still picturing Aphrodite in his mind.

The vision started to fade as he drifted off.

The vibrating of his phone woke him up. He glanced down at Bianca who had fallen asleep on his chest. He tried to reach the phone without waking her, just in case it was Devante.

It was a text message.

A series of images.

Pictures of himself and Devante at the cafe, going into a hotel room, pictures of them inside other hotel rooms, pictures of them having sex, even a shot of him coming from an angle that meant the camera had to be inside the room.

He felt sick to his stomach seeing himself, balls deep inside of Devante.

It wasn't the bodies, not even the hard cocks. It was that look of ecstasy on both of their faces.

It shamed him.

The phone rang.

Bianca stirred.

He looked at the phone. A blocked number.

He answered anyway.

"Hello?"

A deep rumble of a chuckle answered him back, before a smooth baritone said, "I guess you already got my message."

Adonis looked at Bianca again, then slowly moved her over until she transferred her head to the pillow.

Adonis went into the bathroom, closing the door before he whispered hoarsely, "Who is this?"

"Someone who knows, Adonis. That's all you need to know," the voice answered.

Adonis paced the bathroom floor. Frustrated. Frightened. His world was about to come apart, not like the unraveling of a seam, but a fuckin' world destroying big bang.

"Okay, how much money do you want? That's what this is about, right? Money? Name your price."

The voice began to laugh.

"Oh Adonis, you sweet gay fool. You totally don't see the bigger picture, do you? This ain't about how much I want."

"Then what is it about?"

"How much you're willing to lose?"

Adonis' fear began to turn into frustration.

"You're fucking with flames here, you know that, right?"

"Yeah, but I ain't the one who is gonna get burned. That's you, Adonis, unless you do exactly what I say," the voice threatened.

"Then what do you want me to do?"

The voice chuckled. "Soon. Be ready for my call."

Click!

The wedding was one for the ages.

The theme was Old English Royalty, like that one on the TV with the first black princess.

Joe Hamlet pulled out all the stops for his babygirl. He rented out a 52-room mansion and its full estate for the ceremony, and had people arriving in horse-drawn carriages, met by servants in white gloves and tails who bustled about, intent on catering to every detail.

The guests were among the most powerful people in the city. Both realities of the city, legitimate and underworld, came to pay homage to Joe and see his only daughter married. And if money could buy happiness, it sure as hell did in this place; every face smiled joyously, save for one: Cash.

That poor bastard knew his worst nightmare was about to come true.

He had risen in power under Othello, working as his capo, old school, as the last few months had seen him overseeing a large part of the territory allotted to them by The Commission. He'd even taken it on himself to branch out on his own into areas outside of The Commission's domain. It was all about power, money and sex. Right now he had all the money he could spend, all the power to crush the life out of his enemies, and some of the dirtiest downright fucking nasty sex he'd ever had, but it only served to show him none of it was worth a damn without Mona to share it with.

Looking at her now, she still had it to stop his heart with a single look.

She looked gorgeous in her off-white Vera Wang lace and silk wedding dress, a 25-foot long train trailing behind her.

Proper princess material.

Mac and Kandi moved through the crowd taking everything in.

Mac too had matured into a power player. In many ways, he was even more powerful because Kandi got the game and was much more ambitious than either of the men, and kept her forked tongue hissing in Mac's ear, pushing him to grasp higher, further, her greed knowing no bounds. And she was a boss in her own right, with a crew of chicks that did whatever she told them to do. Her instructions were never more complicated than: GET MONEY, BITCHES!

Kandi worked the room, while Mac shook hands with the big hitters.

His eye was taken as he watched Aphrodite move across the room. She eyed him back, one of those *come hither* type glances that promised nothing but trouble, before she moved toward one of the many bars set up around the grounds.

Mac checked around for eyes, either Joe's or Kandi's, but they were otherwise occupied so he made his move.

"Do I congratulate the mother of the bride?" He asked as he reached her.

Aphrodite smiled, holding out a glass of Cristal for him.

"You may."

"Then congratulations."

"Why thank you, Mac. I must say, you are looking mighty fine in that tuxedo of yours. Of course, there is a reason they call it the best man."

"I make everything I'm in look good."

"That is not the reason," Aphrodite remarked, setting him up for the kill shot.

Mac frowned subtly.

"It's an honor."

"No sweetheart, best man means second best, one rung behind the groom, the top man, star of the show," Aphrodite quipped with a sassy smirk.

The jab heated Mac's collar, but he kept his composure.

"I thought we had this conversation before? I'm second to none."

"Well, I need a man for my... non-profit," Aphrodite told him, but the way she used her pauses meant there was way more she wasn't saying.

"Oh yeah? What position you have in mind?" he smirked, relaying his own innuendo.

Her smile said, *message received.*

"Every position."

"Just as long as I'm on top."

She held out her card. "Give me a call. Let's see if I'm right about you, Mac."

Mac watched her sashay away, loving the way her ass bounced, no panty line. "Damn, that's one sexy bitch," he said under his breath.

Mac checked his watch, then looked around for Othello.

He had been chatting with a hustla from St. Louis who wanted a sit down with Othello.

He moved through the crowd, looking for the other man.

He found Cash first.

"Yo brah, you seen O?"

"Naw," Cash responded, turning up yet another drink.

There was something off about the man. He could have let it go, but this was the big day, he didn't need Cash bringing 'em all down. "What's wrong with you?"

"I'm good," Cash lied, then wandered off before he could push it.

He disappeared into the flock of people.

Mac thought about Cash for a moment, then shrugged it off and continued his search. Bigger fish and all that.

The mansion was huge, bigger than the Biltmore Estate.

Mac walked through the place, looking up at the cathedral ceilings and gilded columns. This was serious old money, but without the taint of slavery that accompanied those plantation houses in the deep south. This was regal. The deeper he went, the more haunting and hollow the echo of his shoes became on the polished marble floors.

He emerged near a back patio, spotting Othello sitting with Joe.

Neither man saw Mac approach.

He was about to make his presence known when he heard Joe Hamlet ask, "So, have you decided who you're going to give your connect to? Mac or Cash?"

That stopped him cold.

He stood exactly where he was, waiting for Othello's answer.

Othello sucked in smoke from the thick Cuban in his mouth, then puffed out a smoke ring in the air. He still didn't give his answer. Instead, he made a show of swirling his brandy around in the sifter. He set the glass down. Only then did he respond, "Yeah, I have. Me, Mac and Cash came up together and I love both of them niggas like brothers, but Mac... Mac is too bull-headed, too extravagant. His ambition outruns his discipline. Mac as boss would definitely be too dangerous, so no choice. Cash gets the connect."

The words stabbed Mac in the chest, sharper than any fucking shank.

It was like listening to his woman declare her love for another nigga.

It bit.

After all I've done for this nigga? Seriously? After all my loyalty, holding this nigga down, this is how he sees me? This is how he repays me? With disloyalty and mistrust? Muhfucka, Kandi was right, only be loyal to yourself. That's the takeaway. No other fucker will be loyal to you... I'll show this cocksucker who has the brains to be boss!

Mac's thoughts burned with pure rage.

Incandescent, he stalked away, a man on a mission: to burn this whole fucking thing down if that was what it took to get the throne he deserved.

"He *what*?" Kandi spat, as red hot hearing Othello's judgment as Mac had been.

He hadn't told her until they were back home from the ceremony, not wanting to set her off in front of the wedding party.

Kandi was undressing. There was nothing close to half-naked rage.

"That's some real bullshit!" She exclaimed, popping the backs off her diamond studs. He knew that look. She was wishing she had someone to punch in the face.

"You think I don't know that?" Mac said, only half looking at her as he rolled the blunt he needed to take the edge off his anger.

"You the one puttin' in all the work, while pretty boy Cash just chased fuckin' pussy... it's such bullshit."

"Again, tell me something I don't know," Mac said, lighting the blunt.

Kandi sat down next to him on the bed, stripped down to nothing but her panties.

He hit the blunt, then passed it to her, his mind deep in thought.

"Whatever you do, don't show your hand. You get more bees with honey," she reminded him.

"Yeah, but you get more flies with shit," he retorted, "And what this calls for is shit, and plenty of it!" Mac had a plan coming into his mind, piece by piece.

Kandi smiled as she hit the blunt greedily, blowing smoke through her nose like some raging bull. "What are you gonna do?" She asked.

He told her, and by the time he finished laying it out she had a grin wider than the Joker's.

"We've got a problem," Adonis huffed, pushing past Devante's into the condo.

Devante shut the door, trying to judge just how dark his lover's mood was as he followed him back into the lounge. Adonis hung his favorite burgundy butter leather jacket over the chair, then sat down rubbing at the shadow of stubble on his face.

"This sounds serious."

"It is. Fix me a drink."

Devante crossed to the bar, pouring out two, then handed one glass to Adonis as he sat across from him. Adonis knocked back half in a single swallow, then said, "Somebody's been taking pictures of us while we were fucking."

Devante's eyes got huge. "No!"

Adonis handed him the phone.

Devante flipped furiously through each picture.

He saw the same thing, straight away. "Some of these shots were taken inside the room... But... How?"

Adonis looked at Devante.

"Exactly." A beat.

"Wait. I know you don't think I'm setting you up!" Devante protested. "That shit is poison in your brain. You know I would never."

Adonis sighed, downed his drink and shook his head.

"I don't know what to think right now. This shit is bad, real bad."

Devante slid over closer to him and began to rub his back.

"I would never do *anything* to hurt you, you should know that. I love you," Devante professed. Adonis looked him in the eye. The sincerity he saw, made him feel guilty as hell for questioning him.

He caressed Devante's cheek and smiled.

"I know. It's just... I'm about to be a very powerful man, and if this gets out..."

"I understand. Believe me, we'll find out who is behind this before all that happens, I swear," Devante assured him.

"I hope so."

Devante gently turned Adonis' face to his.

"It will be okay," he whispered, inclining his head slightly, then moved in to meet his lips, tender, his tongue exploring, opening him.

Meanwhile, the camera clicked away silently...

Mac gave Cash dap and a gangsta hug before the pair sat down. They met at a rundown tittie bar not far from their crib. They mockingly called this place the Graveyard, like the Elephant's Graveyard, where hookers went to die. The bitches dancing here had stretch marks and bullet wounds and pussies that stank of skank. It was the perfect place for an out of the way meeting between two powerful lieutenants.

"What's good, yo. What you drinking?" Mac asked as the topless waitress approached.

"Henny straight up."

"Make that two," he told her.

The waitress nodded and walked away.

"Remember her?" Mac smirked.

"Who? The waitress?"

Mac nodded, eyeing him to see if he did.

Cash squinted through the smoky darkness, watching her profile as she waited by the bar. She glanced over her shoulder a couple of times, but her expression was one of pure boredom and utter indifference.

Cash shook his head. "Can't say that I do."

"Kat."

He thought about it for a second, trying to place the name. "Kat?" Saying the word sparked the inner recognition, and he repeated, "Kat as in Kat Kat? Get the *fuck* out of here!"

She returned with their drinks, Cash looked at her with a smile.

"Katrina."

Her smile said she had already recognized them ,but it was nice to be recognized in return. "Cash, how you doin'? I see you still hangin' around with trouble."

Mac chuckled.

"Oh now *I'm* trouble."

"Ever since the fifth grade," she sassed.

Cash's mind went back to simpler times. When candy money and Catch-a-girl-Kiss-a-girl were his only concerns. How the fucking times had changed. Back then, Katrina had been one of the baddest little chicks in school. They'd played the kissing game a few times, not that he remembered how her tongue tasted, probably of Pop rocks or bubble gum. He'd lost contact with her, like most people from back then. Looking at her now, it seemed like she had given up on life. It was weird to find her holed away in a no-name club like the Graveyard. He assumed she was selling pussy and doing whatever else she could to get by.

"I just got out of jail about a month ago," she told them, as if reading his mind.

"You need a job?" Cash asked.

"Not any kind you can give. This may not be much, but it's keeping me out of trouble, you know?" Cash nodded, then pulled out his money, flicked through the roll, counting out some notes, then handed her five hundred dollar bills.

"Welcome home."

She smiled and tucked the money in her boy shorts.

"Still got class, I see. Take care of yourself," she winked, then walked away.

Cash sipped his drink.

"Damn yo, life is crazy. I never expected her to fall off. Of all the old faces, I had her pegged to be a doctor or some shit. You know, the good life. Not this."

"Yeah, one decision can change your whole life," Mac commented. "But yo, I got some big shit to talk to you about."

"I'm listening."

A beat.

"I'm retiring."

Cash looked at him, then laughed. "You *almost* had me, yo."

"Naw brah, I'm dead ass. I'm done," Mac replied with all seriousness.

"Retiring? Why? Brah, we on the way up. We in The Commission. Only way is up."

"No, O is in The Commission. We just on his so-called team," Mac retorted.

"So-called? We are a team," Cash disputed.

Mac shook his head.

"Yeah, well, not no more. It's time I bow out gracefully. I've got plans to start a record label, maybe even do some movie productions," Mac told him. "Do something good with my days. Step away from the hustle."

Cash eyed him levelly. "You serious."

Mac nodded, sipping his drink.

"Fuck. You told O yet?"

"Naw. But yo, he's gonna be stepping back from the game, too. He's going to have to give his connect to one of us."

"Which is gonna be you, Mac. Why walk away now?"

Because it won't be me, Mac thought bitterly, but said, "When a man gets tired, they get tired. Me and Kandi want to have kids. Life is good. But I ain't bringing kids into the game. Don't worry about me, brah, this is your shot to blow. With me retiring, he'll definitely give it to you."

Cash took a sip, not only of his drink, but of Mac's words, turning them into thoughts that danced in his head.

"Brah, this is your opportunity, but I'ma keep it real with you," Mac told him, "O love you to death, but he think you just a pretty boy," Mac informed him.

Cash looked at him, like, "Pretty boy? Fuck you mean?"

Mac shrugged.

"Come on, Cash, you always been more worried about the bitches than the money. Don't get me wrong, we all fam, but bottom line is, to be a boss, you got to be M.O.B, money over bitches."

"Like I don't know that," Cash huffed, caught up in his feelings, just as Mac had known he would be.

"What you need is a muhfucka to holler at him. Convince him that you should be the next boss. Get in his ear, feel me?"

"So you holler at him for me," Cash suggested.

"You know I will, but we both know the better person to make your case is Mona," Mac proposed, the devil hidden behind his poker face.

Just the mention of her name got Cash's total attention. "I can't do that."

"Do what? Ask her to speak to O on your behalf? Why not?"

Cash downed his drink, then raised his hand for Kat to bring another. "It just ain't a good idea, believe me."

"Cash," Mac began, dropping his head for a minute. He needed to play this just right, deliver the coup de grâce, looking him in the eye, "I know about you and Mona."

Cash fronted him.

"I was there, remember? That night at the Waffle House? I got eyes to see. And I also know you never got over her. I don't know what happened between y'all, but it's obvious to anybody watching you when she's around."

Cash shook his head.

"I don't know what you talkin' about."

Mac chuckled lightly.

"Nigga, this *me*. We been down even before O moved to our 'hood. I *know* you. I know you better than you know yourself. I know you feelin' shortie and I know shortie still feelin' you. So let's not beat around the bush here. You wanna be boss?"

"Of course."

"Then I'm tellin' you the best way to make that happen is Mona. She got O's ear... among other things," Mac quipped with a smirk.

Katrina brought Cash's drink.

He took a deep gulp, smacking his lips as he slammed the glass down, empty. 'That obvious, huh?"

"Yeah brah, it is."

"I just don't know what it is about her, yo. Maybe it's just we want what we can't have. Maybe it's because she the only chick that just blew me off. I dunno. Bottom line is, she under my skin bad and ain't shit I can do about it," Cash admitted, scratching at his forearm like an addict, as though just her name was enough to set the withdrawal biting.

"Now who's the sucka for love?" Mac teased him.

They laughed.

"Yeah, you right. Now I understand, yo. Ain't nothin like that special woman."

"Holler at her. She'll put a bug in O's ear. I'll put a bug in the other," Mac assured him, but he just didn't tell him what kind of bug he had in mind.

"Word. Good luck in that new life, Mac. A nigga might even be jealous."

They shook hands.

"Come on, brah. What are friends for?"

"You feel tense," Aphrodite said, her breath warm on Joe's neck as she massaged his shoulders.

It felt good.

Better than good.

He allowed himself to relax back into her touch.

He sat on the edge of the bed. She knelt on the box spring behind him.

"Goes with the territory," he responded, eyes closed.

"Maybe it's time to pull out of that territory," she suggested slyly.

He smiled, keeping his eyes closed.

"Soon," he promised.

"You know I heard that promise a year ago," Aphrodite reminded him.

"These things take time, baby," Joe said, eyes closed. For a moment, he could just wish it all away, the world reduced to the feel of her fingertips on his flesh. "You know that. I can't just walk away."

"You won't be. *Think different*, like Steve Jobs always used to say. Adonis would just be getting on the job training. You'd be his advisor. The voice in his ear." She stopped massaging him and came around to sit on the edge of the bed beside him.

"Truth? I don't think he's ready," Joe confided.

"But ask yourself how will he get ready if he never gets a chance to test himself? You know this world, you get tempered by the fire, it's the only way it works. You gotta get into the fire. Nothing makes you ready."

Joe shook his head.

"I don't know, Aye. In so many ways he's still just a kid. You must see he doesn't have that killer instinct. Nature fucked up. I wish Mona was the boy, I'd leave the family to her in a heartbeat. She's stone cold."

"Not out of the question," Aphrodite countered, like the notion had just occurred to her. "We live in a modern world. What's wrong with a female Commissioner?"

"Nah. The Commission would never respect her, no matter how many bodies she piled up. A woman in this game always has to be more aggressive than her nature intends. She may be good, our girl, but she'd never be accepted."

Aphrodite sighed.

"Adonis is as ready as he's ever going to be, Joe. Besides, there's something dark about this Othello I don't trust."

"He's married to our daughter."

"And I told Mona that was a mistake, but she's your daughter. Hard-headed, doesn't listen to me," Aphrodite remarked and they both laughed at that, because they both knew it was the diametric opposite of the truth. But there was another truth about to be spoken. "How can we trust a man whose father you..."

Joe rubbed his face.

"He doesn't know."

"Are you sure about that?'

"No. But, I know people. If he was going to move, he would've done it by now," Joe surmised.

"Still..."

Joe caressed her cheek.

"I tell you what... I'll start bringing Adonis up to speed on the family business across the board. By this time next year, if he handles shit correctly, I'll step back. You have my word, Aye."

Aphrodite kissed him, looked her man in the eye and told him, "Remember, sealed with a kiss."

Aphrodite stepped out of her convertible Jaguar and headed inside the high-rise apartment building that housed the offices of her non-profit.

As she headed toward the elevator, she passed several people on their way out and a few lingering, including the security guard who greeted her with a smile.

Her stride was firm, purposeful.

She rode the elevator up, then stepped off onto a floor buzzing with activity.

The place was set up like any office, desks inside of cubicles spaced around a large mirrored glass office. That was her domain. Right outside sat her receptionist, and in the chairs designated for visitors, she saw Mac. He was dressed conservatively in a double-breasted Kenneth Cole suit and matching Italian loafers. He looked like he had just stepped out of the pages of *GQ* magazine.

Seeing Aphrodite, he smiled politely.

"Mrs. Hamlet, how are you? Do you remember, you asked me to come by and apply for a position," Mac reminded her, as he stood up, as though she needed reminding.

"Ah yes, Macklin, right? I'm glad to see you again," she remarked, her smile matching the falseness in his.

They were both playing a role for the receptionist, but Aphrodite liked the fact Mac knew how to play the game.

He definitely got points for being smooth.

Aphrodite turned to her receptionist.

"Reach out to that singer, what's her name? Nefertiti?"

"Egypt?" Mac suggested.

"That's her. There could be a business opportunity worth exploring here. I'm told she's looking for a backer to launch her own label after the clusterfuck that was Notorious. I'm thinking we might be able to do something. At the very least we should talk. Two powerful women together, we might just change the world."

"You hear Street Love? That girl was the real talent of that stable, forget fuckin' Power and the QBC, she is the real deal," Mac opined.

"She's got it in her to be a star," Aphrodite agreed. "Make it happen."

"Yes ma'am," her secretary, a young white woman, replied.

Mac held open her door. "Wonderful. Thank you, Mr. Bethel. Shall we?"

"No problem, Mrs. Hamlet."

They entered. Mac loved the place right away.

Once the door closed, the sound from outside disappeared. The room was sound-proofed, and, he was guessing swept for listening devices daily. It was spacious enough for a large oval, mahogany table, complete with twelve high-back swivel chairs around it. Against one wall there was a small wet bar, a couch and loveseat, then her desk and her chair behind, which had an Ernie Barnes original looking over her shoulder. The view through the floor-to-ceiling windows was of the city far below, and the distant harbor, giving the view a feel of infinite vision.

"I love your office," Mac remarked, "It says a lot about you."

"Like?"

"Like, you are willing to listen to what people have to say, which is shown by the round table. No head to a round table, right, so it gives everyone sitting here a feeling of equality. Like you value them being there. Then, you have the more intimate setting over there, the one-on-one with the couches and the bar. Another place to make the elite feel included. But, see, the real importance of the room is right over there, your desk is where the decisions get made, and there, I see only one seat. Yours," Mac explained.

Aphrodite laughed as she sat on the edge of her desk.

"Very perceptive of you. I like men who know what to do without being told," she replied.

Aphrodite moved toward the bar, but Mac stopped her with a gentle touch to her forearm. "Let me."

She smiled, demurred and sat on the couch, crossing her long, shapely legs.

"While you are fixing the drinks, why don't you tell me about yourself, Macklin."

"First of all, call me Mac. All my friends do," he told her, as he poured them both a glass of wine.

He turned and handed her one.

"And what makes you think I want to be your friend?" Aphrodite quipped.

"You chose the couch. If this was a job interview, you would've sat behind the desk," Mac smirked.

Aphrodite nodded. "Perhaps," she said, sipping her wine.

Mac sat down beside her.

"You want to know about me? I'm a man who has a vision... plans. When I wake up in the morning, my first thought is, what's for dinner? I think long-term, everything else is just a means to the end. It's all about getting there."

"I like that. I like that a lot. Yes, I do think you and I can be friends."

"Good friends, or just friends?" Mac flirted.

"Which do you prefer?"

Mac downed his wine in one shot, sat the glass on the coffee table and pulled Aphrodite over on his lap.

"One thing you'll find out about me is, I want it all," Mac

growled, then held her roughly by the back of the neck and tongued her down with gangsta authority.

He knew no other approach would have worked with a woman like Aphrodite. He had read her the first time he laid eyes on her. Joe may have been a gangsta, but he was going soft, a fact proven just by looking into Aphrodite Hamlet's eyes. She was the pampered wife, the cougar waiting on young meat to devour.

But he wasn't about to be the next boy toy. He was going to break her.

Or so he thought.

Because Mac may have been right that Joe had gone soft— and yes that fact was reflected in the hungry look in Aphrodite's eyes, but she wanted more than a young stud. She wanted a pawn in the game. She wanted a young aggressive go-getter to counter the hesitancy she knew Adonis suffered.

Because Aphrodite Hamlet was playing the game too.

She wasn't content being the wife or mother of a gangsta...

She *was* a gangsta.

But at that moment, she let Mac take control, allowing him to ravage her, because she needed a good thug fucking, and feeling the hardness and girth of his thug muscle, she knew she wouldn't be disappointed.

Mac pulled up her dress, slid her panties to the side and began to finger fuck her with two fingers.

Her lips were already soaked, her pussy oozing and as soon as he penetrated her, she let out a loud moan.

"Fuck!" Aphrodite exclaimed, riding the rhythm of his fingers. "Don't fucking tease me."

"What about the people?" Mac huffed, his dick hard as a pole in the winter.

"What about them?" Aphrodite gasped.

The windows from the inside were clear, but looking on from the outside, they were mirrored. Two way glass. No one could see in. Although at certain times in the day, when the sun was just right, you *could* just make out silhouettes inside.

It was that time of day.

But by that time, both of them were undressed, and neither cared if the whole room was watching. It only added to the thrill of the fucking.

Aphrodite's naked body looked like Egyptian gold in the sunshine as Mac ran his hands and tongue all over her.

He gripped the base of his dick then drove it deep inside of her, stabbing her with the sweetest blade in the world.

"*Yessssssssss,*" Aphrodite hissed, the note going on forever as her whole body shivered like she was freezing. Her nerves endings were sensitive to every stroke.

She threw her head back and rode his dick, taking every inch in and matching the intensity of his strokes with her own grind.

"I've wanted to do this ever since the first moment I laid eyes on you," Mac groaned in her ear, loving the way she rode his dick, grinding and gyrating her shapely hips, pussy juices running down over his nuts. It was fucking nirvana.

"Make me cum again, I want to cum again," Aphrodite begged.

Mac sunk lower in the couch and changed the angle of his strokes, using the curve in his dick until he found her g-spot. He knew by the way she couldn't hold her silence and the way her body trembled, that he had found her secret place. It felt too good for her to even moan. She opened her mouth but nothing came out. Behind her closed eyes, she saw bursts of color. Mac was relentless, taking her breath away, until she exploded all over his dick, gasping for air.

"God... damn, I'm still cumming!"

Mac pulled her down and tongued her nipple, bringing another groan from her lips. "I'm gonna make this pussy mine," he vowed, going down to lick his own cum out.

The way her pussy tasted at that moment, he already had.

Othello leaned against the door, watching his wife sleep.

The double doors that led to the terrace were open, letting in the cool Venetian breeze. She looked like a sleeping angel, her hair flared out around her like a halo, that slight smile still on her lips as if she were dreaming of the beauty of her future. Their honeymoon had begun in Bali and was ending in Venice, an ancient city that he had always wanted to visit. In prison, he had seen pictures of the city and read about how it was slowly being swallowed by the sea, and he found a profound beauty in the waterways that served as streets. It was one of the few unique places in the world.

He and Mona had done all the things lovers do in Venice, including taking the gondola ride, being photographed beneath the Bridge of Sighs, being serenaded by a sweet-voiced Italian playing a mandolin, eating gelato and drinking espresso on the palazzo.

They had also shopped hard, feeding the fetish they both had for shoes.

They got shoes and stilettos handmade, along with tailor-made suits.

Before he knew it, Othello had spent well over fifty grand.

But the smile on his wife's lips was worth it.

Standing in the doorway, he couldn't imagine life without her.

He had finally found something he would die for.

Or kill for.

He held a light blue silk scarf in his hand.

It was her favorite color.

He remembered her saying something about a scarf her grandmother used to have. She had described it with so much detail, and he'd listened, knowing it was important to her, so when he had it made, it was easy to duplicate.

He sat on the edge of the bed and began to use the end of the scarf to lightly tickle her face.

Mona wiggled her nose, frowned up and turned away.

Then Othello let it barely touch her cheek.

She slapped at it, slapping herself in her sleep.

He held back laughter as he tickled her ear.

She woke up, confused, but when he busted out laughing, she knew exactly what was going on.

"Oh you wanna play, huh?" She cracked, wriggling around and jumping on Othello, knocking him over on the bed.

Mona began punching him playfully, sticking her fingers in his ears and mouth until he was crying with tears.

"Truce! Truce!" He cried.

"No truce!" She cackled back.

He held up the scarf. "*Truuuuuce!*"

When she laid eyes on it, her heart skipped a beat. She stopped in her play-fight tracks. Her eyes couldn't widen enough. This was her childhood.

"Oh... my god," she gasped, "Where..?"

"I had it made for you yesterday. Remember the old man that made my ties? He said, "For your-ah beautiful wife-ah," Othello said, playfully using a bad Italian accent.

Mona didn't know what to say. She had no words. She didn't need them for him. The tears in her eyes said it all.

"No one's done something for me this beautiful, baby. Oh, I love you so much," she declared, wrapping her arms around him and giving him a big kiss.

"And you know I love you too, lettin' you kiss me with that dragon breath!" He teased.

Mona howled with laughter, while pummeling him with more love taps.

Othello flipped her over and pinned her to the bed.

"You my heart, babygirl," he told her, solemnly.

"And you're mine," she replied.

Their long passionate kiss led to an early morning love-making session.

Venice was like an aphrodisiac for any newlywed couple, so intensely beautiful and headily exotic.

When it was time to go, and they were sat on the plane waiting for it to rumble down the runway, Mona whined, "Do we really have to leave? I love my family, but I could do this for a few more years."

Othello chuckled.

"Soon."

"So what are you going to do now that you're retiring?" Mona questioned.

Othello rested his head against the headrest. "I don't know, but it's good to have choices, you know? Being a Black man with choices feels real good. And rare."

"Just hang around with me at the theater. Maybe we can even turn some of the plays and performances into movies," Mona suggested. "Wouldn't that be something?"

"Not a bad idea. I could be like the gangsta Tyler Perry," Othello joked.

Mona laughed as the plane began its taxi, ready for takeoff to return to their real world.

"Othello's back from his honeymoon," Mac told Cash over the phone.

Kandi drove.

He sat back in the passenger seat.

"I heard," Cash responded, across town sitting on his couch. The TV played in the background.

"So now you can holler at Mona," Mac stated.

"Man, you sure this is a good idea?"

"My nigga, who always keep it real with you?"

"You."

"And I ain't gonna steer you wrong now, am I? Don't worry about O. I'ma take him out the way, you just go over to the theater and holler at Mona. She gonna put in the word for you. Trust me, you'll be boss in no time! Just do me a favor, make sure you bounce by three."

"Okay... Okay, yeah set it up. And Mac, you know I appreciate this."

"I know you do," Mac chuckled then hung up.

"What he say?" Kandi wanted to know.

"What you think he said? He swallowed that shit whole," Mac laughed.

"I gotta give it to you, babe, you a fuckin' evil genius."

"Tell me something I don't know."

The next day.

Mac picked Othello up so that they could make the rounds. It was part of what they did: watching, being seen, which was important across the different spots in their territory. It showed people they were there. Othello leaned the seat back, cracked the window and lit a cigar. He'd picked the habit up from his new father-in-law, always sucking on those thick dick Cubans like some sort of Freudian thing-or was that the one where you wanted to bone your own mama?

"Venus and Milk say shit is rolling lovely," Othello remarked, lips off the cigar for long enough to lay down some wisdom. "Them two of the realest bitches I done met in a minute."

"No doubt, no doubt. But yo, I need to talk to you about something."

"What up, Mac?"

"I'm getting out the game," Mac told him.

Othello looked at him.

"What up, brah? You good? You ain't sick or nothin are you? You ain't got cancer or no shit like that, do you?"

"Fuck is you talkin about? Hell no, I ain't sick. Don't mark me like that."

"Naw, I'm just sayin' you getting out the game is like the sun getting out the sky. Nigga, you live for this shit," Othello pointed out.

Mac shrugged, backing the gesture with a subtle chuckle. "Time to move on, you know? Do some other things. We been hustlin' since we was kids, my nigga, and we've had a good run, you know?"

Othello nodded. "True dat. To be honest with you, I've been thinking along the same lines."

I know you have, you ungrateful ass nigga, Mac thought, but he hid his hiss in a smile and said, "Word?"

"Word. I'm ready to move on, too. Start a family and just chill."

"That's the real life right there. And speaking of chillin', when was the last time you been to Ice's?"

"Ice's? Man, goddamn, it's been *years* since I even thought about that ol' hole in the wall," Othello laughed.

Mac looked at his watch.

"Let's go have a drink or two. I have a surprise for you."

"I'm supposed to go by Mona's theater. She's having some dance exhibit next week and she want me to check out the rehearsal," Othello said.

"Damn, your leash reach to the Southside don't it?" Mac joked.

Othello laughed, but it worked out just the way he knew it would. "Nigga, fuck you. Like Kandi ain't got *you* wrapped around her pinkie!"

"What she got me wrapped wit' might be pink, but it ain't no finger!" Mac joked.

"One drink," Othello agreed.

"Or two."

They arrived at the small out of the way tittie bar, needing to squint back the dark as they entered until their eyes properly adjusted to the gloom of the Graveyard.

"This muhfuckin' place ain't gonna never change," Othello commented, looking around.

"Just like the past," Mac added.

They found a booth, then sat back blowing blunts and watching the bullet-scarred, stretch marked topless dancers gyrate around the half-empty room. There wasn't so much as a dick twitch.

"These bitches couldn't sell pussy in a Mexican whorehouse, yo," Othello cracked.

When Kat walked up, her whole face lit up.

"O?"

Othello looked up. It took a heartbeat, then, "Kat?"

"Surprise!" Mac commented, as Othello got up and wrapped Kat in a big hug, lifting her off her feet.

"What up, ma! Where the hell you been?" Othello asked, looking her up and down, not much liking what he saw.

"Vacation," she chuckled.

"So was I," Othello answered. "How long?"

"Seven years."

Othello shook his head.

"That's some stretch. Sit down. Have a drink with us."

Kat glanced at her manager, who was sitting by the bar watching her.

"I can't, I already took my break," she apologized.

Othello looked back at the manager, "Drinks on me for as long as I'm here, and I'm here as long as Kat can drink," he called over.

The manager gave him a thumbs up.

Kat laughed.

"Bring a bottle of Henny and three glasses, ma," Othello told her.

When she returned, the three of them sat back, drinking and smoking, and reminiscing about old times. For some around the table, better times.

"Yeah, when Mac walked in here a few weeks ago, I couldn't believe it," Kat remarked, knocking back half her a glass in one gulp.

Mac chuckled.

"I couldn't believe it either, believe me, girl."

"So what you doin', Kat? You know you fucked with real niggas all your life. You ain't gotta be up in this joint, scraping pennies."

Kat tapped the blunt ash in the tray and looked at Othello.

"Those seven years broke me, O." She shrugged and it was obvious she was telling the whole truth. "I promised myself I'd never put myself in a position to go back, and I'm not gonna."

"I respect that, believe me. I feel the same way. But I've got a lot of connects outside the game, maybe I can get you a job?" Othello proposed.

Kat snorted a chuckle of self-contempt. "Doing what, nigga? The game is all I know. You think I'd be here if I had job skills? I know what I am, and that's an addict, O. That dog food had me fucked up for a minute, but I go to my meetings, I keep my head down and thank the Lord for another day above ground. I'm good. I'm surviving, and that's more than can be said for some."

"Naw, ma, my wife owns that new black theater downtown. I can get you a job over there. You can learn as you go."

"You have a wife? Not big, bad Othello? Shackled to a ball and chain. Damn I gotta meet the beauty that locked down the beast," Kat laughed.

Othello laughed right along with her.

Cash pulled up in front of Mona's theater, took a deep breath, centering himself, then cut the car off.

He checked his face in the rearview mirror, looking into his own eyes and wondering what the fuck was wrong with him, giving himself butterflies so easily.

"Here we go," he told his mirror self, then got out of the car.

Once inside, he went up to the receptionist desk.

The sister behind the desk, a dead ringer for Jill Scott, beautiful smile, afro and all, beamed, "May I help you, sir?"

"I'm here to see Mrs. *Moore*," he replied, finding it hard to call Mona by her married name.

"She's in the dance studio at the end of the hall. Just keep straight and follow the music."

"Thank you."

"Anytime," she said, with a hint of flirtation in her tone.

Cash headed down the hall, taking in all the artwork on the walls. There were people in each of the rooms, and down on the stage, rehearsing and doing their thing. It felt good to see kids reaching for their dreams.

He reached the dance studio, and stopped, looking in through the door.

She was in there, looking like everything he had ever dreamed a woman should look. She had on a white leotard, and was dancing barefoot, with her hair held back in a ponytail.

Even with no make-up, she glowed.

She was teaching a group of young girls their steps.

He stood in the doorway watching her for a moment, content. She moved with such grace and poise, he couldn't help but imagine that Maya Angelou poem, *Phenomenal Woman*, had been written for her.

One of the little girls saw him, and whispered to her friend, then they both broke into a fit of girlish giggles. The giggles went like wildfire through the tiny dancers. Mona heard them, how could she not? She looked up and was about to chide them when she saw the cause of their distraction.

Her eyes held his for a beat, then she cleared her throat and told the kids, "Okay girls, take five. Five, not six. Got it?"

As they raced off, she walked over to Cash, drying her face with a towel.

"Hey... what are you doing here?" Mona questioned.

"I'm sorry to impose, ma. It won't take long, but I could use a favor," he answered.

She looked at him, like, "A favor?"

"I'm hopin' you'll listen a few. I won't take up too much of your time, if we could go somewhere?"

Mona weighed it out, sighed and replied, "My office."

When they got inside her small, cramped cupboard of a room in the back of the dance studio, she sat on the desk. "Okay, Cash, I'm listening."

He gritted, looked her in the eye. God it was hard. He started, "I know Othello is falling back from the game. He's got good reason to," Cash offered her a compliment. Mona kept her game face, but the inside of her cheeks blushed.

"And?"

"He talked to Mac, but Mac is falling back, which only leaves me. But, O thinks I'm just a..."

"Playboy, womanizer, heartbreaker, stop me when I'm warm," Mona quipped playfully.

Cash laughed.

"Yeah, all that. I'm not that bad, yo."

"No, you're worse. But go on."

"Anyway, I want that connect. He need to keep it in the family, but I'm afraid he'll sell it to someone else on The Commission, someone who won't keep me in the game. I don't want to be frozen out," Cash explained.

"Okay, I can understand that, but what's it got to do with me,

Cassio? I don't have anything to do with how Othello does business. That's all him."

"Ma, that nigga love you to death. Your word matters to him. You don't have to know his business, to put in a good word for me."

Mona looked at Cash. There was a curious expression on her face he couldn't read. It wasn't like she didn't understand how the game was played. She was, after all, her father's daughter, and the apple didn't fall from the tree. Maybe she felt a little guilty for leaving Cash like she did? Maybe she felt like she owed him?

"I don't know how much help I could be, but I'll mention it to him," she promised.

Cash breathed a sigh of relief.

"I really appreciate that, ma."

Mona nodded.

"No problem," she answered, hopping off the desk. "Is there anything else? I've got an army of tiny tearaways waiting out there."

He looked at her. They were alone in a small room. No one would know if he expressed the secret language known only to his heart. The look in her eyes was almost like she *wanted* him to say something else, but the words were never going to come. Both of them were bound by an unbreakable allegiance to the same man for very different reasons.

"No, that's it."

She nodded, then turned to the door.

When she grabbed the knob, he grabbed her arm.

"No, I'm lying. There is one more thing."

"Guess who's home?" Kat said.

"Who?" Othello asked.

"Rihanna! She got out about a month ago," Kat told him,

feeling nice off the three glasses of Henny she'd knocked back and the blunt she had inhaled.

"Rihanna?" Mac echoed, not following. He thought he knew everyone in O's circle.

"Naw, you don't know 'em. Word, that's what's up. I can't front though, scrams go hard. So what up, you gonna ride with me or what on this job thing?" Othello wanted to know.

Kat propped her hand under her chin and smirked. "It better be legit, O."

"Scout's Honor."

"You were *never* a boy scout."

"But I've always had honor," he winked.

"It's good to have family again," she said.

"To family," Othello toasted, and they all clinked glasses.

"Why?"

Mona just looked at Cash.

It was a simple question, the simplest, really, but it demanded a complicated response.

She peeped out at the girls.

They were working through their dance steps on their own with that quiet intensity only little ones can manage. She shut the door, and replied, "Cassio...okay. When my father found out that I had... been with you that night, he told me, if I ever saw you again he would kill you," Mona explained.

Cash shook his head.

"But goddamn, you coulda gave me a chance to make the decision on my own. I didn't need you to think for me," he huffed, heated.

"Cassio, you *saw* how he reacted to Othello. Do you seriously think he would've hesitated making good on that threat?"

Cash sighed hard.

"You left me cold, ma."

"I'm sorry. I really am."

"You broke my heart."

"Don't do this, Cassio," Mona begged softly.

"I'm not doing anything, believe me ma, honest to God. I know where things stand, and I would never violate that."

"I would never let you violate that," Mona stated firmly.

"I know, but still... It don't make it any easier, you know?"

Mona sighed, kissed him on the cheek and told him, "You'll find someone Cassio, I know you will. Just stop running those streets and give her a chance to find you."

"I already found her, ma, ain't gonna find her twice," Cash replied.

Mona fought back tears.

As Mac drove, Othello sat back, hitting a blunt.

"It was real good to see Kat. Hell, I ain't thought about shortie in *years*," Othello said, deep in the reminiscence.

"No doubt. First time I saw her I couldn't help think about that time you smashed her, then a few weeks later, Cash was fuckin' her too! That shit was crazy!"

Mac chuckled.

Othello's brow furled subtly, he'd put it out of his mind, but it was there, locked up in his mind, and had been ever since the time Mac had brought up. Truth was, Othello had never gotten over the feeling he had seeing Kat with Cash that night. It was like a razor to the nuts, opened him up and everything he felt about love unraveled like bloody yo-yo's. It wasn't like she was his girl, but she might have been, and there was a code: he'd always believed that homeboys shouldn't fuck the same bitch out of a gangbang situation. He had never confronted Cash about it, but it went right to the root of his insecurity. It only added to his sense of inferiority, side-by-side with Cash. Cash was the big dick, pretty boy, and what was he? The big, black ugly nigga with the smarts.

Mac knew his dude well enough to know it was a deep scar. He was no mug. That was the only reason he'd wanted Othello to see her again. It was all about dredging up all those old useless feelings so that they could get put to a better use in the here and now.

Mac glanced over at Othello, a sly smirk stealing across his lips.

"Let me find out you in your feelings still about that hood rat."

"Fuck outta here, yo," Othello denied, passing him the blunt. "I wasn't in my feelings then, shit just caught me off guard."

"I feel you. But shit, we grown ass men now, ain't no way that would happen again. That thing that bonds us, thicker than blood."

"No doubt."

Cash watched the girls go through their routine.

It was a hip hop-classical music fusion, where they got to do all of their favorite hip hop dance moves, then morph into a more graceful ballet. Surprisingly, it was a good show, and when they were finished, he found himself clapping for them.

"Ay yo, y'all make me want to get my groove on," Cash joked, doing a mock of a pirouette. He was not graceful.

The girls cracked up, including Mona.

"They're chasing their dreams. I bet you had a dream when you were little," Mona commented.

"I was never little," Cash quipped, with a knowing wink.

Mona couldn't help but blush. "Younger."

Cash shrugged.

"Yeah, I wanted to play baseball."

"I didn't know you were a baseball fan," Mona said, not quite able to mask the surprise in her voice.

"Go Yankees," he replied.

She sucked her teeth.

"Let me rephrase that: I didn't know you *weren't* a baseball fan."

They laughed.

"If it ain't Boston, why bother?"

Mona chuckled.

"Traitor."

They were enjoying each other's company so much, that when Cash glanced at his watch and saw it was 3:05 he felt like Cinderella at 11:59, knowing his carriage was gonna turn into a pumpkin and the whole charade was going to Hell.

"I have to go, yo. Make sure you handle that for me. I owe you, ma," Cash said, as he headed for the door.

"Oh," Mona began, confused by his abrupt departure, "Okay. I will. See you 'round, Cash."

He was out of the room before she finished her sentence. He high stepped down the hall, checking his watch twice more before reaching the front. The receptionist smiled sweetly, but when he didn't return it, she said, "Umm, excuse me."

He stopped, halfway out the door, turned and replied, "Yeah?"

"I-uh usually don't do this, but..." she said, then slid him a piece of paper, looked him in his eyes like a grown woman, and added, "That's my number. Why don't you use it?"

Too flustered to deny or reply, he simply took the number and walked out.

He was so intent on leaving, he didn't look right or left in traffic, he just bugged out.

Had he done so, he would've seen Mac's car coming down the street.

"You see that? Wasn't that Cash bugging out of Mona's theater?" Mac asked, squinting at Cash's car as it merged into traffic.

Othello looked, following the direction of his gaze.

Nice and sleazy does it. Every time.

"Yeah... yeah that's his car right there making a right," he said, his voice carrying a hint of indignation, still half living in the past and old transgressions.

The timing was perfect. Seriously could not have been better.

"Oh," Mac said.

It was a simple expression, not even a word. But, the way he said it—the inflection he put into it—as though implying much more, caught Othello's ear.

"Oh? What you mean, *oh*, nigga?" Othello questioned, the growl in his voice the rumble of a coming storm.

"Nothing, man."

"Naw yo, why you say it like that? What you tryin' to make me think?"

"Like what?" Mac asked, feigning innocent ignorance.

"Lil' brah, I ain't no fuckin' fool, that came out your mouth like pure surprise and like it was something so wrong, so now you got me thinking *why*?" Othello questioned.

Mac chuckled. "Big brah, you ain't makin' no sense."

Mac's chuckle rubbed Othello the wrong way. "Something funny?"

"O, you're reading way too much into this," Mac countered, soberly.

Othello thought for a minute.

"I'ma call him."

He began to reach for his phone until Mac said, "For what? If it wasn't him, he gonna think you on some bullshit, like you don't trust him and he wasn't even there. But if it was him, he ain't gonna tell you anyway if he on some bullshit, feel me? He'll just say it's all good," Mac reasoned.

Othello thought about a moment, seeing the logic in Mac's reasoning, and nodded wordlessly.

Mac saw that he had him, so he continued.

"This what you do. Go in, don't mention it, don't say anything about it. If it was Cash, and there's no big secret, Mona will be all, 'Oh you just missed Cassio,' see? But, if she don't say anything, well then..." Mac let his voice trail off, allowing Othello's jealous imagination to go where it would.

"Then what?"

"Big brah then it's... still probably nothing."

Mac was a master of the meaningful pauses, leaving just enough room for the shred of doubt, and once doubt got its nasty little teeth into a man, that fool will do anything to get out of it, but first they gonna speculate. And speculating just feeds the beast.

Othello, eating his line of reasoning hook, line and sinker, nodded.

"Yeah, I feel you, Mac. Good look, yo. I was about to flip."

"Hey, what are friends for?"

When they got inside, Mona and the kids were practicing the routine, going through the drill. He could smell young sweat. She had the girls looking good, and Othello couldn't help but admire her shapely curves in the tight leotard she wore. He even smiled a bit, thinking he was hot for teacher. Then his mind overheated, because he thought about Cash having just seen the same thing.

She smiled at him as she danced, but her smile looked distorted in his clouding mind.

What does she think, I am a fool? Her smile that used to light the sky, seems to be laughing at me, mocking me and shit! I knew it was too good to be true. A woman that beautiful, that smart and articulate, to truly love an ugly muhfucka like me. Sure, I pull bad bitches, but it's my money, my swag, my gangsta style, but they never really love me! Cash... Cash is what women really want. His looks, his style, his... I don't even want to think about it, Othello fumed to himself, struggling to maintain his composure as Mona came over and gave him a welcoming kiss.

"Hey baby," she chimed happily.

Did she say the same thing to Cash?

It was a dark thought.

"What's good, beautiful? I see you've got the girls looking good," Othello mentioned, giving the little ones a nod.

"What's up, Mona?" Mac greeted.

"Hi Mac," she replied, then added, "I can't wait for the show."

"How has your day been, love?" Othello questioned, subtle, giving her the chance to come out about Cash.

There was no way he could know about the conflict of reason running through her mind as she looked into his eyes: If I tell him Cash came by, then when I speak to him about giving Cash the connect, he's gonna know it was Cash that asked the favor. I want to help Cash. It's the least I can do, but I can't do that if Othello knows I'm trying to help. He's gonna feel played. A man always hates when a woman tries and tells him what to do, so I gotta do what all women do: make him think it was his idea.

Mona said, "Nothing exciting, just been rehearsing all day. How about you?"

Othello looked at Mac out of the corner of his eye.

It took *everything* in him not to ask her about Cash's black ass. "Not... much. Listen, Me and Mac have to go handle something. I'll see you when you get home."

"Okay bae," she smiled, then kissed him again, giving him that look, adding, "Thanks for dropping by. I'll be home first, so I'll make sure I'm naked when you get there."

It should have been the sexiest thought in the world, but her flirtation only served to make his anger turn crimson.

He mustered a chuckle.

"Yeah."

His response threw her off, but she let it go and went back to rehearsal, clapping her hands as she bounced back to the little dance stage.

They watched a second longer as the kids picked up their moves, then hustled out.

Back on the street, Othello slammed the door as he got into the car, fuming.

For a moment, neither of them spoke.

It was Mac that broke the silence, appeasing, "It probably wasn't him."

Othello looked at him skeptically.

"O, I'm tellin' you, Cash would *never* slink away like that because he saw us coming."

The word *slink* stuck in Othello's mind. It was a cold word. Spoke of treachery.

"You're reading too much into this," Mac insisted.

"No, I'm not."

"Yeah you are. I know you, O. I know how you get about bitches, I mean, females."

"Bitches, you had it right. All women have bitch in 'em. Period. They go to bed to work and get up to play. Don't get it twisted, I may love Mona, but my eyes are as open as my nose," Othello assured him.

"I feel you. So just watch them, watch her, and see how she move, how he move, feel me? If it's anything going on, you'll know. Trust me," Mac laid it out there.

Othello nodded.

"Yo, on some real shit, Mac, you my man. You always keep it real. If you wouldn't have been here, I probably woulda played myself, yo."

They shook hands.

"Fam, you already know. I got your back," he winked.

Mac knew he wouldn't have to worry about Cash getting the

connect for a few more days, which gave him time to make sure he never got it at all.

Othello walked into his apartment.

The smell of his favorite meal, fried chicken and macaroni and cheese, filled his nostrils. It was heavenly. The kind of meal men asked for when the warden asked them to fill in the ticket for their last meal.

Mona came walking out of the kitchen wearing only a chef's apron and red bottoms.

"So what do you want first, dinner or..." she purred, untying the apron and letting it fall to the floor so that her goddess-shaped body was on full display, "...dessert."

No matter how mad he was, Mona's magnetism always brought his anger to its knees.

She kissed him deeply, unbuckling his pants with desperate fingers, then dropped down, her legs spread like eagle wings, and took him into her mouth. She bobbed, taking him deep into her throat. No gag reflex. She used her hands to massage his balls while she deep-throated him, bringing him to the edge of ecstasy before getting up.

She smiled at him, his precum wet across her smile.

God what a sight.

Othello picked her up.

She wrapped her legs around his waist, her arms around his neck.

He spread her ass cheeks, sliding two fingers in her ass as his dick slipped inside of her. She began to ride him hard and steady. The fingers in her ass driving her crazy, making her go buck on his dick. This was no old married sex. This was still hot fucking.

"Ohhhh Daddy, right there, right *there!*" She squealed, kissing him on the neck and sucking his earlobe as he pounded her pussy like he was grudge-fucking her, taking out all the frustrations and suspicions of his imagination on her pussy.

And she loved every stroke.

"I-I-I'm about to cum!" she gasped, then she did, all over his dick, juddering and shuddering in his arms.

Feeling her wet juices running down his thigh, Othello couldn't last much longer. He stroked it, pushing in hard, all the way up into her, and came.

"I love you, you know that?" Mona stated, looking him in the eyes.

I hope you do. He thought.

"I love you, too. You ready for dinner now?"

"Maybe a little more dessert first?" she replied, going down onto the carpet and spreading wide. He dropped to his knees and feasted on her juices...

As they ate, Mona watched him gobble down her cooking.

"Damn ma, you know I love your mac and cheese," Othello garbled, between bites.

"Like you needed another reason to love me," she teased.

Othello laughed.

"O."

He looked up.

"Yeah?"

"Have you given any more thought to retiring? I mean, like, what you're going to do?" Mona probed.

Othello wiped his mouth and shrugged.

"Not really. A lot has to happen between now and then."

"You know, I was thinking about it... I watched my Daddy all my life, and you remind me a lot of him. How he moves."

"Yeah. How so?"

"You're loyal to family, which is good. Plus, you can see seven steps ahead of everybody else."

Othello shrugged.

"It comes natural."

"You know who else reminds me of you and my father?"

"Who?"

"Cash."

His ears perked up, right along with that spike in his jealousy, but he held his composure. "Oh yeah? Pretty boy? You think so?"

Mona nodded, taking a forkful of mac and cheese. "He's sharp."

"Sharp don't mean shit in the game," Othello countered.

Mona looked confused.

"You have to be sharp."

"With the chicks maybe."

"I'm not talking about that kind of sharp."

"You sure?" Othello quipped.

Mona stopped eating and looked at him. "What do you mean?"

"Come on Mo, don't tell me you don't think Cash look good," Othello shot back.

"What's that got to do with what we were talking about?"

"Everything. Just answer the question," Othello urged.

Mona shook her head.

"For what?"

"I just want to know. Do you think Cash look good?"

"Forget I brought it up," she waved him off, then picked up her plate and took it to the sink. Othello's worse fear was racing on towards confirmation.

"Yeah, you think he look good."

Mona spun around.

"Okay, yes, sure. Cash is attractive. It don't mean nothing in the scheme of things."

"Fine."

"Othello, you're tripping."

"Because you're making a big deal out of nothing, yo. Aight tell me this. What's your number?"

"What?"

"You heard me. How many people have you had sex with in your life?" He questioned.

"I can't believe you asked me that," Mona shot back.

"It's just a question. We're open with one another, right? I ain't got nothing to hide, ask me, I'm an open book."

Oh my God, did Cash tell him about that night? Is that why Othello is tripping on Cash tonight? Should I admit it? If he already knows, he'll just make a bigger deal, but if he doesn't, this shit could really get ugly. No. I won't tell him. If he asks, I won't lie, but ain't no need in stirring up the past.

"Thousands, O. Is that what you wanted to hear? I've slept with thousands. I've gobbled so much dick I get worried every Thanksgiving I'll be mistaken for a fuckin' turkey. Gobble gobble. Happy now?" Mona remarked, sarcastically.

"I figured that," he spat back coldly.

"Fuck you, Othello," Mona rasped, then stormed out, the tears welling in her eyes made of anger, guilt and frustration. As soon as she entered the bedroom, she grabbed her phone and went straight to her Facebook page.

Did you ever tell him?

It took several minutes before she got a reply.

No. Why?

Don't.

Mona tossed her phone aside, not even waiting for a reply.

Othello walked in almost immediately.

Mona glared out him.

His expression seemed contrite.

"I'm sorry. I was out of order. I shouldn't have come at you like that."

"You damn right you shouldn't have. Look O, I have a past just like you, and I find other people attractive, just like you. That doesn't take away from the love I have for you. You're my husband, I married you. To me, you're all the fine I'll ever need," Mona expressed, no longer able to hold back her tears.

Othello felt like shit.

He went and sat on the side of the bed, taking her into his arms.

"I'm sorry. I just love you so much, sometimes it just makes me a little crazy, okay? Things get in my head. Ghosts, I guess. Whisper in my ear." He told her.

"We're on the same team, Othello. I got your back," she told him. Then kissed him to show things were all good. "And I'm telling you Cash is street sharp."

"What about Mac? He sharp, too," Othello retorted.

Mona looked away.

"What?" Othello asked, sensing something in her silence.

"Look, I know Mac is your boy and all, but..."

"But what?" He pressed.

Mona sighed.

"It's just... look, babe, I don't wanna say, but there's something about him and his wife, Kandi. They just..." Mona said, ending her sentence with a shake of her head.

Maybe it's because Mac is onto your bullshit, bitch, Othello's jealousy darkened side spat.

No, no, she loves us, his softer side argued. "Mac's my boy, ma."

"So's Cash," she shot back. "Didn't you always tell me that Mac is too hot-headed, too quick to move without thinking?"

"Yeah," he admitted, reluctantly.

"Then you already know what I'm saying," Mona concluded, then kissed him on the nose. "I'm going to take a shower."

Othello watched her naked ass prance into the bathroom, and for a moment he was tempted to join her, but feeling too full for another round of her chocolate he laid back with every intention of getting back up, but his stomach overcame his will and he soon drifted off to sleep...

He heard voices.

He lifted his head to find himself alone in the bedroom.

"Mona?" Othello called out, but got no reply.

He checked his watch.

3:33 a.m.

"Damn, I sleep that long?"

The voices, whispered in the wind, hard to discern, but easy to recognize. It was Mona and... a deeper voice. One that was familiar, that he knew as well as his own... but not in the context of the middle of the night.

Othello got up and headed towards the living room.

The voices were no longer saying words, they were making sounds.

The sounds of panting and heavy breathing.

Fucking.

He quickened his pace, but the hallway seemed to just grow longer, like a funhouse treadmill that moved faster as he ran harder. The sounds growing louder, louder, until he could hear them clearly.

"Ohhhh fuck this pussy," Mona called out.

"Whose pussy is this?!"

"Yours!"

"Say it louder!"

"Yours baby, yours!"

"Whose?"

"Caaaaaaaash," she squealed, and Othello knew from the tremble in her tone that she was squirting, her pussy milking his dick and pelvis.

"Nooooooo!" Othello cried, as he finally made it into the living room.

He saw Cash, with his big ass dick, long-dicking Mona, cockeyed, her head thrown back as he blew her back out, her titties bouncing to the rhythm of his stroke.

"His dick is way bigger than yours, baby," she giggled, as Cash smacked her ass, biting his bottom lip.

"Nigga, I'll kill, you."

Othello flew upright in a rage, spinning around, left, right. Trembling. Every muscle fired off trigger warnings, about to do something dumb. Mona was asleep next to him, her face partly glowing with the light of the moon.

He looked at his watch. 3:33 a.m.

His heartbeat thundered out a mile a minute.

He looked into Mona's sleeping face.

She seemed to be smiling, like she was having a pleasant dream.

About who? His jealous mind taunted.

Mac walked into the mosque and looked around.

On the men-only side, several Muslim men were in prayer, as two women, dressed head to toe in black hijabs, burkas, shuffled past him, their beautiful eyes downcast.

Two men approached him.

"I'm here to see Malik," Mac told them.

"He expecting you?"

"Yeah."

One of them left, while the other waited with Mac.

Neither man spoke.

The first man returned a couple of minutes later, hooked a finger and said, "Okay, follow me."

He led Mac down a back corridor with pipes and electrical ducts exposed, to a set of stairs that went to the next floor. They climbed them. On the landing, Mac saw a small studio apartment, decked out with what he assumed were Islamic motifs. There was a thick oriental rug in the middle of the floor. This wasn't his world. He didn't go in for all that religion stuff. He didn't think much of the idea of a higher power, nevermind some great divinity. He was more down to earth in his thinking that all men were gods with the right tools in their hands. They could create, they could destroy. Simple as that.

Malik reclined on an oversized pillow. It was every bit as big as a couch, and looked just as comfortable.

Mac was about to set foot on the carpet, when his Muslim guard stopped him.

"Shoes," he said, pointing at Mac's gators.

"My bad," Mac replied, kicking them off. "No offense intended."

"None taken."

He stepped over to Malik, who rose slightly to shake his hand, then sat across from him on a similar pillow. It was a strange way to live. "Glad you could make it," Malik said, by way of greeting.

"Glad that you were willing to talk."

"A wise man is always willing to talk," Malik said.

"I could use a drink," Mac commented.

"Alas, Muslims do not drink," Malik shot back.

"Far as I'm aware, they don't sell drugs either," Mac chuckled.

Malik laughed.

"I like you, Mac. You get straight to the point. No bullshit. It is an endearing trait."

Malik nodded to one of his bodyguards. They man disappeared out of the room, only to reappear a few minutes later with a bottle of Hennessey and two glasses.

He poured Malik and Mac two fingers each.

"What can I say? I'm just not the kinda guy who likes to deal with facades," Mac told him.

"Understandable. So, given you have come to me, I assume you want something? What can I do for you Mac?"

Mac took a sip, then replied, "Othello is retiring from the game."

Malik's eyebrows lifted.

"Retiring? Unexpected, especially as he just joined The Commission. Are you sure your information is good?"

"It's not his decision. Joe Hamlet made it for him. An ultimatum, The Commission or marrying his daughter."

"I see. So, Othello chose love?"

"He did."

"Will he be leaving The Commission, too?"

"No. He'll be strictly legit, but he'll be in Joe's pocket, and that will be a problem for you," Mac explained.

Malik nodded and sipped.

Mac continued. "What you may or may not know, is that Joe Hamlet is on the way out as well. It'll be his son we'll be dealing with."

"Adonis is soft."

"This is true, but his mother isn't. She's the real power behind the throne."

"Don't worry about that. What I need from you is a guarantee."

"I don't give guarantees."

"First time for everything. I'm fronting to you to cement our relationship. See, I'm going to be filling Othello's shoes. Heir apparent, if you will, and when I am in place I'll be loyal to those who are loyal to me. Right now, I'm simply looking for where those mutual loyalties may be found," Mac stated.

"So you come to me?"

"Exactly."

"So, enlighten me, Mac. What exactly would I be guaranteeing?"

"Your friendship throughout whatever I have to do to claim the seat. With Joe out of the way, I figure you stand to be Commissioner, that is, assuming you have the votes? Mine will be guaranteed," Mac assured him.

Malik smiled.

"A guarantee for a guarantee, huh?"

"You scratch my back, and I'll drag my fingernails down yours," Mac said.

Malik rubbed his chin, then downed his drink.

"Okay, Mac, you've got yourself a deal," he said. The pair

shook on it, old school. But Malik held Mac's hand a little too long and said, "If you become boss."

"Not if...*when*," Mac smirked.

"Damn, you make my pussy wet," Kandi cooed, laying in the stew of their own sexual juices in the aftermath of a marathon fuck session.

She'd been fucked raw pink.

Mac chuckled, feeling himself.

He knew he was on his way up, and he had everybody around him on a string.

He felt like a muhfuckin' puppet master supreme.

"This shit is too easy," he remarked, rubbing Kandi's back.

"So O bit? He really thinks Cash is fuckin' his wife?" Kandi questioned.

"Not fully, he just doubts his own mind. It's in there, eatin' away at him. I don't want him certain about anything yet, 'cause with certainty comes control of your own actions and that nigga needs to be on the edge. Long as he's in doubt, he's open to influence, the wise words of his tried and true friend."

"Oh, you are so bad," Kandi snickered.

He kissed her on the nose.

"You ain't seen *nothin'* yet."

Aphrodite listened to Adonis' explanation, calmly, leaning back in the chair, behind her desk, while he paced the floor of her office, nervously.

"Ma, I'm telling you, I don't know what to do," he admitted, his voice trembling.

"First of all, Adonis, sit down. You're making me nervous with all of this pacing. I can barely think."

He sat down.

She continued.

"Secondly, you need to *think*. How are these pictures getting taken inside the places where you and Devante meet?"

Adonis shook his head.

"There is only one way," she reasoned

"But ma, I love him," Adonis admitted.

"This isn't about love, Adonis, it's about survival. And the evidence would suggest Devante doesn't love you the same way."

Adonis shook his head.

He couldn't say anything because he knew his mother was right.

It had damn near broken his heart when the deep-voiced dude contacted him again, this time with pictures of him and Devante having sex on the couch, taken the same day Adonis had gone to Devante's crib to tell him about the blackmail.

"You gotta use your head. Who else could it be, baby, if it isn't Devante?" Aphrodite asked.

"Nobody," he replied, his heart shattering for the thousandth time with the admission.

Aphrodite stood up, came around the table and caressed his cheek.

"Then you know what you have to do."

Adonis looked at her.

"Me? If I'm a boss, then I shouldn't have to get my hands dirty."

Aphrodite smiled knowingly. "First, my child, you have to *prove* you are a boss, and you do that *by* getting your hands dirty. Taking care of this yourself is the only way to know you have what it takes to be the head of this family. If you can't look Devante in the eye, stare him right in his treacherous face as you take his life, then you don't have what it takes. No one will respect you. Not even me," Aphrodite's voice was as cold as her eyes. Ice.

Adonis nodded, the coldness in her eyes froze the blood to ice in his veins, steeling him against his own emotions. "Okay, ma. I'll handle it," he vowed.

"Today, Adonis. You never give a snake a chance to strike once you know where he's hiding in your grass," she schooled him.

Adonis stood. He hugged his mother. When they broke the embrace, Aphrodite caressed his face again, this time, running her thumb sensually over his lips. "My sweet Adonis, my sexy Adonis. I know this hurts, but believe me, Devante is only your first love... he is far from your last."

The implications in her tone, made Adonis' heart skip with anticipation.

As he began to walk out, Aphrodite said, "Call me when you're done. I'll send somebody to clean up the mess."

He wasn't Jesus, but he wept, all the way down to the car in the underground lot beneath his mother's non-profit office.

He had been being groomed for this moment his entire life.

His father's expectations for his only son had rode Adonis hard since childhood.

Deep down, he didn't *want* to be a gangsta, but with a killer for a father and a devil for a mother, it was hard to escape. He never had a chance at being his own man.

That fact rammed home with the first cock he had dreamed of taking. He was seventeen years old, surfing the internet, searching for porn, and came across a bunch of streams dedicated to trannies.

It wasn't a term he was intimately familiar with, but once he went headfirst down into the rabbit hole, life was never going to be the same again. The first thing he saw was this beautiful Asian woman. She looked just like a real woman, so he was amazed when he saw the little pink piece of meat hanging between her legs. It didn't disgust him, rather, it kinda turned him on. It was the femininity of the transgender that turned him on. After that, he would secretly go to the site and masturbate to videos of trannies being fucked, liking the ones when they were on their backs, and their hard cocks were bouncing against their stomachs. Then he found ones where they came without being touched and his mind was melted. He couldn't get enough. Thing was, he didn't imagine he'd ever have the nerve to actually fuck a shemale in real life, as hypnotic as he found them.

Until he met Devante.

He met him in Cancun, at his eighteenth birthday party.

He was Malik's nephew. Malik, a strict Muslim. Devante carried himself properly in front of the world, the right male front, but the first time he looked at Adonis, Adonis recognized the mask. It was the same one he wore. The glint of mockery in his eye said it all. *I know you see me, and I see you, your mask... I see you.*

Devante was every bit as pretty as a girl, but packaged all boy.

That first time they were alone, Devante smiled that damned smile of his and asked, "I took a birthday picture for you. Wanna see it?"

Adonis nodded. Devante sent him a picture of himself, butt-naked, bent over in the mirror, looking back over his shoulders with a fuck me expression. His face was made up so well, he looked like a sexy young girl. Adonis immediately got an erection. Devante peeped it and giggled.

"You're welcome. Do you want to see more?"

"More?"

Devante eyed him lustfully, nodding. "Everything."

In Devante's hotel suite, Adonis' whole world changed.

They became the best of friends and lovers.

To the world, they were two young dudes, on the prowl for pussy, but behind closed doors, they were free to be who they were. Their own true selves. They both knew the day would come when Adonis would take over the family, and that's when things got out of hand.

Could a true gangsta be gay?

It was a simple enough question, but he couldn't think of a single one. Of course, if any had been gay, most likely they would have hidden the fact, and put on their own mask.

Adonis was two men, and had always been. One him craved the power of a true gangsta and the chance to rule his own life, the other him wanted nothing more than to be free...

Adonis wiped his eyes, took a deep breath and called Devante.

"Hey you," Devante cooed over the phone, "I was just thinking about you."

"Oh yeah? What part of me?" Adonis flirted, his voice firm, even as his heart wavered.

"How you fucked me so good last night."

"Funny, I was thinking about how you fucked me," Adonis replied, Devante unaware of the duplicitous meaning of his words.

Devante giggled.

"You are delicious."

"I'll tell you what, I've got a few hours. Meet me at our secret place in a couple of hours," Adonis suggested.

"I'm on my way. Mwah!" Adonis hung up the phone.

Yeah... you are.

Their special place was a small cabin in the woods, right out on the fringes of the suburbs, way beyond The Commission's control.

It was a place people went to fish, canoe and camp out.

And like Crystal Lake, it was the perfect place for a murder.

Devante was already there when Adonis arrived. He saw his

car parked behind the cabin, discrete. Adonis pulled around back as well. He took a deep breath, looked at himself in the mirror, and said to the man in there, "Choose."

He got out and went inside, not convinced he had actually made a choice.

Devante was already naked. He was in a whorish sprawl across the king-sized waterbed, dick raging in his hand as he peeled back the foreskin, enticing Adonis with the view.

"See anything you like?" Devante sang, his voice husky and wanton.

Adonis couldn't help but get hard.

Devante knew how to turn him on.

On the drive up, he'd imagined it in the simplest possible way: walk through the door, no words, no second thoughts, just pull the trigger, shoot Devante in the head and walk out. The last thing he wanted to do was give him the chance to plead for his life, to beg, claim his innocence, how they were being set up, all of that shit that mocked Adonis' intelligence. But he was smart. Smarter than that. There was zero chance Devante wasn't involved. The places they had gone together, no one knew about except for them. Try as he might, Adonis couldn't imagine a way to clear his lover, but Devante had betrayed him, he had betrayed his love, and for that he had to pay the absolute price.

Devante sensed something was wrong.

He stopped stroking his dick and knelt on the bed, facing him. No sign of his erection fading. It was a beautifully potent thing. How could he be such a bastard?

"What's wrong, Don-don?"

Adonis stepped up to him.

Moved in close.

Devante wrapped his arms around his neck.

Adonis looked him in the eyes.

He couldn't find the words to describe his pain.

Instead, he kissed Devante like he was trying to suck the life out of him, knowing it was a metaphorical kiss of death.

But to Devante's horny mind, it was the kiss of life, a kiss full of such passion that he had never experienced.

He grabbed at Adonis' jeans, fumbling with the belt until his long, hard dick popped out, the veins so prominent, it looked like it would explode.

It took both of Devante's hands to wrap it around the girth of Adonis' dick as he guided it to the welcoming wetness of his mouth. He devoured it like a death row inmate, not knowing that it would indeed be his last meal.

Adonis' eyes welled, overflowing their banks and spilling tears down his face; tears of pleasure, pain and sadness.

He needed to feel Devante's tightness once more, one last time, so turned him around and entered him with such force, his lover who never loved him cried out, "Oh God! Shit, you so deep in me!"

He shivered with the deliciousness of each thrust, loving the way Devante's asshole fit him like a glove. "Deeper Daddy, go deeper. Take me there," Devante begged.

Adonis pushed balls deep, giving Devante every inch of his last request.

The tears poured as he pounded Devante relentlessly.

Devante heard him sobbing, he reached back, trying to run his hand over Adonis' face.

"Why are you crying, baby?"

"Because... I know it was you," Adonis replied, then before Devante could say another word, wrapped both of his hands around Devante's throat and began to squeeze so tight his fingers clawed into his windpipe.

Devante bucked wildly, his last moments trapped in some curious place between life and death, pain and pleasure, confusion and clarity, the cock in his ass taking him to hell and heaven. Adonis continued to ride him, fucking the treacherous bastard unmercifully, pounding him until his asshole was wet with blood.

His grip was too tight for Devante to loosen. He scratched and clawed desperately at his hands, but couldn't break his vicelike grip, and all the while his cock raged harder and harder as he was choked of air like some sick bastard asphyxiation dick play. He tore away strips of flesh from the backs of Adonis' hands, but it was never going to be vital DNA evidence, only a guarantee that his corpse would be burnt, and those burned remains dissolved in acid.

His fight lost its fire, but he kept taking the dick.

Choking.

Right before his lights went out forever, the last thing he heard in this life was Adonis whispering in his fading ear, taking him into hell, "I love you."

Which was every bit as fucked up as being fucked to death.

Devante slumped and he shit all over Adonis' dick as Adonis came hard and long, spurt after spurt until his whole body sagged with sexual exhaustion on top of the corpse of his last and first love.

Adonis pulled out, the sound of extraction resembling the sound of removing a spoon from mac and cheese.

He looked down and the lower half of his six-packed abs and dick covered with shit, cum, blood and death, knowing he'd committed several deadly sins all at once, right up to necrophilia with those last few deep dick strokes.

He looked down at Devante's body.

"How could you betray me? How? What could they offer you that I couldn't have given you? What power did they have over your soul that you sacrificed your heart? I know what it means to be cold now, to know what it takes to be a gangsta, and you did that to me, D. You and your betrayal. How could you?"

It wasn't so much a roar as a wail. Adonis staggered through to the bathroom of their secret place and cleaned himself up thoroughly. Standing under the shower for a full twenty minutes, as he soaped himself, he felt himself getting hard again. Nothing to do with sex, this was all about the thought of the woman filling his mind and how he had sealed himself to her forever in ways that went far beyond blood. Before he realized what he was doing, he bust a nut all over the tiled wall and felt his legs give way.

He sank to the bottom of the shower stall and curled up there, the cum on his knees and the rope of precum hanging from his dick, washed away by the relentless heat of the shower.

He didn't leave until the cold drove him out, and then, naked, he walked through to the lounge and called his mother.

"It's done."

"Where are you?'

He told her.

"The cleaners will be there in an hour."

Othello's connect had hit him with some of the best product in the game. It was so good, it didn't take more than a week for word to spread and Othello's spots to become the biggest ones booming through The Commission's territory.

Everyone was copping from Othello.

His numbers were doubling damn near by the day.

He made so much bank, he might as well have been printing the shit.

Joe Hamlet had been watching his son-in-law steadily grow in power, but it wasn't all roses. He watched the boy with a skeptical eye. He had yet to name his successor, despite his word. And if he didn't retire from the game he'd have to retire him, which wasn't a pleasant thought, as much as Joe enjoyed that side of the life.

So he called him out to the estate, intending to have a little heart to heart with Othello. Drop some home truths on the boy. Remind him.

"Relax O, what are you drinking?"

"Henny on the rocks," Othello told him.

"A man of decent tastes," Joe brought Othello a drink, then sat down across from him on the patio, watching the sun set. "I love sunsets, O. Ever since I was a little kid, I used to love to watch the sun go down from the roof of my building. We may've been poor, but that sunset, that beauty, it was something else. It let me know there was more to life, put simply, there was beauty and money could never buy that. You didn't need the cash to enjoy it, all you needed to do was reach out and go for it," Joe said, making Othello wonder if there was some sort of allegory in his story, some deeper meaning.

"Yeah, I feel you. I always wondered how you could tell the difference between a sunrise and a sunset if you didn't know what time it was, you know? You ask me, they look exactly alike at that one moment in time when the horizon is purple and ready to go either way."

Joe nodded.

"You're not wrong, O. It's that twilight, that time when truth and falsehood are so intertwined you can't tell one from the other. It's like life, in those moments when the next thing you say, the next decision you make, will determine what happens forever."

Othello sipped his drink.

Joe lit a cigar. Sucked on it. Blew smoke. Sighed.

"It's been a while since we had a chance to talk."

"Shit been hectic, Joe," Othello explained.

"True, but you gave your word. So I gotta ask, O, and believe me when I say I hate that you've put me where I have to, but when can I expect you to keep it?"

Othello thought about what he said. Truth was, he knew he should've already retired, but the situation with Mona and Cash had preoccupied his mind, and that made him second guess whether he was making a mistake to give the connect to Cash. Didn't help that Cash had been acting strangely lately. They both had. Mona was still trying to put in his head he should give Cash the connect. She never came right out and said it, but her words all pointed in the same direction, which only made Othello wonder why she wanted to see Cash as the new boss?

The bitch love that gangsta shit. Her father was a gangsta and she married a gangsta. Now you want to retire? Nigga, gangsta is the only thing you got going for your ugly ass. Without that, who are you? What are you except a stovepipe black nigga with a little dough. But Cash... he got it all, no surprise she want it too, then sees herself with him. Power power power.

"I just need a little more time, Joe."

"Time does run out, O. How much are we talking? Days? Weeks? Months?"

Joe Hamlet had eyes to see, and they saw how much money Othello was making and how his power in the streets was consolidating. He was good at the game, and that was a problem, because it wouldn't be long before the whole Commission would be beholden to him. Months? By that time he'd literally choke them out of the street life, which was something Joe Hamlet was not about to accept, even from his son-in-law.

"Joe, look at me, I don't like pressure, okay? I said I would do it, and I will. But in my own time," Othello replied, his tone neutral but his meaning firm and non-negotiable.

But Joe Hamlet wasn't a man to be told that there were boundaries.

He leaned in, blowing more smoke. "Look O, I've been patient, *more* than patient with you, but you need to grasp this truth, son. I'm not the one to be kept on no goddamn leash. Now, I expect you to keep your word, and I expect it to happen soon," Joe spat, tossing down the gauntlet.

"Or what, Joe? Tell me. Or what?" Othello answered, his voice low and menacing.

"Am I interrupting anything?"

Both Othello and Joe looked back to see Adonis come out

onto the patio.

Welcoming the interruption, Joe rose, smiled and shook his son's hand. "Adonis, how are you, son? O and I were just discussing business."

Adonis and Othello shook hands.

"How's my sister?"

"Never better," Othello smiled, as he stood up, then looked at his watch. "I'm sorry I ain't got more time to kick it with you, Adonis. We need to have lunch though, soon."

"Whenever, just give me the word when," Adonis replied.

"Later, Joe," Othello walked out, leaving Joe and Adonis to watch him leave.

"Everything okay, Dad?"

"It will be," Joe Hamlet assured him.

"I think he knows, Joe," Aphrodite read between the lines. She and Joe relaxed in the Jacuzzi in their suite.

"I don't think so, baby. He would've been made his move," Joe countered.

"I dunno. I'm beginning to think maybe Black Sam wasn't his only backer."

Joe looked at her, his shift in expression betraying the fact he hadn't considered that angle.

"Think about it," she reasoned. "He didn't kill Don. Why? Because he wanted to keep him on ice? Then Don comes out of hiding, he doesn't even try to move on Othello after he kidnapped him? It doesn't make sense. Don ain't ever been a pretty boy's bitch."

"Othello isn't pretty," Joe said, and sat back and pondered her words.

He could see her point, but he shook his head.

"No. Don ain't a planner. He's a *doer*, and I've known him long enough and well enough to know he's a secret coward. He talks big, but he ain't no killer. He knows he's exposed, especially after Othello eliminated his heavy hitters. He may be licking his wounds, but he wasn't down from the beginning, that I can tell you."

"Maybe you're right baby, but what if you're wrong?"

Mona, Celeste and Kandi made their way over to the table. The restaurant was crowded. And loud. Five star or not, whether it took weeks to get a table or you could walk in off the street, none of that changed the acoustics. It was loud. And while most of the diners had to wait weeks for their seat, it was different for the wives of the top gangstas in the city. They got a table the same afternoon, like they was on some reality show. Real Housewives of the Underworld, or something.

They had all gone shopping. It had been Kandi's idea, saying she wanted to get to know Mona better. Despite Mona's misgivings, she was wanted it to work, their men were closer than blood so life would be easier if they all just got along. She decided to invite Celeste along. To Mona's surprise, she had a good time. Kandi was funny and had an intoxicating personality. Mona was won over.

By the time they got to lunch, they were like old friends.

"Girl, I'm tellin' you, did you see that white bitch's face when you whipped out that black card on her ass? Priceless," Kandi laughed.

"I thought the bitch's head was gonna explode!" Celeste chimed in, enjoying it every bit as much.

They all laughed as the waiter approached, drinking him in slow, not expecting a white man to be so fine.

"Damn, boy, are you a waiter or a Calvin Klein model?" Kandi half-joked.

He smirked.

No doubt he got that type of reaction all the time. He had a look that most women wanted to worship; dark Grecian features reminiscent of the noblest of ancient blood, square jaw and Mediterranean olive oil skin with eyes the color of the sky. Yeah, they loved him.

"You flatter me. Thanks. Can I take your orders?"

"I'll have you, half an hour, I'll change your world," Celeste blurted out, then gave Kandi a high five.

He took it in stride, smiling along until they finally gave him their orders, then walked away.

"Damn, now that was a fine ass white boy," Kandi remarked.

"Can't disagree with you there," Mona seconded.

"And did you see that print? Shit, I'd definitely give him this pussy," Kandi commented.

Mona looked at her.

"And Mac would kill him."

"Shit, what Mac don't know..."

Mona shook her head. "I could never do O like that."

Kandi looked at her out the corner of her eye, skeptically. "Come on, Mona. You sayin' that for a *hundred million* you wouldn't give another muhfucka the pussy?"

"A hundred million?" It was such an outrageous sum. "Shit the right muhfucka could get it for a hundred dollars!" Celeste joked and they all laughed.

Mona shook her head again. "Y'all are too crazy, but no, I've never been a cheater. Shit, if I'm gonna cheat, might as well leave, you know?"

"I hear you," Kandi replied, sipping her glass of zinfandel, thinking, *Bitch, please. If your celebrity crush comes walking through the door, you'd fuck him on the table and we all know it.*

Mona was wearing her scarf, the one O had custom made from her memories. When Kandi saw it wrapped around her neck she said, "Oh my god, that scarf is *so* beautiful."

Her mind went back to her conversation with Mac.

"The whole purpose of you hanging out with Mona is to get something of hers," Mac had explained.

"What you mean *something*?"

"An article of clothing, some kind of personal item, something he'll recognize. I don't give a fuck what, just make sure it's recognizable."

"You like it? O got it for me on our honeymoon in Italy. It's *just* like one my grandmother used to have," Mona told her.

Perfect, Kandi thought.

"Please please please, don't get mad but I have this skirt that would beautiful with that. I'd kill to wear it, just once," Kandi begged.

"No, I couldn't," Mona tried to protest, but Kandi was all in.

"I *promise* I'll take good care of it. Please."

And being the kind of person who hated to tell someone no, Mona finally sighed, half-smiled and replied, "Sure, but only this time, and you have to swear to look after it."

She untied it from around her neck and handed it to Kandi.

The other woman eyed it greedily. "I can't wait to see how this looks," Kandi finished the sentence in her mind: *when O sees where we put it.*

The three girls continued to kick it.

In the bathroom a little while late, Kandi took a moment to text Mac.

I got it! A blue scarf.

Othello woke up with a start.

He had *that* dream again.

The dream about Cash and Mona fucking.

It was the exact same dream, in the exact same place.

He sat up and rubbed his face, shaking his head, trying to

dislodge it, and unable to get Mona's cum-face out of his mind, the way she looked, that secret look, the intimacy of the ecstasy, on her face when Cash was inside of her.

"Fuck man, it can't be," he mumbled to himself, but then his phone rang and his mind was really blown...

Mac had been planning his move slowly and methodically. He knew each piece and how they built on the last. He was good at this. Better than good. He was a master at putting it all together, in tearing down a man's mind, step by step.

Now, he was about to throw Othello over the edge.

He had gone over Cash's house and found Milk there with him.

Since Othello had gotten married, he had stopped fucking Milk, which left her running back to the superior dick game of Cash.

She lay in the bed knocked out, while Mac and Cash sat in the living room, smoking a blunt.

"Ay yo, that bitch's ass is fat as a muhfucka," Mac remarked.

Cash chuckled.

"Fattest ass on a white girl I've ever seen." Mac inhaled the blunt.

"What up with that thing with you and Mona?"

Cash shrugged.

"I hollered at her a few times. She said she's working on it and to be patient."

Mac secretly hit the send button on his phone, which was already set up with Othello's number.

Othello saw it was Mac's number and picked up.

"Hello?" He answered, but got no response, so he repeated, "Hello? Mac?"

Mac didn't say anything, at least not to him, but Othello could hear Mac and Cash in the background shooting the shit.

He heard Mona's name and got real quiet so that he could hear *every* word.

"That bitch love to fuck, yo," Cash laughed, then hit the blunt. "She like a goddamn nympho or somethin!"

"You blowin' her back out though, huh?" Mac goosed Cash on.

"Shit, you think I ain't?"

"Better not let O find out," Mac warned playfully.

"Ay, pussy pussy, we don't love these hoes," Cash laughed.

Othello threw up in his mouth.

Hearing his heart's name mentioned so flippantly, like a common whore, thinking they were talking about how Cash was fucking her, it was like he had the sight, his dream come true.

He threw up a second time, over the arm of the chair this time, chunks all over the floor, then begin to cry tears of rage as he heard Cash say, "Man, O can't fuck that bitch like me."

Othello's blood felt like lava flowing through his veins.

He had heard enough.

He hit END and staggered down the hall.

When he came across the mirror and saw his own reflection, he shattered it with one blow, then eyed himself through the broken glass.

Mac smiled to himself.

He knew that somewhere in the city, Othello was in a murderous rage. He figured it wouldn't be long before he came over to Cash's house to confront him. It was still too soon for that. Mac knew he had to head him off.

He handed Cash the blunt and stood up.

"Yo brah, I gotta go handle something."

Cash stood and embraced him. "Be safe."

"You, too."

Once he got into his car, he called Othello. It rang several times before it went to voicemail.

"I hope that dumb ass nigga ain't blow his own brains out," Mac chuckled to himself, then called again. This time, Othello answered.

"I need to see you," Othello seethed.

Mac acted like he didn't know what was going on.

"What's wrong, big brah? You sound like you upset."

Mac had to hold back his laughter.

"Just get your ass over here now!"

Click!

"I got him."

When Mac got to Othello's apartment, he hadn't even stepped all the way through the door good before Othello grabbed him by the collar and slammed so hard against the wall, the damned plaster cracked like some cartoon, leaving his imprint there forever.

"Yo, O!" Mac bleated.

His fear was genuine.

He had unleashed a beast that he couldn't control.

He could only hope he made it out of there in one piece.

"You think this is a game? Do you? I'll kill both of you!" Othello thundered, his eyes flashing with the lightning of intensity.

Mac's eyes were as big as plates.

"What the hell are you talkin' about, O? What the fuck I do?"

Nose to nose, Othello's breath felt like the flame of the dragon on Mac's face.

"I *heard* you and Cash talking about Mona, talking about fuckin' Mona like she was some fuckin' whore in the street!"

"Whoa, whoa, whoa! You heard *what*?" Mac asked, feigning bewilderment, seeing that he was slowly reigning control of the situation, because Othello's eyes showed confusion.

"Tell me the truth, Mac, was he talking about Mona?"

"I musta butt-dialed you by mistake, O."

"ANSWER ME!" Othello barked.

Mac dropped his head then slowly nodded.

"I'm sorry, O... yeah... yeah, he was talking about Mona, but nigga, I wasn't laughin', not at you."

Othello roared with such rage, Mac thought he was going to rip open his own chest.

"There's something else you need to know," Mac added.

Othello looked at him, ready to tear his nut sack off.

"When I was over there, I found something I think belonged to Mona. A scarf." Mac said, as if it were a question.

Othello glared at him. "A... silk scarf? Blue?"

Mac nodded.

Othello sat on the couch and covered his face. "I'm done." His tone was so broken, Mac almost felt sorry for playing with his emotions. "I want to see the scarf. If it's hers, Cash is dead," Othello vowed.

Mac looked at him solemnly, but inside, he was gloating with victory. "Brah, we boys. We came up together."

"Tell *him* that!" Othello bassed. "He violated, Mac, and I can't live with that."

Mac shook his head.

"Okay, if it's hers... I understand. But wait until he's not there. We don't need the heat right now. I'll take him on my rounds and while he's gone, you go over there," Mac suggested.

Othello nodded his head, defeated.

He got up and looked Mac in the eyes.

"I won't forget this, brah. Now, I need to be alone."

Where's the scarf?

I got it here.

Meet me at Cash's place, asap.

He knows?

He knows.

Milk answered the door, naked.

She looked like temptation made flesh, but he wasn't biting.

"Goddamn ma, do you ever put clothes on?" Mac chuckled. Even so, he eyed her luscious body.

"Why? It *bothering* you?" Milk smirked.

"Hell no," Mac replied, watching her ass jiggle as she walked away. He was a good liar, but not that good.

She sat on the couch.

"Cash is in the bathroom taking a shower. He said to tell you he'll be ready in a minute. Smoke something," Milk suggested.

"I ain't bring no piff, yo."

Milk shrugged and went back to watching her movie.

"Let me see if this nigga still got my shit," Mac remarked offhandedly. He got up and went through to Cash's bedroom. As soon as he was out of sight he pulled out Mona's scarf and looked around for somewhere to plant it, trying to work out just where it might fall if...

He glanced at the closet. No, out in the open, obvious. He decided to drop it on the floor and half kick it under the bed, just enough that a nigga might miss it, but plenty easy to find if you came in in a rage looking for it.

Perfect.

It was barely hidden before Cash came out of the bathroom, wearing only a towel.

"Goddamn nigga, put some fuckin clothes on," Mac growled.

Cash chuckled. "Muhfucka, what *you* doin' in my bedroom? You pretty an' all, but I ain't doin' ya."

"Lookin for my fuckin' watch."

Cash took the chrome Tissot watch off the dresser and tossed it to Mac. "Now get the fuck out. I'll be ready in a minute."

Mac clipped the watch around his wrist and walked out, smiling to himself.

A half hour later, Othello arrived at Cash's place.

Milk came up the stairs a few steps behind him, key in hand. Her face lit up seeing Othello on landing.

"Long time no see, stranger," she remarked, giving him a big hug that he returned absentmindedly. She scrunched up her face and asked, "You okay, O?"

"Yeah... I'm good. How you been?" Othello responded.

"Bored," Milk snickered, "You ain't got nobody for us to kill?"

"I may have, ma, and to be frank, you might not have to go far," Othello replied sinisterly.

The comment struck her as strange, but she let it go, opening the door.

She called out Cash's name as he followed her inside.

The apartment was empty. It looked like Hurricane Floyd had torn through the lounge. There were pizza boxes and all sorts of other shit littering up the place.

"Needs a woman's touch," Othello joked, looking around the place.

Milk sat down on the couch and hit the remote to turn the TV on.

"So, wanna wait with me?"

She acted like she was completely at home, but then that was how they treated each other's cribs, places to lay their heads or lay low, all friends together.

"Naw, it's good. Just picking up my shit."

"Knock yourself out."

Othello went in the back and headed straight to the bedroom.

Inside, he scoped the place out. He pictured Mona on the bed, naked and wet, bent over and taking every inch of Cash's dick.

Othello's blood boiled as he looked around, lifting up the pillows, kicking away clothes scattered across the floor, even lifted up the mattress.

And that was when he saw it and a little piece of him died.

It was the wink of blue that caught his eye and tore his heart straight out of his chest.

"Why baby?" he groaned, as he bent to retrieve the scarf.

He held it close to his nose.

He could smell her on it, her favorite perfume and her, present in it, and he raged at the symbol of infidelity it had become.

"I gave you my heart, and you tore it into pieces like paper. You went against the grain for a moment in time, when I was promising you forever," Othello shook his head, dismally, then thought of Cash and his anger began to take on hellish depth. "And my friend, my boy, my partner... All my life I've had to worry about your shadow, how women in my life always ended up with you and I never protested because it was money over bitches. But my wife? Now, you will feel what I feel, but in a very different way," Othello swore, not exactly a blood oath, but it was a promise to the god of death.

He lovingly kissed the scarf, then let it fall to the floor and left it where it lay.

7

They called the place the Hanging Gardens of Bali. It was
like nothing else on earth. Adonis stood on the terrace. He
was on the edge, looking out over the lush tropical forest as the
valley below cut a deep V through the world. With nothing but
the moon, the world out there was an inky black nothingness,
with the glitter of faraway stars pockmarking the sky like raindrops on a universal window. The breeze blew across his face,
and with every sensation, he felt Devante near him, haunting
him, reaching out to him.

"Please forgive me as I have forgiven you," he whispered into
the wind.

There were two pools beneath him, one, an infinity one that
seemed to hang out over the cliff, a drop of hundreds of feet
below him. The place had everything two lovers could ever want,
the privacy of the cabanas, the sensuality of the massage tables
and the essential oils. He felt like the only person in the world,
even though there were maybe forty other cabins hidden away
within the trees. The illusion of solitude was perfect.

He'd paid a lot of money to have their table made up in the
middle of the pool, lights lining the way, the water splashing over

the side all the way down to nothing in a fine spray. It was about the most romantic thing he could imagine. The staff had even draped white curtains around the table to give some privacy from certain angles.

But he wasn't hungry.

Bianca stepped out into the night air next to him.

"Oh god, just look at it," she breathed.

"Breathtaking," he agreed.

They had flown in a few hours before, after a luxurious wedding in Jamaica. The Davenports and The Hamlets, two powerful families, joined as one. It was a proud moment for Joe and Wingate, the patriarch of the Davenport clan. Everyone was happy, none happier than Bianca, but Adonis had been distant during the whole ceremony. Troubled.

Bianca wrapped her arms around his midsection.

"Come to bed, baby, we have a marriage to consummate," she cooed playfully.

Adonis sipped his drink.

"Later," he replied brusquely.

Bianca looked at him.

"What's wrong, baby? Are you okay?"

It took Adonis a moment before he answered, "You... have no idea."

She guided his face to her.

"Try me, love. That's what I'm here for. We're a team, right? You and me against the world."

Adonis gazed into her eyes, and for the first time felt genuinely sorry for her.

She was in love, but he couldn't love her back. It wasn't like he didn't want to, or hadn't tried, it just wasn't in him, and out here in what should have been paradise he felt guilty as sin for leading her on.

He turned his body to her, and said, "Bianca. We need to talk."

His tone disturbed her, but she managed to keep her voice steady for the one word response, "Okay."

Adonis took a deep breath.

"I... I don't love you. Not like you love me, I...want to. Honestly, I do. But I'm not the kind of man you need me to be. This... you know... it was about family... our families wanted this union... It was about consolidating power for them, not love. There is no romance in Joe Hamlet's soul, believe me.... anyway... I won't walk away. I won't stop you. We can make some sort of... arrangement," Adonis concluded, hating the way his voice sounded. It was like he was negotiating some backstreet deal.

Bianca fought back tears, but she was stronger than Adonis realized.

"Arrangement?"

"To make it easier on you. On us. You can be with who you want, as long as you are discreet. That is all I ask."

Bianca laughed in his face.

"You don't have the right to ask *anything*! Who the hell do you think you are, Adonis Hamlet? You tell me you don't love me, you slap me in the face on the first night of the rest of our lives, in this place, with such a cold ass speech about power and arrangements, like they are fucking life, then you have the nerve to tell me how and when I can fuck someone else? You can fuck off and die!" She blazed.

Adonis nodded, taking it all in stride. "I understand your frustration-"

"You have no idea what frustration feels like, you motherfucker," she said that last word very slowly, "you spineless cunt of a motherfucker. What if I had a dick? Would you fuck me then?"

Adonis looked at her strangely.

"You think I don't know what's going on? I'm not fucking blind. I know why you don't love me, you fag." Bianca spazzed.

Adonis couldn't believe what she just said.

Bianca was in her feelings and didn't care how it came out.

She had been stupid enough to hope that Adonis had married for love.

Sure she knew about his secret, but she still felt like they had a future.

"*What did you say*?" Adonis seethed, his fist balling involuntarily, itching to strike her down.

"You heard me. You are a fag. I know all about your sick, twisted relationship with that- that... *thing*!"

Adonis felt the rising of an inner tide of raw scarlet rage that he had never felt before. It was red hot lava bubbling up from the very depths of himself. He struggled to control it, fought it with all he had.

"You don't know *anything* about me," he replied, his voice so low, she damn near couldn't hear him over the gentle susurration of wind through the trees below.

He turned to leave the terrace, but Bianca grabbed his arm.

"Don't walk away from me! I'm not finished! I've known about you from day one, but I was still willing to love you, Adonis. So you don't get to lay down the rules of any arrangement, it's my turn now, you give me what I want."

"What do you want, Bianca?"

"A child. You will give me a son, I don't give a fuck about how many cocks you suck as long as I get my boy. That is what I want." She cried, the tears staining her checks as red as his rage.

"I'm going to bed."

Bianca couldn't hold it in anymore.

"I took him from you, you miserable fucking shit," she seethed, her true feelings and her crime out in the open, and the moment those words left her lips, she regretted them.

Adonis stopped in his tracks, then turned back to her.

"What did you just say to me, woman?"

Bianca just looked at him, trembling.

"You heard me."

"Say it again!" He roared.

"You are so fucking stupid, Adonis. Devante didn't betray you. I took him from you, because he took you from me! It was me. I took those pictures!" She screamed, her heart heaving with every breath.

Adonis stepped back out onto the terrace.

"What are you saying? How could you?"

Bianca smiled at him through her tears, chin up, triumphantly. "Your jacket."

"Jacket?"

"You are so fucking blind... you didn't ever think that every time those photos were taken of you fucking your fag you'd been wearing your favorite burgundy jacket? Yeah. Every time. I fitted it with a tiny camera. I took hundreds of pictures, hundreds. You were doing the most vile shit... not just his cock up your ass... I have photos of his fist up there making you cum like a fucking fountain. I have photos of him sticking a metal spike down the center of your cock, then sucking you off with that shit in there and you cumming around it... sick, twisted shit. I've got shots of him pissing in your mouth like a pig. You on your knees... pathetic. You ain't no head of the family, you're the bitch. So you *will* give me what I want. You'll fuck me enough times to put a baby in my belly and then you will never touch me again," she spat, her voice full of pain, the rage a mask.

He couldn't believe what she was saying. How she was taunting him with the fact that he had murdered the only person he could ever have loved, and Devante hadn't betrayed him. He was the betrayer.

It burned him up.

Bianca had manipulated him into murdering his own heart. The thing in his chest didn't mean a goddamn thing anymore.

He looked at her smug expression.

And he hated her.

In her mind, she was untouchable, the golden child. Their marriage was too important to jeopardize. She was his beard.

There was nothing he would or could do to hurt her, so she gloated over his powerlessness.

But she had underestimated how easy it was to kill a second time; the first was hard, it was a moral and ethical dilemma, it posed questions about who you were and what you believed, and even had you wondering about heaven and hell, but the second was easy.

Adonis grabbed her by her throat, squeezing the bones, wanting to feel them snap as he choked the life out of her gorgeous body.

Needing to look her in the eye, to know she was helpless. Desperate.

She clawed at his hand, slapping and kicking, but he was so much stronger. Tears cascaded down her face as she fought air, gasping out two words, "Your mother! Your... mother," she tried to say.

Adonis' nails sank deeper. He could feel the U-shape of the hyoid bone pressing against his palm and knew that all it would take was one clench to break it and rob her of a next breath, but he couldn't do it.

Instead, he let go.

She collapsed to the wooden deck.

He stood over her.

"What about my mother, Bianca?" he spat, both hands flexed like talons.

She looked up at him with a plea in her eyes.

"She's the one... she told me you were gay... She told me that Devante had to go and that if I didn't do something, I would lose you! I did it for you. For us. I wasn't trying to hurt you, I just wanted you to love me!"

Her wretched pleas fell on deaf ears.

The second she had revealed Aphrodite's manipulations his ears had begun to ring with the screams of a thousand cursed souls.

His mind went back to the conversation they had...

"*Who benefits?*"

Now, he saw it so clearly.

She benefited by Devante's death.

With Devante out of the way, she could control him, use his pain as her own tool of destruction. She knew how he felt about her, how tortured he was inside, and she used it, just like she'd used the pathetic Bianca as her cat's paw to toy with him.

But knowing all of that didn't take his rage away.

It didn't change the fact that it was Bianca groveling at his feet for forgiveness, not Aphrodite.

His heart was dead, those two bitches had killed it.

He no longer recognized forgiveness.

Adonis reached down and grabbed Bianca by the hair and hauled her up. He used his other hand to grab her by the pussy, inserting four of his fingers like she was a bowling ball, getting a good grip on her frail, flailing body as he carried her to the edge of the terrace and looked down at the trees in the valley below, their leaves rippling in the breeze.

He lifted her over his head like a weightless dumbbell as she screamed and pissed herself, the steaming yellow urine streaming down his wrist and arm.

She screamed his name as she stared into the abyss of the forest far below.

He felt nothing as he heaved her out over the edge and watched her fall. It took seconds for her body to disappear into the darkness, and more before he heard the rush of it falling through the canopy of leaves, then finally, that a distant, sickening echo drifting back up to him as she broke across the rocks hidden beneath the tree tops.

Adonis turned from the edge and crossed the terrace to the wet bar, poured himself a drink, went to sit with his feet in the infinity pool, watching the sky. The way the moon was almost eclipsed made it look like it was grinning down at him, Jupiter and Venus shining bright like the eyes of the universe.

The gods knew.

He savored his drink, taking the time to really enjoy it before he went through the glass bifold doors into the room to make the call down to the reception in the main building.

"Yes, this is Mr. Hamlet. I need a line to America... Yes, I'll hold."

Several minutes later, once he was connected to his accountant's line, he said, "I need you to get on the phone and have five hundred thousand wired to the Bank of Bali within an hour. Then have someone there get out of bed and bring me the money in cash, right away... Yes, I am well aware what time it is, but, and think carefully before you answer this, do *you* know what time it will be if you let me down? No. Let me give you a clue. Time for you to find another job," Adonis warned, then hung up, sat back and waited for his orders to be executed.

He couldn't help himself.

He felt aroused.

There was no one here.

No one anywhere around, no one overlooking his slice of paradise, so he pulled his shirt off and stepped out of his shorts, and naked and hard, walked over to the edge where he'd disposed of his wife only moments earlier, stroking his erection as he surveyed the most beautiful landscape he had ever seen.

When he came a few minutes later, his cum flew and fell and he couldn't help but smile at the idea that his nut had gone hundreds of feet. That must have been some sort of record.

He swam naked beneath the joker's moon, feeling himself getting hard again.

It would have been a shame to waste a good erection, so he bust another nut, this time in the infinity pool, before he got out, toweled himself off, and went back through to the room to get rest.

Two hours later, the money was delivered by the bank president himself; an older man who shuffled about and seemed to get off on the fact he had a briefcase with half a million bucks cuffed to his wrist and three goons watching over him as he played courier.

"Mr. Hamlet, here is your money. It was an usual request at such a late hour, but we have done all we could to accommodate it," the man said smoothly, taking the key from his pocket to release the cuff before he handed Adonis the briefcase full of money.

"Thank you. If I may, I do have one more request."

"Anything we can do to be of service," the man assured him

"I need to speak to the chief of police. My wife is... missing."

"Of course," the man assured him. "I trust she will turn up soon. Perhaps she went to explore our beautiful countryside?"

"I'm sure she did," Adonis deadpanned.

It didn't take too long for the chief of police to arrive, despite their seeming remoteness.

He was a younger man, though he was graying at the temples.

No nonsense. They shook hands. Before they broke contact, the chief said, "I understand that you would like to report that your wife is missing?"

"Ah, actually, I found her."

"Very good, I trust you will enjoy the rest of your vacation."

"I found her," he repeated, "but unfortunately, she's dead." Adonis eyed the other man's reaction.

The Police Chief looked at him.

"If you will forgive me saying, you don't look... particularly distraught, Mr. Hamlet."

Adonis popped open the briefcase.

The Police Chief looked down at the stacks piled neatly upon stacks of valuable American currency.

"Neither should you," Adonis said, and with those three words the chief understood it all. Enlightenment was funny like that in the face of half a million answers. He pulled out a small notepad. "And how did she die, Mr. Hamlet?"

Adonis shrugged. "I assume she fell. It is a terribly long way down, and that railing is very low."

The Chief closed the pad after writing those few words.

"Then I have concluded my investigation. The official findings will be misadventure, Mr. Hamlet. A pleasure doing business with you, and may I assure you, you are most welcome in our province at any time."

The Police Chief smiled.

Adonis returned the smile with one of his own, but inside he wasn't smiling.

He was thinking of his mother...

"I want you to kill Cash," Othello told Mac, no bones, no bull, straight out asked him to do the deed as they drove through the old neighborhood in Othello's car. They were trolling the streets, reliving the old hustla days, when everything was scratching and ducking and just trying to stay alive. The days when they were brothers and betrayal seemed unimaginable.

Mac shook his head.

"O, don't ask me to do this. Please, anything else," Mac begged, his voice fucked up as he pleaded for Cash's life. It was a mask, and a fucking convincing one. Deep inside, he was ecstatic. Fizzing. "I'm not going to lie, brah. I don't think I can. I mean... I know he did you wrong, real low, but something in me just won't let go. Look out the window, this was our place, O. This was us. Our blood is in those bricks out there, in the cracks in the pavement. We're like this place. Battered, seen better days, but still standing, you know? Side by side, like always. Give him a pass, O. Cut him off, banish him from the streets," Mac suggested, offering an alternative he knew O wouldn't take. Cash had to go, though, because if he stuck around, eventually Othello would confront him, no matter how deeply he tried to bury his hurt. Then all of the truth would come out.

If that happened, it'd be Mac on the chopping block instead, no second chances, no remorse.

Othello shook his head.

"I can't do that, either. I need you to do it," Othello said.

"O..."

"Listen, you do this, and the connect is yours. Period. My word. I'll make you the boss when I retire."

Mac thought his heart was going to betray him. It was howling with laughter at O. Dark as the muhfucka was, it had found its desire, accomplished the cold win. Done. But Mac kept his game face on.

He sighed hard.

"O, you askin' a lot, brah. What about Mona?"

"I haven't decided."

"You kill her, and it's war with Joe, you know that, right?" Mac warned.

"I'm already at war with Joe," Othello revealed.

Mac looked at him, confused. "What you mean?"

"History, Mac. Joe killed my father," Othello told him.

"What?! How you know?"

"Black Sam's brother told me years ago."

"And you believe that nigga?"

Othello nodded. "He knew too much, the circumstances around it, stuff only someone there would know. Bottom line is: I've been waiting for my opportunity, and for the longest time the only thing making me hesitate was Mona. But now..."

"Damn," was all Mac could say.

"So what up?" Othello wanted to know.

Mac looked him in the eyes, and replied, "I got you, big brah."

Othello just had no idea what he really meant was *I got you.* Same words, double entendre.

Adonis returned to the States a different man.

Tempered by tragedy. Forged in fire. Ready to rule.

First stop, less than an hour after touching down, was to see his mother at the estate.

He knew his father wouldn't be home, he'd planned the visit to coincide with a Commission summit. He'd deal with him later. Right now, walking across the gravel driveway in the shadows of the mansion, Adonis didn't know what he would do when he laid eyes on her, but trusted he would once he was inside.

He moved through the mansion like a wraith, climbing the marble stairs, ghosting past the expensive art and ancient vases and other excesses, listening for sounds of life.

He found her in her bedroom.

She was getting her game face on, slapping on the makeup that would hide her emotions as she played the latest political gala for her best needs. This one was for the Mayor they'd bought earlier in the year.

Adonis stood in the doorway, watching her. There was no denying her beauty. It was flawless. It was hard to imagine something so attractive on the outside could be so rotten to the core.

She eyed him through her vanity mirror.

"You're home early, baby," she said, not turning.

"There was an accident." It was a truth of sorts.

Now she did turn.

Aphrodite looked at him.

"An accident?"

"Yeah... it's called marriage," he spat.

Aphrodite frowned.

"Baby, what are you talking about? You aren't making any sense."

Adonis stepped further into the room, closer to his mother, closer to a point of no return.

He felt the rush of arousal, and knew he wasn't gay. He had never been gay. That was too simple a label for what he was.

"I killed her, mother. I threw her off the balcony," Adonis explained, emotionlessly.

Aphrodite took the revelation in her stride.

"Because?"

"Let's not play games," Adonis growled, his voice dangerously edged.

Aphrodite stood.

"What do you want to say?"

Adonis stepped in close, within striking distance of his mother, feeling his dick rage in his pants. He could just bend her over and fuck her before he killed her. No one would ever know...

"No," he said, "why don't *you* do the talking, mother? Why don't you explain why I had to kill that bitch."

Aphrodite smirked subtly.

"I told you baby, this is a grown up's game. There's no room for weakness. None."

"And you thought me being gay made me weak? Is that it?"

"You weren't weak because you like the cock, honey. I like the cock and I ain't weak. You hadn't shown me you have what it takes. So I took away your little boy toy because playtime is over. I wanted you to experience a pain you didn't think you could bear, something that would either break you or make you," Aphrodite rasped, coldly.

Adonis smiled, but it was more of a devilish leer. "You still think I'm weak?"

"Maybe weaker than I ever feared, Devante's dead, by your own hands, and your wife, too. You were a tool, Adonis, a tool of your own anguish!"

It was the laugh that took him over the edge.

He back-handed her so hard, she staggered back, her legs buckling around the shape of the bed, and fell back onto the mattress, stunned, and face on fire.

"Adonis!" She gasped, her voice colored with surprise and fear.

"Bitch, you want strong? I will show you just what you made, mother."

"Adonis, please!"

Adonis smacked Aphrodite again, this time with the full force of his fist. She spat blood, trying desperately to scramble away, but he grabbed her by the ankles and yanked her to the foot of the bed.

Her skirt rode up, exposing her gash. She was not wearing panties. Her pussy sat out between her legs, fat and juicy, some twisted sexual pout just goading him on.

Adonis' blood was filled with fire and fury.

He would show her the monster he really was.

She would understand that *gay* had never been the label for him. Never.

He snatched a fistful of her hair and brought her face to his.

"Look deep into the eyes of what you've created, bitch!" He seethed, then he gripped the back of her neck and tongued her down.

There was hesitation, a moment of apprehension followed by a decision she thought might buy her life; she returned the kiss just as violently and passionately.

He spat on his hand then grabbed both of her ass cheeks and spread them, feeling the wetness from her pussy on his fingertips as he worked his saliva into it.

Aphrodite reached down to unzip his raging hard on, already bigger than he had experienced in any moment of arousal before the murder of Devante, a match even, for the incredible length that came with Bianca's death. She squeezed and stroked his dick, looking him in the eye, needing him to believe she wanted him, that this was all she had ever wanted, but he didn't give a shit. It wasn't about her. It was all about the monster inside him. Adonis spun her around, closing both hands around her throat, echoing the death fuck that had ended Devante, and rammed his dick into his mother with so much force it was as though he was trying to rip her pussy apart with it.

"Ohhhhh fuck," Aphrodite moaned.

"You wanted strong? Is this what you wanted, mother? Is it! Is it?!" Adonis gritted.

"Yes, oh yes, oh yes," she moaned, biting the pillow so she didn't summon the entire staff with her cries.

The sounds of skin smacking skin filled the room.

Adonis pounded Aphrodite relentlessly, jackhammering her pussy until she fear-came back to back, dripping with juices around his meat, her heart beating so fast it felt like it would rip out of her ribs.

"I-I can't... please," she begged, but whether she was begging him to stop or to cum didn't matter. He continued to punish her pussy unmercifully.

"Shut the fuck up, mother! This is what you asked for!" Adonis growled, feeling that familiar rumble in his stomach.

He didn't want to bust in her cunt. That would be too easy. He wanted to violate her. To mirror Devante in every way. He spread her ass cheeks wide, took his dick out and hammered it balls deep in her asshole, no lube, no gentle easing through the sphincter, just rammed the full length of it all the way in in a single brutal thrust.

Aphrodite screamed out, howled, pure agony ripped from the mouth, and collapsed on the bed, the pain shivered through her as he deep dicked her asshole, stroke after humiliating stroke until he exploded in her, his body jerking uncontrollably as his legs buckled beneath him and fell forward across her back, pinning his mother to the bed, his cock still deep inside her ass.

As his sober mind returned, he felt a self-disgust for himself that went beyond words.

This was the monster he truly was, the freak, the creature, and it was so much worse than he had ever feared. He was a beast. A thing of fucked up desires. He felt his soul seeping away, out of his body, the goodness that had once lived inside him banished, leaving behind a cold empty space where he would always be this vile fucked up monstrosity.

He shook himself, then got up, his dick still hard and throbbing, a physical sign of the insatiable nature of his budding desires.

He looked down on his mother's ravaged body, stroking his shit covered dick.

She laid on her stomach, her body wracking with sobs.

"'Bitch, you disgust me," he spat contemptuously, still stroking the raging hard on that just would not die, "You wanted to create a gangsta? You didn't. You gave birth to something far worse.... believe me, far worse." Adonis came again, five strings of cum shooting out across his mother's face.

He stared down at her.

He was a monster.

Cash and Mac rode along in an eerie silence.

The full moon loomed above, always there, watching as Cash drove. Mac stared straight ahead. Out beyond the streets they were out of their natural habitat. The silence got to be too much for Cash. He felt something in the air like Phil Collins.

"What up, yo? You good?" Cash questioned.

"Huh? Oh yeah, yeah brah, I'm straight. Just thinkin', you know, about what I'm gonna do after I retire," Mac lied.

Cash chuckled.

"I can just see you gettin' some old steel fishing boat and spending your days out on the water like some ol' country ass nigga!"

"Naw, I don't know, maybe I'll head out to Hollywood. You

know, be an actor, give Denzel a run for his money," Mac quipped.

"Nigga, don't quit your day job."

"Ha!" Mac barked out a laugh. "Right here, right here, cut down this side road," Mac instructed, pointing.

Cash did as he was told, squinting into the darkness as the car rumbled down the narrowest of narrow lanes. No lights, it was just a darker scar on the landscape.

"Goddamn, it's so fuckin' dark, I damn near missed it. How far?"

"Not much further. Pull up down by the lake."

They rode the last stretch down, taking the pothole-pitted track with care. Even so, it still punished the suspension on their wheels. Out here, they might as well have been hanging out on the edge of the earth. It was beyond dark, and so secluded it would take a year for some hiking party to stumble upon a corpse. It was a good place for smugglers looking to get product moved from one city to the next without worrying about the law.

Cash and Mac got out of the car.

The lake was a shimmer of unbroken glass, reflecting the moon.

"These niggas always late," Cash remarked, not hearing the churn of powerboat engines out on the water.

"Yeah, they gonna be late for they own funeral," Mac retorted.

He pulled out his gun.

Cash didn't see him at first, but when he heard the hammer click in the darkness, he looked at his man.

"What up, brah? Expecting trouble?"

"Not much," Mac replied.

Cash still hadn't caught on, but his street senses began to buzz with warnings he really didn't want to believe.

"Then why the gun?'

"Ay yo... shit is crazy, but it's O."

"O?"

"He has this crazy idea in his head that you fuckin' Mona. It's fuckin' with him, man. Told me to bring you out here."

"Fuckin' Mona? Fuck he get that idea from?" Cash said, but then it all came to him, and he answered himself with, "From you..."

Mac smiled.

"You catch on quick, brah. Of course from me. I played y'all niggas like a Steinway," Mac laughed.

Cash tried to creep his hand around to the small of his back and get his gun, but Mac cut that move short.

"I get it, nigga. You're gonna die anyway, so might as well try, huh?" Mac smirked, not that Cash could see his face in the dark.

Cash stopped and dropped his hands by his sides.

"Why, Mac? We family!"

"Times have changed. You've got O to thank for this, by the way. See, the crazy part is, the dumb muhfucka was going to give *you* the connect over me. Like I could have that. So I needed you to over play your hand. Nothing major, just enough to get his jealousy going. I told you to holler at Mona to put you in the game. Then, it was just a hop and skip into making O think you were fuckin' his lady, being you *did* fuck her, after all," Mac explained.

"What's going to happen to her?" Cash asked.

"Who knows? More importantly, who fuckin' cares? Only thing that matters is I know exactly what's gonna happen to you."

Buck! Buck!

Mac put two in Cash's chest.

No more words.

No more taunting. They were brothers, after all.

Cash staggered back, slumped to his knees, then toppled, lying on his side in the dirt, snuffling and grunting in pain as he sucked in air. "You a piece of shit Mac. Always have been, always will be," Cash cursed, a dead man's naming, marking Mac for eternity in the eyes of the almighty.

"Yeah, but at least I'm alive."

Cash laughed.

"Fuck is so funny, dead man?"

"You, nigga! You killin' me for something I *didn't* do, but you so fuckin' dumb you never guessed the pussy I *did* do!"

"Fuck you talkin' about, Cash?"

"Ask Kandi, bitch ass nigga! Ask her about this dick!" Cash cackled, grimacing through the pain as he bled out.

Mac put him down.

Buck! Buck! Buck! Buck!

Four in Cash's face, making a bloody mess not even his mother could recognize.

But, the damage had been done.

The same seed he had planted in Othello, was now taking root deep inside him, and he could feel it growing greener and greener...

Cash's death rippled through the city, the reverberations rocking the underworld.

Othello used his death as a convenient excuse to wage war on his perceived enemies, quelling the streets, and leaving them awash in the blood of the fallen in the process. He was a brutal overlord. Worse than any of them might have imagined even when he exploded onto the scene with those early kills.

Even The Commission watched on nervously, their own hitters on high alert, ready for the moment Othello's power became absolute and they had no choice but to fight or die.

Everyone came to Cash's funeral to pay their respects and to pledge their allegiance to Othello's factions.

Plain and simple, if you didn't come to bend the knee, you looked guilty as sin and nobody wanted to face O's wrath over his man's slaughter, so crews came from far and wide to make sure their names were on the right side of the ledger.

Mona was distraught with grief. It tore her up in ways that only could've happened if everything he'd feared was true, so O felt good about the order, even if it meant that whore's heart ached. Let her fuckin' dream of what might have been.

Othello watched her with an eagle eye, his own heart breaking a little more with every tear she shed over Cash.

Still, it was done.

They could move on.

Find peace.

"I'm sorry about your friend," Joe Hamlet told Othello, shaking his hand with the coffin as a backdrop. "If there's anything I can do, please just say the word. Your grief is my grief, son," Othello nodded solemnly.

"Thank you, Joe. His death has forced my hand, decision made and all that. I'm leaving Mac in charge and giving him the connect. I am ready to step back."

Joe took the news in stride, but there was relief in the knowledge that Othello was finally honoring his word. He didn't want to see Mac in charge any more than anyone else, but if it kept his babygirl safe it was a sacrifice worth making.

"It's your call, son, and I respect your decision," Joe replied, hand on his shoulder. "It will be better from here on, trust me."

Across the way Aphrodite was commiserating with Mac.

"Your skirt is showing, Macklin," she remarked.

Mac noticed the bruises around her throat, but said nothing about them.

"I wasn't aware I was wearing one."

"You know what I mean. Your fingerprints are all over this. Believe me, I applaud you. It was a masterful performance, but I know Cash was supposed to take over, and here you are, heir apparent. I don't believe in coincidences."

The older woman was sharp.

"You'll appreciate the encore, I'm sure. Tuesday good for you?"

Aphrodite looked at him, the red hue of barely suppressed lust in her gaze, and answered, "Anytime is good for you."

She walked off, the sway in her stride, subtle but unmistakable.

Whatever had happened to her, she was definitely the Queen Bitch in the game.

Kandi didn't miss it either.

As soon as Mac approached her, she grilled, "Who was that?"

"Joe Hamlet's wife," Mac answered.

"Hmm-mmm, I don't trust the bitch. She got snake written all over her slither," Kandi remarked.

Mac side-eyed Kandi.

Takes one to know one, huh? He thought.

No matter how hard he willed those dying words out of his mind, he just couldn't purge himself of Cash's taunt. Half of him desperately wanted to believe it was a bluff, just words that Cash hurled because he had no other weapon. But the other half of him *believed* him.

Mac, like Othello, had always felt inferior around Cash when it came to the women. And when it came to sex, penis envy was an inadequate assessment. It went much deeper.

"Why you lookin' at me like that?" Kandi asked.

"Just tired. Let's get the fuck out of here. Funerals depress the shit out of me. Especially when it's my best friend in the box."

Othello shut the front door behind Mona as they walked in.

It felt good to be out of the church, but not right to be home.

He wasn't sure anything about this place would ever feel right again.

Her eyes were red-rimmed and puffy from her tears.

"I... can't believe he's gone," Mona commented, going through to the kitchen to brew coffee.

Othello tossed his suit jacket over the arm of the couch.

"That's the game, yo. Here today, gone tomorrow." It was too dismissive, like he didn't care.

"That's why I'm glad you're getting out of the game, baby," she called through. "I couldn't stand to lose you, too."

He joined her in the kitchen.

"Too?" Othello echoed, looking Mona in the face. "What do you mean too?"

Mona looked confused.

She hadn't thought at all about her choice of words.

It was just a comment comparing the two deaths, not equating them.

"It was nothin', a comment comparing two deaths, not equating them, baby. I just can't imagine life without you. You are my world, baby."

"No," Othello huffed, his anger building steam, "You said *too* like you lost him. So tell me, what the fuck am I supposed to think that means?"

Mona stared at Othello like he was a stranger.

She knew just how dangerous her love was, and how dark a place his mind could be.

She couldn't wrap her mind around why a word so small and simple could set him off in such a way, unless... It hit her then—the full force of the realization—he had to know about her and Cash. She bit back on the urge to deny, to say *it was just one time, before we even...*

"Othello, what is wrong with you?" Her tears returned, but for an entirely different reason.

"Oh, now you gonna play with my intelligence? I know exactly what you meant by *too*."

"Othello, if you have something to say, then just say it," she said, finally ready to get everything out in the open.

"You fucked Cash didn't you?"

His words were like a slap in her face—a slap of her own reality, her own guilt, her own responsibility that she had ducked for too long. All she had to do was own it, tell the truth. It was history. It had no bearing on them.

"Yes, Othello, yes! Okay? Does that make it better I had sex with Cash?"

That was all she got out before Othello smacked her so hard, he damn near knocked her out, blood and teeth flew from her mouth. She hit the wall so hard it would have set the big one off in LA.

Mona came down hard, sprawled across the coffee table. The glass shattered under her weight. She fell through it to the floor.

Othello stood over her.

"You ho ass bitch! I *knew* it! I fuckin' knew you were nothing but a bitch ass cunt, just like the rest of these dog ass bitches in the street! You fuckin' *whore*."

She stared up at him, desperate, pleading, needing him to believe, "It was before you, I swear! I didn't know you then!"

"Bitch, you lyin'! I saw him when he left the theater, and you didn't say a thing about it! Then I heard him talking about you, how he was blowing your back out and you loving it! Then, on top of all that you nasty no good slut, I found your scarf, your *scarf* in his fuckin' crib!" Othello raged. He hammered a kick into her ribs so brutally it lifted her off the floor as if to punctuate his last word.

The pain made Mona see stars, all the heavens, and hell waiting for her on the other side.

She heard her ribs crack.

Felt the unbelievable stab of pain.

"Please, O! I swear I didn't have sex with Cash while we were together!"

"You lying!"

Another brutal kick, this one to the side of her head.

It took her out, the pain was clouding her mind. She couldn't think. She needed him to believe... to understand... The scarf.

"O, I gave that scarf to Kandi. I let her borrow it, I swear, ask her! Ask her! I've never been to Cash's place!" She sobbed.

Othello's chest heaved as he stood looking down on her.

"Bitch, you better not be lyin'. You lie, you fuckin' die, understand? You really want me to make the call?"

"Ask her!"

"Fine." Othello snatched up his phone and hit the contact.

Kandi picked up.

Othello put her on speaker.

"Kandi."

"Who this? O?'

"Yeah."

"What up, booboo?" She greeted.

"Ay yo, let me ask you something, truth. Has Mona ever given you something to hold?"

"Not that I can remember? Like what?"

"My scarf, Kandi! Tell him! Tell Othello I let you borrow my scarf!" Mona yelled from the floor.

"A scarf? Naw baby, that wasn't me. What kind?"

He didn't need to hear anymore.

He killed the call.

"She's lying, I swear to god," Mona sobbed, her voice hoarse with desperation.

Othello grabbed her by the throat, snatching her off the ground.

The pain in her ribs shot up to her head.

"Bitch, as much as I loved you, I hate you now even more. You better walk on goddamn egg shells around me, because if you don't your whole goddamn family dead!"

He threw her away like the trash she was.

Mona only heard half his words. The pain was so intense, she floated between consciousness and oblivion for a moment before succumbing to the darkness.

Adonis sat in the bar, alone in the corner booth.

He was a changed man in every single way bar one, he still loved a dead man and there was nothing he could do about it.

The place was a frequent spot for the LGBT community. It wasn't somewhere he went often, but the music was good, the atmosphere was better and his discretion was growing weaker by the day. He could have gone back and fucked his mother again. Part of him wanted to stand over her and just piss on her face, completing the ultimate degradation, but he knew that going back there, deep dicking her again, that went from monster to Greek tragedy, and he wasn't ready for that yet.

He had already drunk four shots and was nursing a glass of VSOP when the front door opened.

Devante walked in.

He knew it was his ghost that came to taunt him, all beautiful and dead, and remind him what he could have had, but Devante didn't disappear when he tried to blink him away and clear his half-drunk vision.

It was Devante, only it wasn't. He wore women's clothes, and his shape was more feminine. There were proper breasts, too. Rising proud.

Their eyes locked.

Even in his drunken mind, he *knew* this couldn't be real, that he *had* to be seeing things. There was no way Devante was still alive... he had killed him... been inside him when his sphincter collapsed, shitting himself into hell, his hands wrapped around his neck. The clean-up crew chopped the body up and dissolved what was left of him in acid, making sure there was nothing but the residue in the tub and even that was cleaned up with bleach. There was nothing left of Devante apart from the memories in his head.

So could a memory come to life and sashay in through the

door of non-existence to taunt him with tits and teeth?

He felt sick.

Lost.

Broken.

The closer he came, the wilder Adonis' heart beat until the ghost in drag walked right up to his table, smiled and said, "Looking for me?"

Adonis was dumb founded. "I-I'm sorry."

He smiled.

"I mean, the way you were eyeing me when I walked in, I was sure I was the one person you were waiting for. True love. My name's Rihanna."

Adonis blinked again, this time as he reached for his glass to down what was left of his drink, his vision reset and he was able to see that it wasn't Devante come to drag him all the way to hell with him, but there was an uncanny resemblance.

"I'm Adonis. Join me?"

"Sure, sugar," Rihanna sat down across from him.

"What're you drinking?'

"Whatever you're buying."

Adonis smiled, then waved down the waitress, ordering Rihanna a drink.

The waitress disappeared through the crowded bar.

"So, let me guess, I look like someone you know," Rihanna teased.

"Is it that obvious?"

"You have a real pretty poker face."

They both laughed.

"How come I've never seen you around here?" Adonis asked.

"I just came home a few months ago."

"Came home? Were you in the army?"

"Close. Prison," Rihanna replied, eyeing his reaction over the rim of the glass, "Does that bother you?"

Adonis shrugged.

"You'd be surprised... I've done things... so, no, it doesn't."

"Good, because I like talking to you," Rihanna flirted.

Adonis raised his glass. "The night is full of possibilities," he toasted.

Clink!

"I see you don't waste time getting to the point?" Rihanna remarked, enjoying the way Adonis was looking at him.

"Life's too short, and I'm a man that knows what he wants."

"My kind of guy."

"Shall we?"

"We shall, again and again and again. It's gonna be a good night," Rihanna promised, then downed his drink and walked out and into a whole new life...

Mona felt like shit.

Worse than shit.

Every part of her hurt, inside and out.

Heartbroken, ribs fractured, pride was shattered and her mind was frazzled and guilt ridden.

She had brought this all on Cassio and herself.

She had done this.

Killed him.

If only she'd told Othello the truth from the beginning, Cash would still be alive her marriage intact.

They were victim's thoughts.

Victim's rationalizations.

She sat in the hospital room, her ribs bandaged up, woozy from the pain medication.

Her face was bruised and scarred where the glass from the coffee table had lacerated it, but she was numb to it all. The doctor walked in, an older black woman with gray dreadlocks and pity-filled eyes. "Do you want to file a report?"

Mona couldn't meet her gaze when she answered, "File a report from what?"

"Sweetheart, I see everything on any given night, and believe me, I know what abuse looks like."

"It... wasn't like that," Mona tried to respond.

"Oh? Really? Then what was it like? Trust me, if he hits you once, he'll hit you again and he'll keep right on hitting you until you're either dead or broken, and sometimes dead is better."

Mona looked at her with tears in her eyes.

"It wasn't his fault. I... I lied."

Mona fell into the doctor's arms and cried cathartic tears.

The woman held her, letting her get it out.

After the initial torrent of tears had subsided, the doctor said, "Baby, we all make mistakes. But no one, and I mean *no one*, has a right to put their hands on you because of it. Now... I'm gonna ask you again, do you want to make a report? There are people out there who can help you."

Mona thought about Othello's words.

Bitch, as much as I loved you, I hate you now even more. You better walk on goddamn eggshells around me, because if you don't, your whole goddamn family is dead!

She knew if she made any sort of report, the police would get involved, and nothing could be worse than having the police involved in family business. That had been drilled into her head since she was knee high to Joe Hamlet. Besides, then her family would know what happened and her daddy would to go war with O and everybody would suffer.

Mona took a deep breath, knowing it was better to suffer a few broken ribs over a broken family.

"No... No, I'm okay. It'll get better, I know it."

The doc knew there was nothing she could do. Even so, she said, "You are wrong sweetheart, it never does. Now, if there isn't anything else...."

Mona slid off the table.

"Thank you."

"I'll be praying for you."

Mona walked out, looked back with hesitation, wondering if she was making a mistake, but took a deep breath and walked out.

By the time Mona got in her car, her head was literally spinning.

The pain meds had her feeling floaty and free, like the buzz of a blunt of exotic or a couple of glasses of Hennessey.

She wasn't usually one to drink and drive, but she didn't have anyone else to drive her. And the first person she would have called to help was O, and she couldn't call him, and the second was Cash, and he wasn't there anymore. Calling Celeste or anyone was putting them in the mix and she couldn't do that to anyone she loved, so she got behind the wheel, looked at her own eyes in the rearview, and told herself, "We can do this."

She looked at her swollen eyes, her bruised cheek, all of those little glass cuts and her busted lip and hated herself.

No man had ever hit her before, and up to that point, she had sworn no man ever would, but now she saw how easy it was to become *that* girl.

"Lord, help me," she prayed, but the gods of whoever looked after gangstas' girls weren't listening.

She started the car and drove off.

The trip home wasn't that far, but because of the rain, her visibility was cut to almost nothing.

Mona turned on the radio, but her spirit rebelled, needing silence, like a funeral procession. She turned it off. Her thoughts were jumbled and fuzzy. Lacking shape. She put it down to the medication, but she knew her mind was caught up in a whirl-wind of emotions that went way beyond any cocktail of pills.

The nurse was right.

Of course she was.

Othello would only get worse. He was violent by nature. She

saw it in his eyes every time she looked at him, but up until now there had been love to balance it out.

If she walked out on him, Joe Hamlet would burn the streets down.

Or try to.

He was an old man. He played a different game now. O was something else. He had grown so powerful, too many people had pledged allegiance to him in the wake of Cash's murder, no one would go out on a limb for Joe any more knowing O would be waiting for them to fuck up.

Mona swerved.

Not a lot, but her drowsy mind had dozed for a split second. It was almost enough.

The only thing that brought her back was the blare of an oncoming horn.

"Shit," she said, sitting up in the seat, but it was no use.

The medication was too strong for her to be driving.

She thought about pulling over, but she reasoned that wasn't much farther to her home.

Home...

That one safe place...

What she and Othello shared was a space, it would never again be a home.

He would never forgive her and she would never feel safe in the hands that had brought her so much pain.

Leave him, her mind urged, *just get on the highway and don't look back. Go. Now.*

For a moment, it seemed like the thing to do.

It would be easy.

She had her own accounts, easily over half a mil in them. More than enough to buy a new life somewhere Othello could never find her.

But that would leave her family in danger.

Was she prepared to risk it all?

Mona felt trapped, beyond trapped, like she was heading toward her own slow, tortuous death. Dead woman walking. Being battered, abused and humiliated wasn't a life worth living. It would diminish her, fist by fist, draining her away until there was nothing but a shell where a strong, determined, happy young woman had been.

Her lids grew heavy...

Rest...

The word echoed in her mind, like an invitation to the perfect answer.

Rest...

It would be so easy.

She felt her body begin to relax as she embraced her own peace.

The medicine lulled her deeper, like the song of a siren in the wind, promising a place where it would all go away.

She closed her eyes, and whispered, "Forgive me, Lord."

The car gently crossed the yellow line, the rain beat down on her windshield, the shadow of the raindrops looking like tears streaking her calm face.

The last thing she saw were the headlights of the truck coming at her going sixty miles an hour. The lights looked like the warm beckoning illumination of the rising sun on a new day.

The blare of the horn blurred in her drugged mind.

Mona didn't feel the impact.

The truck crushed her car head on.

She didn't feel the heat of the explosion that ripped her body into thousands of charred scraps, strewn across the blacktop.

She didn't feel anything but the all-embracing awareness of total and complete peace, then...

Her spirit rested.

EPILOGUE

O nly hours after Mona's death, Adonis ordered a hit on the entire Davenport family. Every last one of them save for the grandmother, Edna.

His reasoning was simple: neither family knew of Bianca's death. Only Aphrodite knew. No one else. And certainly no one else could ever know the truth of what he had done. But he knew once it was out there, the fragile political peace it had forged between their houses would be torn asunder. That would mean war, even if it was a righteous war born out of grief. That was something he couldn't have.

So the easiest thing in his mind was to ensure the rest of her family joined her.

But first, a proper celebration. After all, they had a wedding to celebrate.

He gathered them all, promising a feast. It was a family tradition, the entire clan enjoyed Sunday dinner together. It wasn't about religion, it was about family. Both of Wingate's sons, his daughter, wife and mother gathered for one last meal.

The cooks were the first to die.

The hit team entered the mansion through the kitchen.

Automatic gunfire rang through the air like the ringing of trumpets. The family didn't have time to react, or weapons at hand to save themselves. This was their sanctuary, their one safe place. This was their home, and they were gathered to celebrate the homecoming of the happy couple. No one brought weapons to such a joyous occasion. And that was the death of them. Heads exploded from the barrage that peppered the table, splashing blood, guts and brain matter everywhere. It was nothing short of slaughter.

A brutal blow to the back of the head knocked dear old Edna Davenport out cold, and she didn't awaken for several days, in a hospital room. For the longest time, Adonis was worried the old bitch wouldn't make it, that he'd hit her too hard.

But she opened her eyes.

"Mother Davenport, how are you?" he asked, stroking her leathery skin. He sat beside what could easily be her death bed.

She looked around, confused.

"Where am I? I don't... How did I get here?"

Adonis dropped his head, solemnly. Practiced. He had gone over these lines so many times in his mind, but needed to deliver them just so.

"I... I don't know how to tell you this... It... It was horrible... a tragedy... The whole family is gone. Dead."

She drew in a gasp. "Lord, no!"

"You don't remember?"

She shook her head, blue eyes still sharp as steel. "I only remember being at the table, looking around at all the faces..."

"You do remember me and Bianca, coming to join you at the table? She was so pleased to see you..."

The old woman looked at him as if she were trying to do just that, but couldn't find the image in all the horrors stowed away in her mind.

Adonis continued, "I was sitting on your right, with Bianca to my left. The gunmen came in from the kitchen. I grabbed you and Bianca and pulled you both under the table," he lied. "You hit your head... the bullets were flying, tearing up the room. It was a hit. They came for Wingate, but they took every last one of the family. I'm so sorry... I let you down. I failed you all. I tried... but..."

Edna, her mind putty in his hands, squeezed his hand and blurted out, "Bless you, young man... bless you for trying. Is Bianca coming to see me soon?"

Adonis shed crocodile tears.

"She didn't make it, Grandma. You and I were the only ones who made it out of the celebration alive. It should have been the happiest time..."

It was.

THANK YOU

We truly hope you enjoyed this title from Kingston Imperial. Our company prides itself on breaking new authors, as well as working with established ones to create incredible reading content to amplify your literary experience. In an effort to keep our movement going, we urge all readers to leave a review (hopefully positive) and let us know what you think. This will not only spread the word to more readers, but it will allow us the opportunity to continue providing you with more titles to read. Thank you for being a part of our journey and for writing a review.

KINGSTON IMPERIAL

Marvis Johnson — Publisher
Kathy Iandoli — Editorial Director
Joshua Wirth — Designer
Bob Newman — Publicist

Contact:
Kingston Imperial
144 North 7th Street #255
Brooklyn, NY 11249
Email: Info@kingstonimperial.com
www.kingstonimperial.com

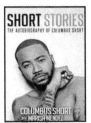

CPSIA information can be obtained
at www.ICGtesting.com
Printed in the USA
JSHW011050081020
8549JS00006B/6

9 780999 639016